The **CATE CARLISLE** Files

Isla Whitcroft is a journalist who writes for national newspapers including the *Daily Mail*, the *Mail on Sunday* and *The Times*. She lives in Northamptonshire with her husband and three children.

The CATE CARLISLE Files

DEEP WATER

ISLA WHITCROFT

PICCADILLY PRESS • LONDON

To my mother Eileen Whitcroft (nee Arkless).
A remarkable woman who gave me endless love
and freedom and surrounded me with books.

First published in Great Britain in 2011
by Piccadilly Press Ltd,
5 Castle Road, London NW1 8PR
www.piccadillypress.co.uk

A catalogue record for this book is available
from the British Library

ISBN: 978 1 84812 155 3 (paperback)

3 5 7 9 10 8 6 4 2

Printed and bound by CPI Group (UK) Ltd,
Croydon, CR0 4YY
Cover design by Simon Davis
Cover illustration by Sue Hellard

PROLOGUE

It was sundown at the turtle sanctuary. The newly lit campfire was giving off a green, smoky haze and several of the younger volunteers were bustling around, preparing supper or securing tents for the night ahead. Someone was strumming songs on a guitar, the gentle sound blending perfectly with the lilac light of the fading Australian sun. Two teenage girls, bronzed from weeks by the ocean, sat quietly chatting. Food and then bed – it would be an early start the next day, as it always was at Snapper Bay.

No one noticed as the white-haired boy crept away from the group, and made his way onto the soft sand of the beach that had been both his home and his work place for the last two months.

The boy, just eighteen, had things on his mind, things he needed to work through and decisions to make, and there was no one at the camp he could confide in. Not yet anyway. It made him feel lonely, scared even, and so he would do what he always did when he was craving peace of mind. He would go swimming, immersing himself in the warm waters of the Pacific Ocean to wash away his fears and clear the nervous chatter from his brain.

He knew the dangers, of course. Everyone at the sanctuary had been told the rules the day they arrived and number one was 'No swimming alone and certainly not after dark'. He remembered Jacob, their Swedish leader, speaking in loud and impeccable English: 'Swimming at night is a high-risk activity. Sharks feed at night, jellyfish are impossible to spot, and you can't see the rip tides which can take you out to sea in seconds. Needless to say, if you get into trouble, it is much harder to find you than in daylight.'

But he didn't care. Not tonight. Tonight there seemed to be more dangers on land than at sea. As he reached the water's edge, the boy unrolled the lycra body suit he had been carrying under his arm. Much as he wanted to swim in just his trunks, he knew that he needed protection from the ever-present and often lethal jellyfish, which spent the summer months in this beautiful part of the world.

He edged into his suit, pulled on his swim shoes and stood at the water's edge, feeling his body relaxing at the first gentle touches of the water, so different from the icy northern seas he had braved as a child. He entered the sea in slow motion, causing no ripples, no sound.

He paused as he reached waist height in the water and turned round to look at the camp. The fires were burning brightly now, standing out against the gloom, and he could no longer see faces, only silhouettes of the people sitting close to the heat. A few lanterns attached to the tents glowed steadily;

there was no breeze tonight. He heard laughter and winced, his blue eyes filling with sadness. Everyone else at the camp was so happy, so upbeat, so up for a laugh. Why was he the one who had to carry such a burden?

He watched for a few seconds and then turned back to the sea and struck out in the direction of the towering islands that lay just a few kilometres offshore. His strokes were regular and economical. Like all strong swimmers he hardly made a sound as he powered through the water. One hundred metres passed, then two, then three hundred metres, and he was almost ready to turn back to shore when he felt a strong nudge against his left leg. Surprised rather than panicked, the boy's first thought was that he had swum into one of the hundreds of submerged sandbanks that littered the bay, and caught out many an unwary sailor. But as he put his right leg down to check, it seemed that there was nothing below him, only water.

Perhaps he had imagined the nudge, but even so, he now began to regret his bravado, his stupidity at ignoring the shark warnings.

He looked around him and at first could see nothing. He paused, instinctively keeping quiet as his heart hammered inside his chest. Then he saw the small fishing boat, its prow facing away from him. He almost laughed out loud with relief. Of course, he had swum into its anchor rope.

He was tempted to climb onto the boat, to lie back and watch the clouds scudding across the moon. But he knew he should really swim back to the beach, and so he trod water for a few minutes, waiting while his heart stopped racing and his breathing returned to normal.

He was just about to turn for home when he felt something

strike his right leg, the blow pulling him under the water. He opened his eyes. There was no denying the shape darting away from him – this time it really was a shark. And it was coming right back towards him.

He lashed out, somehow finding the strength to kick the shark in the gills, making it turn away again as he pushed back up to the surface. The boat was now lit up and closer to him, the two men on board silhouetted against a lamp swinging from the cabin hatch. Relief washed over him – he was saved.

He wanted to call out, to scream for help, but his voice was frozen, paralysed with fear, and the only sound that came out was a desperate whimper. The men looked up from their task. They were dropping something into the water – something so big that it needed both of them to lift it. They didn't seem surprised to see the boy in the water, but nor was there any sense of urgency in their movements. Even in the midst of his terror the boy was puzzled. Surely now they could see him they would rush to his aid?

He slowly began to swim towards them, desperately trying not to think what would happen if the shark returned. After what seemed like hours, one of the men threw him a rope with a buoyancy aid attached. He grabbed it, and felt the utter relief of being towed through the water and yanked onto the boat, where he lay like a helpless child, as his blood seeped slowly out into a warm pool around him. He gazed up at his rescuers, who were staring down at him. Their faces bore no shred of concern, no pity at his plight.

'Please,' he began in a low voice. He tried to gesture towards the shore but he was feeling light-headed now, confused. 'Take me to my friends.'

The taller of the two men squatted down and inspected his leg. 'It's only a graze,' he said roughly. He threw a towel onto the boy's leg. 'Press on the wound. You'll be OK.' The man stood up and spoke angrily, almost to himself. 'Now what? How are we going to clean up this mess?'

'We should have left him in the water.' The smaller man was speaking now. 'The sharks would have finished him off in no time.'

The boy looked from one man to another. The pain was subsiding now, his body releasing endorphins that were taking the edge off his agony, leaving room instead for a gnawing, gut-wrenching feeling of fear. Something was wrong. Badly wrong.

'Thank you for saving me,' the boy said, desperately trying to placate the two men. 'Now, please, can you just take me back to shore? My friends will be concerned for me.'

The first man laughed. It was an empty, angry sound and gave no comfort to the boy. 'Your friends are the least of your worries,' he said. He put out a huge hand and jerked the boy effortlessly to his feet, then nodded towards the small opening through which a set of stairs led to the bowels of the boat.

'Down below, now.'

The boy was about to argue, to protest, to take his chances and scream for help. His friends would surely hear him from the shore. But before he could muster the energy, he felt a hard, sharp object pushed painfully against his neck.

'I'd do as my friend says, if I were you.' The short man was talking again, quietly but with a menace that cut through the night air like his knife. 'It's either that or taking a night swim with the sharks. With both hands tied behind your back.'

CHAPTER 1

The pile of clothes on the bed was growing larger by the minute, the duvet cover slowly but surely disappearing under a pile of cashmere jumpers, jeans, woolly socks and snuggly snoods in a range of bright colours.

Cate Carlisle sighed as her glance moved from the overloaded bed to the one disappointingly small suitcase that was somehow supposed to hold everything she needed for her week away. It was the same dilemma every year. Skiing needed so much stuff, not just to wear on the slope but also in the evenings off-piste. And everything was so large and bulky. How was she ever going to get it all packed? If she wasn't careful she would end up having to wear four layers of clothes on the plane and she wouldn't be able to move along the aisle, let alone sit down in her seat. The thought made her giggle and, cheered up, she picked up the first pair of jeans – her prized pair of Miss Sixties – and started folding them.

'Cate, aren't you packed yet?' said a voice from the doorway.

'Honestly, mine was done ages ago.' Her brother Arthur bounded into the room, made for the bed and then, seeing the mayhem, changed his mind and plonked himself onto her dressing-table stool instead.

'It's all right for you,' grumbled Cate. 'You're a boy. All you need is a couple of pairs of jeans and a few tatty jumpers and you're done. You don't care what you look like.'

Arthur grinned at his sister. 'Well, more fool you,' he said cheerfully. 'Why are you worrying about your image anyway, when your boyfriend isn't even going to be there? In fact, shouldn't you be in purdah or something in case you turn the head of another man?'

'Very funny,' said Cate, laughing despite herself. 'But actually Michel isn't really my boyfriend any more. After the summer he and I agreed that it wasn't sensible to carry on a relationship, what with him living in the South of France and me back at school in London. We're just going to take it as it comes and maybe meet up again in the spring. We're just good friends.'

'Yeah, yeah, yeah,' said Arthur. 'I believe you, Sis, millions wouldn't.' He turned to the mirror, pushed his dark, floppy hair behind his ears and deepened his voice. *'Je t'aime, ma cherie. Je t'aime.* Mwah, mwah.'

A ski glove whizzed past his ear and skidded over Cate's precious collection of Bobbi Brown make-up, a present from Monique, her dad's girlfriend. 'Right, Arthur, that's it,' said Cate, waving the other glove at him and pretending to be angry. 'Out of my room.'

Arthur raised his hands in mock surrender and made for the door. 'OK, OK! But seriously, Sis, you can't leave your packing much longer. Our flight to Geneva leaves early in the morning. I've already got my GPS tracking system working out the best way to avoid the rush hour traffic and I've hacked into air traffic control to see if there are any expected overnight flight delays. There aren't, by the way.'

Just for good measure, Cate threw the other ski glove after her departing brother, laughing inwardly at how his obsession for all things technical could slip into just about every conversation they had.

Two years younger than sixteen-year-old Cate, Arthur was a computer whizz, gifted beyond his years and his talents had been essential at getting Cate out of a particularly tight hole during her adventures in the summer. Having taken a holiday job on a yacht moored in Antibes in the South of France, Cate had been caught up in a vile scheme involving endangered animals. To save them she'd been recruited by a shadowy security organisation, the International Maritime Investigation Agency – IMIA – and had witnessed murder, beatings and very nearly lost her own life.

All these tumultuous events had happened at the beginning of the summer but then there had been weeks of fun, sunshine and camraderie as Cate worked on the yacht and partied with local boy Michel and his friends. While her family had found out the truth, Cate had promised IMIA that she would keep her adventures secret and she had – she hadn't even confided in Michel. As summer had drawn to a close, she had said her reluctant goodbyes to her newfound friends, and, even more sadly, to her summer romance with Michel and returned to London, school, and – worst of all – the start of her A-level courses.

She was still in touch with many of the people she'd met. Cate and Nancy Kyle, the supermodel who owned the boat that Cate had worked on, texted each other regularly. One of Cate's jobs in the summer had been to look after Nancy's five adopted children and she made sure she still spoke to them on the phone every couple of weeks, enjoying hearing their news and listening to their adventures as the children of one of the most famous women in the world. She even still received the odd cryptic text from Marcus, an officer with the IMIA who had recruited Cate to help on the case, and of course she and Michel tried to talk at least once a week, sometimes for hours at a time.

Cate smiled to herself. It had been a mad summer, but boy it had been exciting. It had been a real effort to keep her vow of silence when she went back to school in September, but gradually, as the weeks passed, it almost seemed as if the adventures had happened to someone else, like something she'd seen in a film.

And now it was nearly Christmas and Michel was in a remote part of Australia where internet connection was sporadic at best. He was with his cousin Noah, a professional eco-warrior who flitted around the world as the fancy took him, his chaotic lifestyle funded totally by his doting and very rich mother. One day Noah might be leading a protest march against global warning, the next he would turn up on the nightly news as part of a group trying to board a Japanese whaling boat.

But he was passionate and committed, and so, when Noah had decided that his latest project would be to work on a turtle conservation project on the north-east coast of

Australia, Michel decided that it would be interesting to join him before going to university in Paris. 'I get to save turtles and escape the European winter,' he said to Cate when they were discussing the trip. 'How cool is that?'

Looking out through the bedroom window of her West London home, Cate could see fairy lights twinkling in houses up and down the quiet street and a sprinkling of snow lay on top of the cars parked outside the Georgian terraces. She sighed happily. She loved this time of year: the run up to Christmas with all the parties with her school mates, shopping in Sloane Square, spending hours in Selfridges with her best friend Louisa, admiring the amazing seasonal displays and then scooting off for hot chocolate and ice-skating at Somerset House overlooking the Thames. Now that she had broken up from school, she and Arthur were off for their annual skiing holiday with their father, a United Nations diplomat, and his long-time girlfriend Monique, a linguist who worked as a translator. Cate had skied since she was a toddler and was addicted to the feeling of freedom that it gave her. That, she grinned to herself, and the amazingly calorific lunches on the mountainside. She could hardly wait.

Lost in excited anticipation of the week ahead, Cate didn't at first register that her phone was ringing and by the time she managed to locate it under a pair of pyjamas she thought the caller might have rung off.

'Cate? Cate, it's me.'

Immediately her heart began to race. 'Michel,' she said. 'It's great to hear from you.'

'I'm so glad I got through. Cate, I have to ask you something, and I need to know the answer right away. I know you're about to go skiing but this brilliant opportunity has come up.'

He paused for a second and Cate held her breath. What on earth was he talking about?

'The thing is, Noah's mum was going to fly out and see him for Christmas but her new boyfriend wants to whisk her off to Gstaad and so there's a first class return ticket going begging. Fully transferable. Shame to waste it.'

It took a few seconds before his words sank in. Then Cate gasped. She could hardly believe what she was hearing. 'Michel, are you saying that you want me to come out to see you? In Australia? This Christmas?'

'Why not, *cherie*? I've told you how amazing it is here. You'll finally get a chance to see the huge beaches and amazing forests and the wildlife. It's so different from Europe. And you'll love the guys I'm working with – they all really believe in what they are doing. We're doing some great work too – we must have rescued dozens of turtles already.'

Michel paused, and continued almost shyly. 'I'd really love to see you. Actually, I really wish you were out here with me now.'

Cate still wasn't used to the way in which, compared to the boys she knew in London, Michel spoke his mind and revealed his feelings with complete honesty, and she felt herself blushing.

'There's been a bit of an incident here and it's kind of shaken us all.' His voice changed, he sounded tense and strained. 'This boy, Rafe, well, he's gone missing. Overnight really. One minute he was there and the next morning he was gone, without leaving a message or even saying goodbye. His tent was empty, cleared out. Just like that.'

'Did you call the police?' asked Cate. She was curious now.

'*Mais oui*,' Michel replied. 'Of course. We were worried sick. But once they'd seen all his things had gone, they said he'd just left – travelling or gone home. That he would be in touch when he wanted to.'

'Well, then,' Cate said, 'he probably did go off. Didn't you tell me Australia is full of people on the move, looking for new experiences? Perhaps he got fed up with life on the sanctuary and wanted a bit of new excitement.'

Michel sighed. 'But he loved it at the sanctuary . . . He did seem to have something on his mind that day, but, well, I just think it's odd, that's all.'

He paused again and Cate could picture him making a visible effort to cheer up. 'I'm sorry, Cate, I don't mean to be gloomy and put you off. It's brilliant out here and I'd love to show you around. What do you say?'

Cate's mind was whirling. She looked at her luggage and then at her watch. Surely it was too late to change her plans?

'Cate Carlisle,' Michel boomed in a fake American accent, 'this is a once in a lifetime opportunity.'

The huge engines on the wings of the Qantas jet roared through the early morning sunshine. Inside the massive two-storey airbus, the lights, which had been dimmed for the passengers to sleep, were switched back on and the clank and hiss of a coffee machine coming to life could be heard from the galley at the rear of the plane. Waking in her window seat, halfway down the roomy cabin, Cate removed her earplugs and pushed aside the blanket which had been covering her as she did her best to sleep through the ten hour flight from Bangkok to Sydney.

Shortly after breakfast, Cate pulled up her window screen, peered down at the view and gasped. She had heard about how beautiful Sydney was, seen it on TV and in films, but nothing had quite prepared her for the incredible sight that met her eyes.

The plane was flying directly over Sydney harbour, a great rocky gash that separated the two halves of the city. Below her, the blue water sparkled in the sunlight and, despite the early hour, it was already scattered with craft – sailing boats, green liveried ferries and the odd white giant of a cruise liner. Cate even thought she could see someone waterskiing.

Numerous inlets lined the vast waterway, most of them crowned with neat-looking beaches. Those inlets that were without beaches had been utilised in other ways – Cate counted at least a dozen marinas, crammed with sailing boats and motor yachts and the odd huge villa.

As the plane headed further in towards the city, the harbourside was becoming more built up. Many of the bays and inlets were now edged with buildings, some close together, others separated out with huge gardens and swimming pools.

Most exciting of all, up ahead of her, in-between the city skyscrapers, Cate could see the unmistakable outline of the world famous opera house and, next to it, the iconic Sydney Harbour Bridge stretching confidently between the north and south shores of the city.

Her tiredness forgotten, Cate sat back in her seat and grinned to herself. This was going to be amazing, well worth the long journey, not to mention the hassle of convincing her dad and Monique to let her come to Australia to see Michel, rather than go skiing with her family.

'No way, Cate,' had been her dad's first reaction when she had told him about Michel's call. 'This is our family Christmas, our special time. We do it every year and I really look forward to it.'

That was so typical of her dad. He just wanted his family around him for Christmas. He wasn't at all bothered by the fact that Cate would be travelling all the way to Australia by herself, or going to a strange country where she knew only about three people. No one knew better than he did how independent his daughter was, indeed how adept she was at looking after herself wherever she was in the world.

When Cate was just eight years old, her father working abroad on yet another peace initiative, her glamorous mother had, without prior warning, vanished for a new life in America, leaving a bewildered Cate and Arthur in the temporary care of a neighbour.

Her father had flown home immediately to his grief-stricken children and, rather than dumping them in boarding school as some of his colleagues had suggested, or taking a desk job in London, he brought them along with him as he travelled the world. Those years spent globe-trotting had been the making of Cate. She had picked up several languages and was completely comfortable jumping on and off planes. Finding her bearings in new environments felt like an exciting challenge, rather than something to be frightened by.

Most importantly, she had learnt from that early age how to think on her feet and take care of herself in situations which may well have proved too much for people several years older than her. All these attributes had proved essential during her adventures last summer and Cate did not regret one thing about her childhood.

In the end it had been Monique who, as always, had provided the voice of reason that had convinced her dad to let Cate go to Australia. 'She isn't a child any more and it's natural she wants to be with her friends.' As always her Dutch accent was more accentuated when she was arguing. 'We see Cate all the time and there will be many more family Christmases. She won't get chances like this very often. Let her go and we'll all go skiing again at half-term.'

Cate had held her breath as her father looked from his daughter to his girlfriend. 'OK, Cate,' he had sighed, 'but you have to swear to keep up with your homework schedule.' He smiled then and enveloped her in a huge hug. 'Boy, I'm going to miss my daughter on Christmas morning.'

Cate had felt a sting of tears behind her eyes then. She loved to be with her family at Christmas too, but she remembered how she felt when she heard Michel's voice, how long it had been since she'd seen him and most of all she knew she needed another adventure.

The wheels of the giant airbus skidded onto the shimmering tarmac, and Cate, pinned back into her seat by the reverse thrust of the engines, smiled. She really couldn't wait to see Michel again.

A few minutes later, the plane was at a standstill by the terminal, the doors were open and Cate was shuffling impatiently down the aisle, past the pretty air hostesses smiling their goodbyes, eager to be out in the fresh air again. As she stepped through the door and onto the top of the narrow metal stairway, she was struck simultaneously by a blinding light, a sensation of heat washing over her body and an almost overpowering smell of what she thought was pine. She stopped and breathed deeply, momentarily forgetting about the people behind her in the queue. Her body, deprived of sunshine after a cold winter, suddenly felt lighter, more relaxed, more human.

'It's the eucalyptus trees you can smell, love,' said a woman standing close behind her. 'Gorgeous, isn't it? It's the smell of Australia. Now, I know I'm home.'

Cate looked back at her and smiled. Then she pulled down her gold-rimmed Ray-Bans over her eyes, slung her faithful Mulberry rucksack over her shoulder and set off down the steps. It was only a few metres to the terminal and Cate paused outside, not yet ready to leave the sunshine behind.

As the other passengers passed in front of her she switched on her phone and texted her dad, Arthur and Louisa to let them know she had arrived safely. That done, she reluctantly headed into the air-conditioned building to begin the long and tedious process of clearing immigration and passport control.

In contrast to her usual experience, all was calm and peaceful inside the first class waiting area. A smiling hostess had welcomed her in, taken her bag from her and directed her into the lounge, which was liberally scattered with reclining soft leather chairs and sofas. Along one wall was a bar fitted with drinks and several coffee machines, and a few men in suits were helping themselves to a pile of appetizing-looking snacks placed at intervals along the glass top.

Cate walked over to the bar and poured herself some sparkling water and cranberry juice and chose some prawn blinis and a gorgeous mini tarte tatin from the buffet, then sat down in one of the huge leather chairs and flicked back the seat just for the heck of it. She would eat, Cate decided, then, once her luggage arrived, go and shower and maybe even have a sleep. She wasn't due to catch her connecting flight up to the Friday Islands until lunchtime the next day and Noah had given her directions to the headquarters of the Australian Eco Trust where he assured her she would be given food and a bed for the night.

'It's nothing smart, Cate,' Noah had said when he had called her just before she had boarded her flight to Bangkok. 'We eco-warriors don't waste money on material comforts.'

Cate stifled a snort, remembering the top of the range BMW he drove back in France and the designer grunge wear he was so fond of sporting at weekends.

'Miles, who runs the trust, is a great guy,' Noah had continued. 'Aussie, really cool. He was up at the sanctuary a few weeks ago – he often drops by when the fancy takes him. He's not usually around during the day, but Matthias will definitely be there. He co-ordinates all the protests. He's one smart dude. He'll look after you, maybe take you out and show you a few sights before you head up north to us. Tell you what, I'll text you his address and mobile number and I'll call and tell him you're on your way.'

Cate was jolted back to the present by a commotion at the entrance lobby of the lounge. She turned to see a large stack of leather luggage appearing on a trolley pushed by a very sweaty and harassed-looking porter, and oblivious to the quiet hush of the lounge, someone was talking in an Essex accent so loud that Cate could hear every word she was saying.

'Look, babe.' The voice rose even higher. 'What's going on? Are you telling me that the band still haven't arrived? I've been waiting for over an hour now. Can't you do something? Ring the pilot of their plane or something and find out when it's going to land.'

Cate stood up and peered over the teetering luggage. The tall woman was standing with her back to her, her platinum-blond hair almost luminescent against the low lighting. She was wearing a strapless sundress, which clung to her hourglass shape in the distinctively bold colours of a Versace design, and toweringly high gold roman sandals which accentuated her endlessly long legs.

It had been over three months since Cate had last seen her in the South of France but, even though back then her hair had been a shocking red, there was no mistaking her.

'Nancy!' Cate called out almost in disbelief. 'Nancy, what on earth are you doing here?'

The woman turned round, lifted up her giant sunglasses to reveal huge green eyes, and stared at Cate for a few seconds. Then she let out a shriek so loud that several dozing businessmen sat bolt upright in amazement.

'Cate? Babe!' she screamed, charging past the luggage and sending the top two cases plummeting down onto the thick pile carpet in the process. 'My God! It *is* you, babe. What on earth are *you* doing here?'

CHAPTER 2

Before she knew it, Cate had been enveloped in a huge hug followed by two lipsticked kisses planted firmly on each cheek. Nancy Kyle was clearly very pleased to see her.

'I'm on my way to see Michel,' Cate began. 'He's up north, working at a turtle sanctuary.'

'Is he, babe? Good for him.' Nancy plonked her long frame down into the seat next to Cate and helped herself to one of Cate's snacks. 'I hate being on my own in these places,' said the supermodel cheerfully. 'Full of sad business types. Never anyone fun.' She brightened up. 'But still, babe, you're here and my lovely new boyfriend will be too, any minute now.'

'Is that Lucas Black?' Cate asked. 'From that indie band – Black Noir?' As well as their texts, she had kept up with Nancy's colourful love life via the weekly celebrity magazines and her curiosity had been further piqued by the fact that Black Noir was rapidly becoming one of Cate's all-time favourite bands. She had every song on her iPod and was already planning to go and see them on their upcoming UK tour.

'You betcha.' Nancy pulled out a mirror and began expertly reapplying bright red lipstick to her wide, generous lips. 'He's a babe, babe. He's The One. Definitely The One. We're all going up to a fab island where Lucas is playing a birthday gig for some Arab billionaire sheikh dude. Lucas and the band were offered squillions to play. They've been recording in Bangkok and I was seeing some perfume people in LA so we all decided that we would meet in Sydney and fly up north together.'

As always when listening to Nancy talk about her exotic lifestyle, Cate's head began to whirl. 'Naomi C has been there and she was telling me all about it,' Nancy continued. 'This island is super-fab – it's got private spas, infinity pools, butlers, the works. Naomi said it made Richard Branson's Necker Island look like a First Choice all-inclusive.'

'What's the name of it?' asked Cate. 'I'm headed up that way too. I'm going to Snapper Bay, on the mainland just opposite the Friday Islands.'

'Really?' said Nancy. 'That sounds familiar, but you know me, geography isn't my strong point. Hey, babe!' she called to a hostess who was walking through the lounge. 'Bring us a map of Australia, there's a good girl. Quick as you can.'

Cate and Nancy poured over the leather-bound atlas that was fetched. 'Here's Snapper Bay,' said Cate, pointing to a stretch of sand at the end of a wooded peninsula, 'and there are the Friday Islands. They're really close.'

According to the map, the Friday Islands lay scattered in roughly parallel lines about four or five kilometres off the coastline. There were easily fifty or more, some tiny little specks in the vast ocean, others, Cate estimated, at least twenty or thirty kilometres in length.

She began reading off the names of the larger islands. 'Victoria Island, Albert Island, Edward Island, Elizabeth Island,' Cate recited. 'Gee, they like their royals out here. Plymouth Island, Portsmouth Island, Purbeck Island —'

'That's it!' Nancy reached down into her large Hermès bag and waved her travel itinerary in the air triumphantly. 'Purbeck Island, that's where we're going. We're flying up by private jet tomorrow to some weird-sounding airport – Passande, is it? I so can't wait to get there, kick back, relax, have a massage, watch the sun go down over a cocktail or two . . .'

Cate stared at the map and then at Nancy. 'Purbeck Island is one of the closest islands to shore and look, Snapper Bay is only about twenty kilometres from you over the water. You're there and I'm here. We're practically neighbours!'

'A-maze-ing!' Even Nancy was impressed by the coincidence. 'Hey, Cate, why don't you come out and visit me? You know, take a few days off from saving the whales and have some real luxury.' Nancy was on a roll now. 'And why don't you fly up with us on the plane tomorrow? Meet the guys in the band, have a bit of fun? In fact, if you wanted, you could even stay at our hotel tonight – I've got a massive suite with a fab pool, right on the waterfront by the opera house. Go on, it'll be cool – a great chance to catch up.' She lowered her voice. 'Between you and me, Lucas, well, he likes to hang with his band, drink beer, read books. I get a bit, well, you know . . .'

'Lonely?' Cate asked. Poor Nancy, she thought, she had a complete talent for picking the wrong type of guy for her.

'I guess. Bored too,' said Nancy glumly. Then she brightened up. 'Cate, you're one of my oldest friends now and it would be fab to hang out for a bit this holiday.'

'Thanks, Nancy, that's really generous of you,' said Cate, trying not to smile at the thought of someone she had known for only a few months calling her one of her oldest friends. In truth, she was genuinely touched by Nancy's generosity and was very tempted indeed. A night in a fabulous hotel versus kipping on a spare sofa in a grungy eco-den? It was, as Arthur would say, a no-brainer. But on the other hand, Cate had promised to meet up with Noah's mate Matthias, and he would be expecting her.

The sight of a porter pushing a trolley into the lobby told Cate that her luggage had finally arrived and she made up her mind.

'Nancy, I've already got a flight up with Quantas but I can't resist your private jet.' Cate grinned happily. 'And you try and stop me from visiting you on Purbeck Island. But I've promised to go and meet some friends of Michel's tonight. I don't want to be rude and bump them at the last minute. I'll call you later and get the flight times.'

'OK,' said Nancy. 'You've got my number. Oh and give my love to your dishy dad when you speak to him and your cute brother, Arthur. My boy Oak always talks about Arthur. Thinks he's some kind of god, the way he can do all that computer stuff. By the way, the nanny's bringing the kids over after the gig.'

'Well, I'll definitely come and see you if your lovely children are there too,' said Cate, giving her a quick hug goodbye. 'Make sure you tell them you saw me and that I was asking after them.

Now, I'm off to take a shower, otherwise I'm not going to be welcome anywhere.'

The mention of Arthur's name reminded Cate of his glum face as she broke the news that, for the first time ever, she and he wouldn't be spending Christmas together. Like the sweetie he was he hadn't tried to talk her out of it but, as usual, he couldn't resist giving her some advice. 'Take care out there. I've got some online mates in Australia and they all talk about how you have to be careful away from the cities. Snakes and spiders and getting lost in the bush and all . . .' As they'd said goodbye, Arthur had handed her a tiny bright red rectangle. 'A super-sensitive dongle that can use even a distant signal. Think you might need it,' was all he said.

'Thanks, Arthur.' Cate hadn't known whether to laugh or to cry at her brother's kindness. 'I'm gonna miss you so much.'

'Me too.' Arthur stared hard at Cate through his glasses, as if trying to imprint her face on his memory. 'You being in France all summer was bad enough but that was only a short plane ride away. Australia – that's just so far.'

'I know,' said Cate. 'I'm sorry. But I'm taking my laptop and with that boosted dongle we'll be able to Skype every day wherever I am – yes? And this time it's only for three weeks. I've got to be back in time for school next term.'

Half an hour later Cate was showered, refreshed and raring to see this new city. As she took her leave of the ever-smiling hostess, Nancy was nowhere to be seen.

Just then, there was a chaotic arrival of black-clad young men and various musical instruments all crowned by a hub-bub of English accents. Instantly Cate was forgotten as the hostess rushed to hold the door open for them. As she did so, Cate glimpsed a throng of teenage girls pushing up against the glass wall and heard the chants of 'Lu-cas, Lu-cas,' before the door was shut firmly in their faces.

Open-mouthed with starstruck admiration, Cate watched as the four members of Black Noir brushed themselves down, straightened their sunglasses and set off through the lobby and into the lounge as if they owned it. The lanky figure of lead guitarist and singer-songwriter Lucas Black was leading the way, and bringing up the rear was the red-haired drummer Pete Simmonds, known in celebrity magazine speak as the hell-raiser. As he sauntered past Cate, he lifted his Ray-Bans, looked her up and down and gave her a broad wink.

A few seconds later, Cate heard the familiar scream. 'Babe!' Nancy had obviously spotted her boyfriend. Cate grinned to herself and, taking a deep breath, slipped out through the doors into the throng of crying, screaming girls.

'Did you see him?' A girl with Lucas's name written across her forehead in black ink was clutching at Cate's arm. 'Did you see Lucas Black?'

'Can you get me in there?' asked another. 'I can pay you. A hundred bucks, and I'll give you my iPad. Straight up.'

Cate looked around at the anxious, hopeful faces and shook her head in bemusement at the fan frenzy. She liked Black Noir, but this was ridiculous. 'Sorry,' she said, as she pushed her way out to the blazing heat of the Australian sun. 'Got a bus to catch.'

CHAPTER 3

Cate queued patiently in the dusty heat for the buses to the city. She had stowed her luggage away in a locker in the first class lounge and was now travelling light, her rucksack containing just enough for an overnight stay, and, of course, her beloved running gear.

As the blue and white bus clanked and ground its way into the city, Cate looked around her avidly, trying to acclimatise to this new world. At first it seemed weirdly familiar. The cars were driving on the same side of the road as they did in the UK and the dual carriageway was virtually identical to any back home.

But there the similarities ended. Giant eucalyptus trees towered above brightly coloured parakeets, which were clinging at bizarre angles to the spindly branches. Enormous bright green cacti lined the roads, along with trees bearing strange-looking spiky leaves and enormous fat flowers that curled like giant hands against the vivid blue sky. Even the grass on the verges seemed different somehow, more coarse, less lush.

From the electric blue of the sky and burnt red of the soil, to the pinks, purples and blues of the bougainvillea blossoms which ran riot over fences and up walls, everything seemed to be imbued with vivid colour, like a child's painting of a summer's day. Cate, starved of warmth and colour as she had been for the last few months, felt as if she had been transported not just across the world, but to another planet entirely.

As if to emphasise the point, out of the corner of her eye Cate suddenly spotted a flash of brown fur leaping easily from some scrubland and out along the kerb for a few metres before disappearing again. A kangaroo, thought Cate excitedly. Just here, on the street. Awesome. Now she knew she really was in Australia.

All around her people were striking up conversations with total strangers, swapping stories of endless flights, travel tips, and asking about plans. At every stop the driver shouted out the name of the destination and waited patiently while people got on and off, cracking jokes with his passengers. It was a far cry from London, Cate thought, where people sat in silence on public transport and even making eye contact with some-one was considered to be borderline weird.

No sooner had she thought that than a couple of teenage girls sitting with enormous backpacks on their laps opposite Cate, smiled at her.

'Where are you headed?' The girl nearest to Cate spoke with a mid-western American twang. 'You travelling on your own? We're going to a hostel near Bondi – you'd be more than welcome to join us.'

'Thanks, but I'm visiting friends. I'm off to the Parramatta Road. According to my directions I get off at Circular Quay and change buses there.'

'The Parramatta Road?' She looked at her guidebook, frowning.

Cate smiled at them ruefully. 'It's just for one night,' she said. 'Then I'm headed up north to the Friday Islands.'

'Nice,' said the other girl. 'We'll maybe see you there. Once we've done Sydney and Melbourne and seen the Aussie tennis Open.' She pointed out of the window. 'Circular Quay. All change.'

The bus pulled to a halt and the hydraulic doors swished open. Cate's body was still insisting that it was the middle of the night, but she thought she should get something to eat, and she was desperate to at least take a quick look at the harbour and its famous landmarks while she was there.

Waving goodbye to the Americans, she followed the smell of the sea coming in on the light breeze, and headed down towards the water, leaving the city skyscrapers and the office workers behind her. A hundred metres later, Cate stopped dead still in shocked wonder. There, looming above her, was the awesome structure of Sydney Harbour Bridge, the metal framework glinting in the sunlight, the perfect archway spanning over one thousand metres of water. As if this wasn't spectacular enough, to her right stood the Opera House, rising out of the water like a shimmering space-age sailing ship.

To see these two icons in real life was incredible, like finally meeting a world famous celebrity in the flesh. 'Excuse me,' she said to a young Japanese couple. 'Could you take some pictures of me on my phone?'

She would send the photographs to Louisa and to several other of her friends and family as well when she got back to the bus terminal. They were going to die with envy, she thought wickedly.

It was a different crowd on the bus out west to Parramatta. No tourists now, just a few gum-chewing young mums with babies in pushchairs and the odd pensioner quietly reading the paper. Cate got out her phone and composed a polite text to Matthias to tell him she was on her way. The bus passed through the central shopping district, the streets crammed with chic-looking boutiques and vast department stores, the windows looking faintly ridiculous with their Christmas displays of snow and reindeer in the shimmering heat.

Soon the shops and office blocks had been left behind and the monotony of the wide, straight road was broken only by a variety of fast food outlets and car lots. It was a depressing sight, and Cate found it hard to believe that the splendour of Sydney city centre was just a few kilometres away.

The lots began to space out, the odd bungalow appeared and down the side streets Cate could see rows of terraced houses. The bus stopped and started, the young mothers climbed off, no one got on and soon Cate was one of the last few people left on board.

She checked the address. *128 Tremlott St, Parramatta Road.* 'It's the stop after the Big Benny Burger outlet,' the driver had told her.

Just as Cate was wondering if she had missed her stop, the driver caught her eye in the mirror and nodded to her. 'Tremlott Street,' he said shortly and pulled the wheel sharply to the left.

Cate headed for the side road where a dirty sign confirmed she was in the right place. She glanced down at her phone but there was no reply from Matthias yet. She hoped he had remembered that she was coming.

There was no pavement here, just a verge that had once been all grass but now, at the height of summer, only a few sturdy clumps of coarse grass remained, clinging bravely to the hard-packed reddish brown soil. The houses had seen better days. Some just needed a coat of paint, others with broken window frames and tiles missing from the roof looked like they needed a major overhaul.

The further away from the main road she went, the larger the buildings became, some two or even three storeys high. The gardens were wider too, separated by fences and hedges to give more privacy and there were even names on some of the gates – Avalon, Good Rest, Holly Cottage – that hinted at a once genteel past for this now unkempt neighbourhood.

Finally she reached the peeling gate of number 128. It was a large brick house, three storeys high with a steep sided roof. The wooden veranda, which ran along the entire front of the house was decorated in a patchy, sullen grey, sections of it hanging at a dangerously steep angle. Several windows had been broken and boarded up.

The drive was empty, but parked outside on the road was a black Japanese saloon car with blacked-out windows.

Perspiring in the dense heat, Cate thought longingly of Nancy's harbour-side suite. She could be by the pool now, lying under the cool shade of a parasol, wearing her treasured Maaji bikini and sipping a fruit cocktail.

Cate made up her mind. She would go in, say hello, but

make an excuse about being unable to stay the night and head back to the city instead.

She pushed open the rickety gate. The garden was large, the nearest neighbours a good twenty metres away to either side and the high hedges gave the house a withdrawn and solitary feel. The front door was covered in graffiti sprayed in a vivid red paint. *Ferals out*, one slogan howled. *Rich scum go home*, ranted another, scrawled roughly alongside a primitive portrayal of a hangman's noose.

She was just about to knock when she noticed a printed sign telling callers to go around the side of the house for *security reasons* and headed off in the direction of the arrow.

A few concrete steps led up to a narrow wooden door on the frame of which was bolted a metal security entry code pad. She pressed the red entrance button and up above her a small security camera whirred and clicked into action, pointing its long lens towards her face.

There was silence. Cate tried the buzzer again, then thumped loudly on the door. Still getting no response, she walked to a nearby shuttered window, banged on it and shouted. Somewhere, in a house further down the street a dog began to bark, the only living sound in the stillness of the afternoon heat.

She pulled her phone from her pocket and rang Matthias's number. She listened intently, and from somewhere inside the house could hear the faint sound of a ringtone that carried on until she cut the call.

Strange. Noah had sounded so certain Matthias would be there, and according to him these activists were glued to their phones – they were a lifeline keeping in touch with

31

their network across the world and allowing them to organise rallies and demos at a moment's notice.

She shrugged. Perhaps he was in the bath, or asleep, or had his headphones on. Or maybe even he had simply forgotten Cate was coming, gone out and left his phone behind by accident.

The front door only had a swipe card access point, and was edged in reinforced steel. The large metal hinges looked as if they wouldn't give way to a battering ram. Cate gazed up at the windows at either side of the door and realised, with a start, that they too were shuttered up. This place was like a fortress.

The silence was unnerving. No sound from the houses around her now, no traffic on the street outside, not even birdsong in the trees overhead. It was spooky and it was making her anxious.

Suddenly she heard a noise coming from inside the house. Two sharp sounds, one after the other, like a hand clap, then silence again. Deep down, she knew something was wrong.

Cate froze and listened closely, but there was nothing more to hear. Her heart was racing and she couldn't help feeling uneasy.

'Only a fool ignores their gut instinct,' Marcus, her contact at IMIA, had always said. 'That's the first thing they teach you in subterfuge training. Listen to what your gut is telling you, treat it like another sense and use it in conjunction with your sight and hearing, smell and touch to evaluate the risk.'

Cate moved around the house, sizing it up, looking for any chink in its armour that might allow her to look inside. But to her frustration every single window was blocked.

She reached the far side of the house and walked right into

jungle. Some sort of vine with long, drooping leaves had gone completely wild, covering most of the walls and windows, forming skinny bridges between the house and the branches of the eucalyptus trees which overhung the path to next door's garden.

It was hopeless. There was no way in. But just as Cate was about to give up, one small window up on the second floor caught her eye. Partially obscured by the vine, a corner of glass had been broken away. It was her only chance.

She reached into the rucksack for her tracksuit bottoms, pulling them up underneath her skirt to give her legs as much protection from the rough branches as possible, and swapped her sandals for trainers. Ready for action, Cate eyed the tree nearest the window. Taking a deep breath and giving thanks for the years she had spent climbing trees as a kid, she reached into the branches and pulled herself up. The branches were surprisingly strong and, in less than a minute, Cate was ensconced in the upper branches of the trees directly opposite the broken window.

She looked curiously through the window into a small room containing just a low couch with a sleeping bag on it and a small sink. Pretty basic and not very clean by the look of it.

The window was nearly two metres away from her and she was a good five metres in the air. Now all she had to do was work out how to get in without killing herself.

As she hesitated, Cate heard a door slam and the noise of heavy footsteps coming along the path. Looking down between the leaves, she saw two men appear from the back of the house. They pushed their way through the vegetation, spreading the vines apart, peering into the undergrowth.

'I thought I heard someone at the door.' The man was speaking Spanish – one of the many languages Cate knew. 'We have to check it out.'

The men were standing directly beneath her now. Cate froze, hardly daring to breathe, thankful for the curtain of vegetation that made her all but invisible. As quietly as she could, she slipped her hand into her pocket and pressed the *off* button on her phone. These men could be perfectly harmless but better to be cautious.

She couldn't see much, just the top of their heads. Both were heavily tanned and balding, one with a scar running from the middle of his head down around to his left ear. The other man stood for a few seconds to light a cigarette and she saw his right hand. It was burnt, the two middle fingers missing and, despite the heat of the afternoon, Cate felt suddenly cold.

They gave one last look up and down the alleyway before moving off to the front of the house. A couple of minutes later she heard a car start up and drive off at speed.

What was it she had heard? A crack of a whip, the slap of a hand hitting a face? Maybe her imagination was running away with her, but those two men had been real enough.

Cate's mind began to race. Perhaps Matthias was still inside, injured and in trouble.

Reaching above her head, she grasped a couple of the thicker vines that had spread from the house to the trees and tested her weight on them. One snapped and she grabbed another, which instantly felt firmer, and pushed herself off from the branch with both feet. Her swing propelled her towards the broken window, the thick soles of her trainers hit the glass, instantly shattering the rest of it, the momentum carrying her through to the wooden floorboards on the other side.

She raced across the room and opened the door cautiously. As soon as she did, she smelt it. At first she thought it was the smell of a cigarette, but it was too strong, too powerful for that. She peered out carefully onto the landing and, to her horror, she saw thick tendrils of smoke. Fire!

Every fibre of Cate's body was telling her to get out of there, call the fire brigade and leave it to them. But she knew that by the time help arrived the whole house could be up in flames. If Matthias was in there and in trouble she would never forgive herself for leaving him. She had to act now.

She reached into her rucksack, brought out her clean T-shirt and headed to the small sink in the bedroom, wetting it thoroughly before winding it around her nose and mouth. She took the main stairs two at a time down to the ground floor, all the while shouting for Matthias at the top of her voice.

The source of the fire wasn't too hard to spot. At the bottom of the heavily barricaded front door, was a pile of smouldering rags, the deadly smoke rising up the stairs towards her.

A curtain was hanging from a rail over the back of the door and above that a thick wooden beam supported an open ceiling which reached up to the roof of the house. Once that curtain caught fire, thought Cate in horror, there would be no stopping it.

When Cate had been in Serbia with her father she had witnessed a house being torched by locals; the owner was rumoured to have collaborated with the enemy during the civil war. The fire had taken a few minutes to take hold but then, like a mythical monster awakening from its lair, the flames had exploded into every crevice of the building, the owner and his family lucky to get out alive. Cate knew she didn't have much time.

She tugged on the curtain, desperately trying to move it away from the flames. Cate felt her legs scorching, the soles of her feet hot through the trainers, gave one last despairing yank at the curtain and felt it come away from the door.

Struggling to breathe, her eyes watering in the smoke, she threw the heavy material down over the flames and then ripping off her trainers, began to beat down on the curtain.

For several minutes she worked frantically, pushing the material down, cutting off the oxygen supply to the flames each time they reappeared, coughing and choking as the smoke rose in gusts. Then the flames finally died out, and the smoke began to clear.

Cate sat back on her heels panting both from relief and from the sheer effort. Now she needed water to really finish the job off. There had to be a kitchen around somewhere.

She stood up slowly, wearily, and turned to look back down along the corridor. As she did her heart gave a massive jump, and she let out a yelp of fear and surprise. There, just a few metres away from her, at the end of a corridor, was a young man, tied to a wooden chair. His head lolled from one side to the other and tears streamed from his half closed eyes. His nose was bloodied and bruised, a rag was stuffed into his mouth and on his face was a look of sheer terror.

CHAPTER 4

Cate moved slowly towards him, almost smelling the fear coming from his tensed-up body and, as she reached out to touch him, his bright blue eyes opened wide and stared into hers with a mixture of relief and pain.

'Matthias?' she whispered.

He nodded.

Cate pulled sharply at the thick black tape that was holding the gag in place. Matthias breathed in deeply then spat and coughed, a wracking cough that shook his whole body. Cate reached into her rucksack and pulled out a bottle of water, which she held to this mouth. He tipped his head back greedily, the water dribbling down his chin and into his long hair as he drank.

'Am I pleased to see you!' His accent was Scandinavian – Danish, maybe Swedish. 'Whoever you are.'

'I'm Cate,' said Cate warily. 'Cate Carlisle, Noah's friend.' She reached into her pocket. 'And I'm calling the police.'

'No!' he shouted, vehemently between gasps and coughs. 'No police. No! Wait!'

Cate looked at him in astonishment.

'Please, just get me out of this chair. In my pocket, there's a penknife. You can use it to cut me free.'

Reluctantly Cate put down her phone and slid her hand around the back of Matthias's broad torso and into his pocket. The penknife was tiny but sharp and made quick work of the nylon rope.

'Right,' she said, as she finished her work, 'take it easy, and don't get up straight away. I've got to get some water on that fire just to be sure it's out for good. Where's the kitchen?'

'Behind us, at the end of the corridor,' said Matthias, rubbing hard on his wrists and ankles. He stood up gingerly, and almost immediately fell against the wall. Cate rushed to his side and he slipped one arm around her shoulders, leaning his weight onto her. He was well over six feet to Cate's five foot five, and Cate winced and staggered slightly under his weight as he grinned down at her ruefully.

'Sorry, Cate,' he said gently. 'That's a fine way to treat the girl who saved my life. Go on, I'm fine now. Get that water.'

Cate hesitated and then nodded, sliding away from under him and heading down the corridor to find the kitchen. Like the hallway, the room was in semi-darkness and Cate had to feel along the wall by the door for the light switch.

Light from a single bulb revealed a large but makeshift affair, an old-fashioned cooker set into a tiled recess, some plastic pine cupboards on the wall and, in place of work surfaces, a thin pine table that by the look of the cutlery upon it evidently doubled as an eating as well as cooking surface. Noah had been right:

creature comforts obviously didn't mean much to these people.

Cate dashed over to a large metal sink which stood under the boarded-up window and ran the taps, filling a bucket which appeared to be there to catch drips from a leak. She ran back down the corridor and poured it carefully over the embers, taking grim pleasure from the resulting hiss.

Suddenly she heard the sound of a heavy door slamming somewhere in the house behind her, then footsteps running towards her, a deep Australian voice exclaiming in surprise. 'My God! What the hell happened here?'

The man had thick, curly ginger hair, and a look of horror on his pale face. He surveyed the scene in silence – what was left of the curtain, the smoke-blackened paintwork and the water which was now running down the hallway.

He turned to Cate. She noticed his hands were shaking. 'Who are you? And where is Matthias?'

As if on cue, the blond man appeared. He had cleaned himself up, changed his shirt and washed the blood from his face. Only a slight limp gave away the ordeal he had just gone through.

The ginger-headed man rushed towards him. 'Matthias, buddy, thank God. What happened?'

Matthias gestured towards Cate. 'She saved my life,' he said simply. 'This girl saved my life.'

Two sets of eyes turned towards Cate.

'I'm a friend of Noah's,' she said. 'I thought you were expecting me. I was looking for a way in when I heard strange sounds from inside. Then those two burly guys came out. I was worried about Matthias so I broke in.'

Matthias's face relaxed into a smile. 'I'm glad you did, Cate.

And I'm sorry. I forgot I was expecting visitors. But under the circumstances I hope you can forgive my rudeness.'

He gazed at the remnants of the fire. 'They burst in and took me by surprise,' he said quietly. 'They tied me to that chair. For hours.' He rubbed his face carefully. 'I wouldn't have had a chance if that fire had got going.'

'I got a warning.' The ginger man was almost talking to himself. 'An anonymous phone call. It said I had to get back to HQ within ten minutes.' He swallowed hard. 'I must have broken every speed restriction in Sydney. I just didn't know what I was going to find.'

There was silence, then Matthias spoke again. 'Cate, this is Miles Finlay.' He made a mock bow towards him. 'Long-time eco-warrior and the esteemed leader of the Australasian Eco Trust. Miles Finlay meet Cate Carlisle, the girl who rescued me and who is now, not surprisingly, very keen to call the police.'

There was a sharp intake of breath from Miles. 'Listen, Cate,' he said urgently. 'You can't. I mean, if I was in your place I would think the same. But please, please listen to me first. The eco network, well, we often do things that aren't quite within the law, bend the rules a bit – always to do good, you understand, but sometimes the police don't quite see it like that. If you report this . . . event, it will be a great opportunity for them to find out more about us. They will come to the house like a swarm of bees and they will go through our computers . . . Nothing will be left unturned.'

'Miles, Matthias,' said Cate, looking from one to another. 'I *don't* understand. Some people break into your house and set fire to it with someone in it and you're worried about the police? These guys have to be stopped.' She looked Matthias straight in the eye. 'They could have killed you. What if they do it to someone else?'

'That won't happen. They're not after anyone else,' Miles said. 'It was a warning to us, to the Eco Trust. Think about it. If they really wanted to kill Matthias they wouldn't have sent me that message to come here. Whoever it is just wanted to scare us.'

'Well, they certainly succeeded in scaring me,' said Cate, folding her arms. 'And you looked pretty freaked out to me as well, Matthias.'

The two men looked at each other.

'The thing is, Cate,' said Miles slowly, 'there are names on our computers and in our files of brave people who work in government and newspapers all over the world, who tip us off and help us out at great risk to themselves. People who work for our sworn enemies, like the whaling companies, the rogue oil companies, the corporations that persistently ignore all the environmental and moral rules that the rest of us take for granted. If the police get hold of that information our network will be finished, and so will the careers of a stack of really good, decent people. Please, Cate. Think of them.'

A year ago, before her experiences in the South of France, Cate wouldn't have hesitated. She would have rung the police and reported an attempted murder. But now she had learnt that things weren't always that simple, that sometimes doing the right thing meant bending the rules.

She blew out her cheeks, buying time and then looked at Miles, who was gazing at her with a worried expression. 'Please Cate,' he said. 'Don't wreck years of hard work over one incident.'

41

At the penthouse suite of the Ridgeway Boutique Hotel, the party was in full flow. The glass doors, which ran the length of the long sitting room had been pulled wide open to provide access to the huge balcony and the large marble swimming pool that took centre stage within it. Chinese lanterns swung in the light breeze, their gentle red glow standing out against the gathering dusk. Cate had been let in by a butler and now stood taking in the city view, breathing the jasmine-scented air, the events of the afternoon a million miles away.

Nancy, resplendent in a bright red string bikini, was dangling her long tanned legs into the turquoise water. Lucas was sitting cross-legged beside her, jeans rolled up above his bony knees. He was strumming a guitar, seemingly oblivious to the R & B music belting out from some invisible outdoor speakers. Nancy, her sunglasses pushed up over her head, and a pile of celebrity magazines next to her, looked bored. Although the two of them were sitting closely together, it seemed to Cate as if they were a million miles apart.

At the side of the pool was a swim-up bar, with a barman expertly juggling bottles and glasses to the delight of his audience. The pool was packed with the other members of Black Noir and some gorgeous Aussie beach-babe types whom Cate recognised from her favourite Australian TV soap opera.

The balcony jutted out over the water providing an utterly breathtaking view of the harbour. People had finished work and were now making their way to their sailing boats, jet skis and surfboards. The water was crammed full of sails of various different shapes, sizes and colours, the gently ruffling breeze

42

enough to send them briskly on their way.

Cate could have stood watching for hours but Nancy was waving frantically at her to come over. Cate grinned back and she picked her way through the abandoned towels and wooden sun loungers to greet her.

'Hey, Cate, great to see you!' Nancy stood up, pulling a gold-threaded shawl around her waist and tying it into a sarong. As Cate reached her she sniffed. 'God, Cate, what have you been up to? You smell like you've been standing over a bonfire.' Her gaze travelled down to Cate's denim skirt and T-shirt and winced. 'And, babe, I know you like to rock the casual look but this might be taking it a bit too far.'

'Nancy, I'm so sorry.' Cate was mortified, the more so because Lucas Black was within hearing distance.

After she had agreed to secrecy about the fire, Cate had done her best to clean herself up, washing her face and hands and rinsing out her hair in the filthy little bathroom at the Eco HQ. Miles and Matthias had run her back into town in Miles's battered old car, Matthias insisting on stopping at a sports shop to replace her ruined running gear.

'Thanks for everything, Cate,' Matthias had said, as the pair stood outside Nancy's hotel. He hesitated and then gave her a massive hug. 'I still can't believe what you did today. You're an amazing girl.'

'What will you do?' asked Cate. 'You can't be thinking of staying here in Sydney? What if whoever was after you decides to have another go?'

He shook his head. 'You're right, this was a pretty heavy scene and I'm not that keen on hanging around for a repeat. I'm going back to Europe for a while, just until things calm down.

My folks haven't seen me for a few months so they'll be thrilled to have me back for Christmas. I can't persuade Miles to leave though.'

Miles stuck his head out of the window. 'Hurry up, Matthias,' he said. 'We've got work to do.' He nodded to Cate and put out his hand to shake hers. 'Hey, Cate,' he said. 'Respect. Tell Noah I'll call him as soon as. And maybe I'll see you one day up at Snapper Bay.'

Nancy wandered off to join the party at the bar and Cate sat down by the pool. When someone sat down next to her it took her a while to register it was Lucas Black! When she did she felt like pinching herself. Lucas Black was one of the hottest rock stars around, an ex-soldier who had fought in the Middle East. He had been commended for bravery but gave it all up to become a musician, reaching number one with his first record, a love song written to a beautiful Iraqi girl who had died in suicide bomb attack.

Since then his career had gone stratospheric, and now he was pictured in just about every celebrity magazine, week after week, with a succession of gorgeous models and actresses.

Cate was itching to take a picture of them together with her phone and send it to her friends but somehow she didn't quite dare.

'What's going on, Cate?' Shocked to be spoken to, she looked up to find Lucas staring at her, his sharp brown eyes boring into hers. Close up, his shiny black hair and prominent nose gave him the look of a crow, slightly scary, missing nothing. For a few seconds she found herself wondering if he was always that intense and if so, how he and Nancy found a balance between their two opposite personalities. 'Nancy said you were hanging out with some eco-warriors today.'

Cate nodded, suddenly tongue-tied.

'I'm guessing from the look on your face and the state of your clothes that you didn't have the best time with them, right?' He plucked a small tune on his guitar, looking at her thoughtfully. 'It's none of my business but I've got a kid sister not much younger than you and I'd like to think someone would give her a word of advice when she needed it.' He paused, choosing his words carefully. 'These eco-warriors like to think they're always on the side of right and I know most of them mean well. But some are just in it to cause trouble and they don't give a damn about who or what gets hurt.'

Cate began to protest, but Lucas shrugged. 'Whatever, Cate. Feel free to disagree. All I'm saying is, don't take anyone on face value. And watch your back.'

Cate woke early, stretched and pulled open the shutters. She'd started falling asleep halfway through the evening meal with Nancy and the Black Noir members the previous day, but was so excited to be there with them that she had forced herself to stay up late anyway.

Before she went to bed she had tried to Skype her family but there was no reply. It would have been late morning in Switzerland and Cate suspected that they would already be on the slopes. For a few minutes, she desperately wanted to see them, wishing that she could somehow teleport herself across the world. She imagined racing her dad down a black run, throwing snowballs at Arthur and going window-shopping with Monique.

But now, after a deep, refreshing sleep, Cate felt cheerful

and excited again about the days ahead. For half an hour or so, she lay watching Sydney harbour coming to life then, at six a.m., she got out of bed, splashed her face and brought out her brand new running gear. She grabbed her belt bag, chucked in her phone and bottle of water and crept out of the penthouse and down to the hotel lobby where a young night porter sleepily waved her off.

Cate loved running, and found it the best way to explore new places. She marvelled at the vivid colours she passed, the bright blue jacaranda trees, the deep green tropical ferns and the neon colours of the birds that flashed and darted around as she ran.

Despite the early hour, a few shops were already open. Cate could smell coffee and bacon coming from a café, and the mouth-watering aromas made her stomach grumble. She breathed deeply, enjoying the feeling of crisp, clean air against her face and bare arms.

She reached the water's edge and looked down over the stone wall into the harbour. The clear water was completely calm, lapping quietly at the flat stones that edged the wall. Up ahead, a ferry steamed past, a few early bird commuters out on deck clutching coffees and newspapers. The searing heat of the day lay ahead and for now it was the perfect temperature to be out.

Cate sprinted for a kilometre or so and then, momentarily exhausted, she sat down on a park bench and lazily watched an olive green helicopter circle overhead before dropping in to land close by. Mindful of the ever-strengthening sun, Cate reached into the small belt bag for her suncream. As she did she noticed her phone flashing with a message from Arthur.

Interesting fact number one about Snapper Bay. See link. Xxxx

Cate grinned to herself. She could just imagine Arthur sitting in his ski chalet burrowing about on the internet for facts and figures about the place where his sister was going. He had probably Google Earthed it already as well. She followed the link. It was a report from a newspaper called the *Friday Island Herald* dated a few weeks earlier.

> *Last night an attempt by a mystery consortium to buy the expired lease for the coastline north of Passande Airport running up to and including Snapper Bay was turned down by the Friday Islands Local Authority.*
>
> *The consortium's bid was largely anonymous and was applied for via a firm of local solicitors. All bids for the lease were confidential but our exclusive information suggests that the anonymous bid was around twenty times larger than that of the Australian Government, the previous leaseholder.*
>
> *On a presentation to the hearing, a spokesman for the consortium said that, as well as a very generous offer, his clients had also made substantial guarantees for the preservation of the coastline.*
>
> *However, the Local Authority was adamant that the Australian Government, with its record of protecting and conserving the unique beauty of their coastline, should continue as the leaseholder. The motion was passed unanimously.*

Good for them, thought Cate, as she finished the report. How brilliant that they put their environment before making money.

Back at the hotel the young porter had gone, replaced by a

middle-aged man whose formal attire perfectly matched his slicked-back hair and smooth skin. Cate asked for her room key and as he reached for it he pulled out a note from her pigeonhole.

'You are Cate Carlisle?' he said. 'There is a message here for you to go to the roof garden as soon as possible. Lucas Black is doing a photographic shoot right now and he wants you to help him.'

Cate blew her cheeks out. Lucas Black asking for *her* help! 'I'll just grab some food.'

The man smiled at her. 'Madam, I happen to know that a breakfast buffet was delivered to the roof terrace not less than ten minutes ago. Take that lift over there and press the button for the twenty-fifth floor. When it opens turn to the left and then left again. You can't miss it.'

Cate stepped into the lift and hit the button for the top floor. Within seconds, the doors were opening on to the roof terrace. She turned left as instructed and, a few metres on, stopped in her tracks. It was quiet. Far too quiet. Cate had been expecting to see bustle and activity, hear voices shouting instructions from the shoot, maybe even spot the odd band member wandering around eating breakfast. She sniffed. The porter had said that breakfast had just been sent up and yet all she could smell was sea air and a faint smell of diesel fumes.

She was puzzled now and slightly wary. Perhaps it was some kind of practical joke, the band having a good laugh at her as they ate their breakfast round the pool just a few storeys below.

She walked up to the entrance of the terrace then poked her head cautiously around it. Her heart turned a somersault.

There in front of her was the olive green helicopter she had seen flying over her just a few minutes earlier. Standing by it, looking tense and alert, were two beefy men, both sporting short back and sides haircuts and dressed in anonymous green boiler suits. They looked tough, fit, not to be messed with.

Inside the front window of the unmarked chopper a pilot sat still, his helmet and goggles just about discernable through the dark tinted windows. Ready for a quick take off, Cate thought with a shudder. Then she heard one of the men talking.

'If she is not here soon we'll go and look for her,' he said. 'They told us she might be tricky.'

The other man laughed. 'She's a sixteen-year-old kid,' he said. 'How can she be a problem for us?'

The first man shrugged. 'Anton said he saw her go into the lift. So where is she now?'

Cate flattened herself against the warm wall, her heart racing. Someone had set a trap and she had walked right into it.

CHAPTER 5

Cate raced through her options. She could try the lift but she had heard it whirring downwards as she left and by the time it came back the men would have found her. There were bound to be some stairs, but she didn't know where they were.

Her heart began to race. She reached into her pocket for her phone. She couldn't call for help – she would be heard. She considered texting Nancy – but the supermodel probably wouldn't even be awake. She sighed and switched her phone to silent. For now she was on her own.

She edged back towards the lift – her only option. She pressed the button, her heart pounding as she heard the whirr of the lift coming up towards her. Cate looked around, searching in vain for anything she could use to protect herself. There was nothing. The corridor was sterile, immaculate. In desperation she looked down at her clothes. Her hands brushed against her belt and within seconds she had whipped it off, wound the thin leather around her wrist and clasped the buckle in her fist, the point protruding through her fingers. It wasn't perfect but it was better than nothing. She looked down through the glass panels and could see the top of the lift just seconds away from her. There was a quiet beep and the doors swooped open.

'There you are, Cate Carlisle,' said the porter from inside the lift, his pale face and black outfit giving him the look of an undertaker. 'We thought you'd got lost. We can't have that now, can we?'

Cate stared up at him, her heart pounding partly with fear, partly with anger. Whatever these men wanted with her, she wasn't going to give herself up without a fight.

Still staring into the dark eyes of the man in front of her she brought her right hand up hard. Expecting a blow, the man brought his left hand up to stop her, leaving his face open and defenceless as the buckle slammed into the corner of his eye. He grunted, instinctively bringing his hands up to his face and Cate, seizing the opportunity, brought her knee up hard into his groin. He bent double, gasping for breath and with a strength she didn't know she possessed, Cate grabbed his thick hair and rammed his head hard against the inside of the lift. The man groaned and fell down onto the floor in a heap. Cate pressed the ground floor button and, just as the doors were closing, stepped quickly out of the lift.

She silently turned right, and right again to get back out into the roof garden away from the men. Beside her was the back of the lift shaft. She looked up at its roof, took a few steps back, then ran and leapt at the wall and somehow her fingers found the rough edges of the roof. She hung there painfully for a few seconds before she pulled herself up half dragging, half rolling herself onto the hot white surface. She lay flat on her stomach, panting quietly, scanning the terrace below.

She could see the top of the helicopter and one man talking on a mobile. He looked angry. Had the porter called him? He finished the call and motioned to the other man with hand signals that she had seen British soldiers use.

She watched as they split up, each going one way around the lift shaft. Cate held her breath, praying they wouldn't look up.

Who on earth would want her so badly that they would send three men and a helicopter to capture her?

She slid her phone out of her pocket. She had to get help somehow. Nancy. The police. Anyone.

Suddenly, the phone vibrated and a message flashed up. It was from Marcus at the IMIA.

Cate was confused. Could the man smell trouble from the other side of the world? She opened the message and nearly dropped the phone.

Cate, get down from your perch and come for a helicopter ride.

Cate looked at the message again and then back over at the helicopter. The pilot had taken his helmet off and was standing by the helicopter, waving at her cheerfully.

'Marcus!' she yelled, half angry, half relieved. 'What the hell are you playing at?'

'Well?' shouted Cate crossly, trying to make herself heard over the noise of the helicopter as it flew swiftly out over the blue water of the harbour. 'What's all this about? Honestly, Marcus, you frightened me to death back there.'

Marcus turned to her, a huge grin on his face. 'All in good

time, Cate. But I must say, I was impressed with the way you dealt with poor old Luigi. He's got one heck of a headache and he'll have a real shiner in the morning.'

Cate scowled at him. 'You set me up – with your own men. Don't even ask me to work that one out, Marcus.'

'Nearly there now,' Marcus said, ignoring her grumbles as he lowered the chopper so that it skimmed the top of the water. He pointed up ahead. 'Your destination awaits you, madam.'

As the helicopter circled the small, diamond-shaped island, Cate picked out a few long, low buildings amongst the densely packed trees. The corrugated iron roofs and faded tarmac squares gave the game away. *Army quarters*, thought Cate, sitting up straight in her chair.

The helicopter dropped gently downwards, landing with a jolt on a small patch of ground. As the blades slowed to a stop, Cate could see a man standing, still and watchful, in the doorway of a shabby prefabricated hut. His dark skin, bold nose and squat powerful body weren't that distinctive, but Cate recognised him immediately from the way he stood. Even from that distance she could sense his power, his authority, his utter self-confidence. What on earth was Henri Sorenzki, the head of the International Maritime Intelligence Agency, doing on an island in Sydney Harbour?

Cate undid her harness, pushed the door open, stepped down onto the hot concrete and marched angrily over to him. 'Henri,' she said, ignoring his outstretched hand. 'What's the deal? You haven't sent three heavies and a helicopter to get me because you're missing my company. And why heavies in the first place? Just the helicopter and a polite request would have been far more effective.'

'Now then, Cate, that's a fine way to greet an old friend,' said Henri. He was dressed immaculately as always, in perfectly pressed navy blue chinos and a dazzlingly white shirt and blue tie, his tanned face inscrutable behind his sunglasses. 'Welcome to Diamond Island. I told you when we said *au revoir* last summer that we would meet again soon and, well, here we are, meeting again soon.' His voice took on a mock hurt tone. 'I thought you'd be pleased to see me.'

Cate glared at him. 'You haven't answered my questions.'

Henri looked at her calmly, then nodded. 'OK. I'll tell you why. We wanted to know whether you still had the guts that you showed us last summer, the ability to handle yourself in certain situations. After all, you might have returned to that girls' school of yours and gone soft on us.'

Marcus had caught up with her and Cate looked at both men calculatingly. If she had learnt one thing from her adventures with Marcus and Henri last summer, it was that there was never any point in losing your cool with them.

She took a deep breath. 'Well, now you know. So you've had your question answered. And now I can go back to my friends and get on with enjoying my holiday. Marcus – do you mind?' She turned towards the helicopter.

Henri looked at Marcus. 'She hasn't mellowed, has she?' he said. 'Is that good or bad?'

'Good – I think,' said Marcus, grinning. 'Look, Cate, before you go charging back to the mainland the least we can do is offer you some breakfast. I hear you missed out on yours.'

Cate, who was already walking towards the helicopter, stopped in her tracks. She was starving, it was true. She also had to admit that despite her bravado, she was curious, very curious. The IMIA had brought her here for a reason and now, dammit, she had to know what it was.

She looked down at her watch. It was only just gone ten o'clock and she doubted that Nancy had even registered that she had left the penthouse. 'It had better be a good breakfast,' she said.

After the bright sunshine, the interior of the brick shed was dark and gloomy, the atmosphere cool, almost clammy. It didn't help that the windows were tiny and placed high up in the eaves, any natural light more than overpowered by the fluorescent striplights, which seemed to pick out the stained paintwork and tattered linoleum on the floor.

'It's the damp,' said Henri, noticing Cate's expression as she looked around. 'This place was built on a swamp.' He slapped at a mosquito that was buzzing around his face. 'But beggars can't be choosers. It's really good of the Aussie military to lend us this place at such short notice.'

But if the surroundings were shabby, the equipment was clearly state of the art. Tiny computers with large flat screens sat underneath a row of huge screens, one of which was showing a continuous loop of shots of Diamond Island, from the air, from the sea and even from inside the huts.

On the opposite side of the shed, radar and sonar equipment were bleeping gently as they surveyed the surrounding waters. A printer was spewing out an endless stream of paper covered in what looked like map co-ordinates, and, high above them, lodged underneath the corrugated iron roof, Cate spotted the continuous movement of surveillance cameras.

At the far end of the shed, a small section had been walled off to form a couple of small offices. Henri led the way, stopping only to ask a woman if she could bring them some breakfast.

The woman nodded, then looked at Cate, clearly taken aback to see a teenager with her boss.

She doesn't know what I'm doing here or who I am, Cate realised. *Whatever it is that Marcus and Henri have in mind for me, they haven't told their colleagues about it.*

The three of them walked into a small office, and Marcus shut the door firmly behind them. 'Sit down, Cate,' he said, gesturing to a grey office chair. 'We just wanted to bring you up to speed on a couple of things, plus we owe you an apology. We should have been, how shall I put it – a little bit clearer about our personnel policy when we recruited you to help on the animal smuggling case last summer.' He sighed. 'The truth is, Cate, like it or not, once an IMIA agent, always an IMIA agent. When an assignment has ended you can't just go back out into the civilian world as if nothing has happened. You might need further debriefing, for example, or, heaven forbid, some protection. We were dealing with some pretty heavy criminals in the summer after all and we'd hate you and your family to suffer because of your bravery. So, to cut a long story short, we've been keeping a friendly eye on you. An insurance policy for us and for you. That's all.'

'Spying on me,' grumbled Cate. She wasn't sure she liked the way this conversation was going. 'So have you bugged my bedroom? Got people listening in to my mobile calls?' Her face burnt as she thought what the faceless IMIA agents would make of the nonsense she spouted with her girlfriends most nights as they chatted away about TV shows or gossiped about the latest celebrity stories on the internet.

'Cate!' Henri sat down on a large chair behind the heavy oak desk. 'Of course we wouldn't do that. That would be outrageous. And against the law. You deserve privacy. No, it was far less complicated than that. You're on a passport alert list. That's all. Perfectly standard. As soon as your passport was scanned at Heathrow airport we knew that you were on your way to Sydney. Then, I admit, we did check up on your phone records and discovered you'd been taking a few calls from somewhere quite close to the Friday Islands. That was when our ears really pricked up, I must say. But we mustn't get ahead of ourselves. Ah, here's breakfast. Marcus, will you serve?'

As Marcus put sizzling bacon and sausages onto plates and poured freshly squeezed orange juice into tall frosted glasses, Cate tried to compose herself. She wasn't really that surprised to learn that the IMIA had been keeping tabs on her. Last summer had been an education, not least in learning how a secretive organisation operated. Indeed, the IMIA didn't seem to exist. It didn't appear on the internet and, although Cate had twice visited their underground base in the South of France, she had never been told of the location of any others. Marcus and his colleagues, mostly ex-SAS or counter-intelligence, operated entirely independent of government interference, working without formal regulation or control, doing the jobs that other better known investigative agencies couldn't or wouldn't touch. Admittedly this meant that they sometimes bent the rules – recruiting a school kid to spy for example – but from what she had seen, the IMIA got results. One thing was certain: if both Marcus and Henri had made the journey all the way from Europe then something pretty big had to be going on.

'Better?' asked Marcus kindly as Cate finished off the last of her bacon sandwich and turned to the plate of croissants. While she was wolfing down her food, Henri had been bustling around switching on a computer and, up on the wall behind him, a cupboard door was sliding slowly open to reveal a large screen.

'Right, Cate,' he said briskly. 'If you don't mind giving us a few minutes of your time we'd just like to talk a few things through with you.'

Not waiting for an answer, he waved a remote control towards the TV screen which flickered into life. 'South America.' An arrow began to move across the screen. 'And see this country?' The arrow came to rest on a tiny strip of land, sandwiched between the borders of Brazil, Columbia and Venezuela.

Cate shook her head. 'Sorry,' she said. 'Don't know it.'

'Well, not surprising,' said Marcus, opening up a black glossy laptop and powering it up. 'Not many people do. It's Cotia, a tiny state, smaller than Wales. It used to belong to Columbia but broke away after a bloody war and formed its own government, which is now effectively a dictatorship. It has no minerals, no natural resources to speak of, and for the first thirty years of its existence, Cotia was completely poverty-stricken, almost totally dependent on foreign aid. But suddenly, in the last ten years or so, it has zoomed up the economic league and is now one of the wealthiest countries in the developing world. Why, Cate, do you think that is?'

Cate looked up at the map. 'Well, bearing in mind its location, right next to Columbia and not too far from Mexico,

I should say either drug smuggling, gun running or money laundering. Possibly a mixture of all three.'

'Spot on,' said Henri triumphantly. 'Today Cotia is ruled by five different families who have, after a bloody turf war, signed a truce which basically carves up the country between them. Each family specialised in something. The Garcias took on the money laundering in the north of the country, the Ibanez in the south, the Gutierrez family control gun smuggling into Columbia while the Lopez clan have the exclusive on Venezuela, and the Torres are heavily involved in the drug trade. Because the government is so corrupt, criminals from all the surrounding countries come in and out of the country pretty much unchallenged, to launder their money, buy guns and set up drug deals. But the Cotians are more than a match for them. They are the hardest, most ruthless bunch out there. Even the Columbians are wary of them. They have a saying, "Never turn your back on a Cotian or he will steal your kidneys".'

'Ouch,' said Cate. 'Not good.'

Henri looked directly at Cate. 'Last year a Mexican judge and his entire family, including his elderly parents and young children, died when their private jet was shot down over Cotian airspace. He had been brought into the country to preside over a tax evasion trial involving the Gutierrez family. They never did find anyone to take his place.'

'God,' said Cate shaking her head. 'How awful. Henri, Marcus, this is incredible stuff, but what exactly has it got to do with me?'

There was silence. Somewhere in the room a mosquito was buzzing angrily.

'I'll tell her,' said Marcus at last.

Henri nodded gratefully.

'Cate, as you can imagine, along with the CIA, Mossad and MI6, the IMIA have been keeping a very close eye on these families. We can't control what goes on inside Cotia itself, but maybe we can prevent the tentacles from reaching over the borders to other countries we're helping. And up until now we haven't had too much to worry about on that account. The Cotian families have concentrated on building up their empires at home, consolidating their loyalties and taking out their enemies.' His laptop bleeped and he hit a few buttons then pushed the screen over to Cate. 'But three weeks ago this guy arrived at Sydney airport.'

Cate stared at a picture of a young man with dark curly hair, wearing sunglasses and carrying a small, expensive looking suitcase. He looked suave, urbane, a businessman. Cate would never have thought of him as a crook.

'Carlos Ibanez. Youngest son of the head of the Ibanez clan, who hasn't been out of Cotia since he was born. So why did he turn up in Australia of all places? And, more importantly, why, the very same day, did he take a private jet up to the Friday Islands and then pretty much disappear into thin air? Now look at this man.' Another picture flashed up on the screen. The man was much older, a baseball cap pulled down over his hair, his skin pockmarked, his eyes flat and lifeless.

'Not a pretty sight, is he?' said Marcus cheerfully, handing her another croissant. 'He's a Gutierrez, and he arrived a week after Carlos Ibanez. Same journey up to the Friday Islands then not seen again. Followed shortly after by a member of the Garcia clan, the oldest Lopez son and a particularly nasty piece of work from the Torres family. Not to mention a couple of lawyers and accountants who work for the families. All arriving separately. None, so far as we know, have left.'

'Didn't you put a tail on them?' asked Cate curiously.

Both Henri and Marcus looked slightly offended.

'Of course, Cate,' said Marcus. 'But these guys either knew or expected to be followed. He pressed the remote again and pointed his finger at the aerial view that appeared on the screen. 'The Friday Islands and surrounding coastline. As you can see, it's a maze of tracks and wilderness, huge forests and vast groves, not to mention over one hundred small islands in less than a fifty-kilometre radius. Searching for someone who is determined not be found is, well, like looking for a needle in a million haystacks.'

He paused as if considering what to say next. 'When Fernando Gutierrez arrived the Aussie secret service put two of their best men onto him. These guys were complete professionals who know that part of the world like the back of their hands. They tailed him for half a day, until Gutierrez boarded a large unmarked powerboat. The secret service men tried to follow him in another boat.' He sighed. 'They found their bodies a few hours later. They had been cut to pieces by a boat propeller. Back and forth over them a few times by the look of it. That was when the Australians called us in.'

Suddenly the room seemed very hot and stuffy and Cate felt as if she could hardly breath. Perspiration was making her tracksuit bottoms stick to the seat of the chair.

'Sorry, Cate,' said Marcus seeing her expression. 'Nearly finished now. We decided that we couldn't risk any more good men. We called in the techies, an IMIA agent got a job as a baggage handler at Sydney airport and hey presto! The Cotian boys were bugged up to their eyeballs. To be precise, we put tiny GPS trackers into the heels of their shoes and sewed bugs into their jacket linings, but they were ahead of us again. Within hours the bugs were removed or destroyed. It was incredibly frustrating. After three weeks' work we were still no nearer to knowing who or what these people were coming to see.'

'Didn't you find out anything?' asked Cate. Her nausea had gone, replaced by a feeling of excitement which was, she knew, directly as a result of seeing the IMIA agents again, hearing about their undercover work. 'Surely the trackers must have given you some clues as to where they were going?'

Henri coughed. 'Actually they did. Before he discovered it in the lining of his jacket, the concealed GPS told us where Miguel Lopez headed just after he landed at Passande airport and how long he was there for.' Henri looked directly at Cate. 'According to the GPS, sometime around nightfall, Lopez was at the Snapper Bay turtle sanctuary. Right where you, Cate, are going.'

CHAPTER 6

The Gulf Stream jet was far more spacious than it had looked from the viewing window of the VIP boarding lounge. Cate, the first to board, was seriously impressed. The main cabin smelt of expensive leather and exotic spices, the burgundy carpet was thick and deep and, although the plane was undoubtedly compact, every inch of the interior had been designed to give the feeling of space and light. It was furnished with a scattering of wide, white leather sofas and armchairs, each with a footrest and individual racks containing a TV screen and games console. A walnut table, polished to a mirror-like sheen, ran the entire length of one wall, holding a small assortment of crystal carafes, several cocktail shakers, numerous bottles of spirits and a large LCD TV which was currently showing coverage of Black Noir's latest tour. The front of the plane was converted entirely into a smaller, more private cabin which contained a couple of extremely comfortable-looking beds and one large double sofa.

She heard the clatter of the band climbing noisily up the metal stairway and bagged herself an armchair by a window just as they began to file onto the plane.

Pete the drummer led the way, with Daniella, the Aussie soap star that Cate had seen the night before, clinging to his arm. She was sporting a top so tight that Cate could practically count her ribs. Daniella spotted Cate and bared her teeth in a semblance of a smile before planting a possessive kiss on Pete's stubbly cheeks. Pete caught Cate's eye and winked broadly before pulling his new girlfriend down onto a sofa with him. Not at all offended, Cate grinned back.

The rest of the band bustled in behind them, calling for drinks from the stewardess and squabbling over storage space for their instruments.

Suddenly Cate realised that Lucas was beckoning her sharply towards him. 'Have you seen Nancy?' he said, crossly. 'She disappeared after breakfast. She should have been here half an hour ago.'

'She was last seen heading off to Paddington with a driver and bag carrier in tow,' said Cate, trying her best not to smile. 'Apparently the most amazing boutiques are there. She said she needed a few things for Purbeck Island.'

Lucas groaned theatrically. 'Jeez, Cate, why the heck didn't you stop her?'

Cate did laugh then. 'Me stop Nancy Kyle doing something she wants to do? Not likely, Lucas!'

He smiled suddenly. 'Fair enough, but do me a favour – you be the one to tell her that there aren't any malls within a fifty kilometre radius of Purbeck Island.'

Cate grinned and looked out of the window at the airport.

The viewing balcony was filled with people pushing and crushing against one another in a frantic bid to get a last glimpse of the jet that was bearing their idols away from them.

'How do you cope with all that?' She nodded towards the fans.

Lucas sat back in his seat. 'Try to think of it as part of the job, I guess. When I was writing songs in the middle of the desert, boiling hot and either bored or frightened witless, I used to dream of this: girls chasing me, photographers wanting my picture, being recognised in restaurants. Hell,' he laughed ruefully, 'I even used to practise my autograph on the army loo roll. Now, well, I've realised fame isn't quite what it's cracked up to be. In fact, it's a complete pain. But, as my dear old mum keeps telling me, I can't have my cake and eat it. And you know, it has its compensations. I can afford to hire planes like this for a start.'

As if on cue, the pilot came towards them. 'We'll be ready for take off in approximately ten minutes, Sir,' he said to Lucas politely. 'Is that OK?'

'No, it bloody well isn't,' said Lucas, his earlier good mood suddenly evaporated. 'My flaky girlfriend has no doubt forgotten the time. I've a good mind to leave without her.'

'You can't do that, Lucas,' said Cate in horror. 'She'll – she'll go mad. She'll call her agent and probably the newspapers while she's at it. You'll never hear the last of it.'

'Like I care,' said Lucas. 'She's always late.' He picked up the latest copy of *Condé Nast Traveller* and began flicking through the glossy pages.

The Aussie pilot didn't flinch. 'No problem, Mr Black,' he

said good-naturedly. 'I can always cancel the flight plan. Just let me know when Ms Kyle arrives.'

Just then, there was a squeal of brakes and a gleaming black Jaguar pulled up alongside the jet. The chauffeur jumped out and raced around to open the passenger door. A long pair of legs encased in very tight white jeans and impossibly high stilettos appeared, followed by several huge shopping bags, which were handed out to the chauffeur.

'Miss Kyle, I presume,' said the pilot, his face deadpan. 'I'll get the plane prepared for take off.'

A blond head appeared at the top of the stairs and Nancy Kyle stepped gracefully into the aisle. 'Hello, darlings,' she called sweetly. 'Pressies for everyone and a huge hug for my darling, handsome Lucas.'

Cate eyed the designer names on the bags enviously. She had brought very little with her for her stay at the sanctuary – a few pairs of shorts, changes of swimwear, hiking trousers in case they went bush walking, and some sandals.

Cate allowed Nancy's chatter to wash over her as the engines started. She sat back deep into her chair and closed her eyes. She was tired, still suffering from the effects of jet-lag she guessed, but her mind was racing, going over the events of the morning.

'Cate, it's not like last time.' Marcus was using his persuasive voice. 'We're not expecting you to risk your life. We just need you to keep an eye out at the camp, see if any of the eco-warriors have potential links to the Cotians. Maybe that GPS reading was deceptive. Maybe Lopez got lost on his way to somewhere else. But perhaps he was meeting someone there. If so, we need to find out who.'

'You're asking me to spy on my hosts.' Cate was horrified. 'It makes me feel . . .' she shrugged. '. . . disloyal. Dirty.'

Henri made a snorting noise. 'Cate.' Clearly his patience was running thin. 'You have to think of the greater good. If the Cotians start operating in this part of the world, for whatever reason, the consequences could be disastrous. Just look at this.'

He pointed his remote control at the TV screen and suddenly Cate was watching a video of a gun battle in what looked like the high street of a small town. Women and children were running and screaming, trying to take cover. The film was jerky, erratic, but clear enough. Cate stared, horrified, as a young man half-crawled, half-rolled over the tarmac and out of the line of fire, blood seeping onto the back of his white T-shirt. Every few seconds, Cate could hear the unmistakable whipping sound of a sniper's bullet arching towards yet another helpless target, and saw the terrified faces of a group of small children as they huddled in a doorway. One child, tears streaming down his face, was trying to comfort another smaller child. Cate thought she had never seen anything so sad.

Suddenly the street seemed to rock, flames shooting upwards and a hail of concrete raining back down on the terrified bystanders. Then the film ended.

Cate took a deep breath, trying to hide her shock.

'Sorry,' said Marcus. He suddenly looked tired and old. 'Sorry to show you this, but it's the reality of life for so many innocent people caught up in the drug wars in Cotia and the surrounding countries. And if the Cotians get a foothold in our backyard, if they are planning some kind of drug war, then God help us as well.'

Cate thought of her friends at school. A few of them had talked about smoking a joint at weekends, one or two had even boasted about trying harder substances. Cate had never bought into the idea that drugs were fun or cool. In her experience, the girls who boasted about experimenting always seemed to be the unhappiest ones, discontented with their looks, their parents, their lives. In any case, Cate had seen far too many casualties on her trips to visit her mum in LA. Once clever, talented people could now hardly string a few sentences together. They had lost wives and children and even their homes because of their addictions. And now she had another reason not to take drugs – the savagery of drug wars carried out in far away countries which made the lives a misery for so many innocent people.

'OK,' she said, nodding slowly. 'Whatever you want. I'll do it.'

'Wicked!' said Marcus, giving her a high five.

'Well done, old girl,' said Henri, shaking her by the other hand. He went behind the desk and pulled open a drawer. It squeaked angrily as if it hadn't been opened for a while. Marcus winked at Cate as Henri pulled out a washbag decorated with large pink roses. 'We don't like to send any of our agents out without basic equipment, so Cate, we took the liberty of preparing a small package of things that might come in handy in a place like Snapper Bay.'

'Thanks,' said Cate, impressed. Gadgets always cheered her up. She took the bag, unzipped it and looked inside. It contained a toothbrush, toothpaste, soap and a hairbrush.

'Look again,' said Marcus, laughing at her puzzled expression.

She felt around the inside of the bag, running her fingers along the zip and into the tiny interior pockets. 'You've done a really good job,' she said. 'I can't feel a thing.'

'Don't just look at the bag,' said Marcus. 'And that's the last clue I'm giving you, superspy!'

Cate thought for a few seconds and then grinned. She picked up the hairbrush and began twisting the handle. There was a tiny click and the head of a brown pen appeared.

Henri took it and waved it at her. 'This is a small but incredibly powerful camera. It's got infrared to take pictures at night, can be used underwater and has a one-hundred-metre zoom. It's solar-powered too, so you don't have to worry about batteries.'

'Wow,' said Cate. 'Smart.'

'Now take a quick look at the other stuff. There are bugs stored in the handle of the toothbrush, and the tracker devices slot rather nicely into the back of the soap holder. There's money in the base of the bag – a good amount of US and Australian dollars. Buying your way out of trouble is often the simplest and least painful way to be a spy.

'Last but not least, the latest secure mobile numbers for Henri and me,' said Marcus. 'If you do need us, just call and no one will be able to trace our conversation either from your phone or ours.' He held out a piece of paper. Cate took it and went to put it in her pocket. 'Not so fast,' said Marcus. 'I said they're secure numbers. You can't write them down. You need to commit them to memory before you leave this room.'

Cate was grateful her dad had taught her a foolproof method of remembering numbers no matter how long they were. You broke them down into small recognisable sections, for example people's birthdays, ages, dates from history. Much easier to remember than a string of random numbers.

A minute later, she handed the paper back to Marcus who dunked it in his glass of water. As Cate watched the numbers dissolving into a meaningless blur of black ink, she managed to work out just why she hadn't put up more of a fight before she agreed to work with the IMIA again. The truth was, several times over the last few months, when she had been sitting bored in class, or enduring another endless traffic jam on the bus home from school, Cate had relived her adventures of the summer, relishing the feeling of adrenalin pounding through her veins. It had been a terrifying time, but Cate had felt more challenged, more alert, more alive than she had ever done in her life before and she knew she wanted – needed – that feeling again.

She also wondered if she should tell the IMIA about the attack on the Eco Headquarters, but she knew she wasn't ready to break her word to Miles and Matthias. Not unless it was absolutely necessary.

The band members were quiet now too, either dozing in their seats or gulping down copious amounts of coffee. Not only were they still suffering from the effects of the flight from Thailand the previous day, but apparently the pool party hadn't broken up until four in the morning.

Yet somehow Nancy looked as beautiful as ever as she snuggled up next to Lucas. She must have sensed someone was staring at her for she opened her eyes and smiled blearily. 'Hey, babe,' she said, reaching down into one of the shopping bags. 'I saw this fab outfit and I thought of you. Go on, try it on.'

'Oh Nancy,' said Cate. 'Really, you shouldn't have. I'm meant to be travelling light.'

'Oh go on, Cate,' said Lucas, mimicking his girlfriend. 'Try it on.'

Flushing with embarrassment, Cate reached out and took the clothes, then bit her lip as she saw the label. 'Nancy, I can't take these. They're Armani. They must have cost a fortune.'

Nancy smiled a wide, contented smile. 'Babe, when you're Nancy Kyle, the fashion world is your very own great big fat oyster. If Nancy Kyle wants, Nancy Kyle gets.'

Cate was helpless to resist. She went to the bathroom near the front of the plane and locked the door. The shorts reached elegantly to just above her knees. The linen felt like silk and the narrow leather belt soft and supple. Cate pulled it tight around her waist and eagerly slipped the V-necked top over her head. It was fitted, but not tight and Cate had to admit that the khaki suited her dark blond hair and accentuated her green eyes.

At the bottom of the bag she found a pair of high, wedged sandals, with delicate straps made of the softest brown leather woven through heavy brass circlets. Gucci. A work of art. She put them on, enjoying being several inches taller, but the shoes still felt incredibly comfortable and secure.

She stared in the full-length mirror, marvelling at how different she looked from the girl of a few minutes ago. She didn't look older, but more sophisticated somehow, more confident. Looking at this stranger staring back at her, she could see how people got hooked on fashion.

Before her courage failed her, she picked up her discarded clothes, took a deep breath and opened the door. A loud wolf whistle greeted her, followed by a cheer from the back of the plane.

'Hey, Cate,' called Pete. 'You look amazing.'

'Hot hot hot,' called Paddy, the bass guitarist who had woken up from his nap. 'Dinner tonight?'

'Leave her alone, you lot,' Nancy trilled. 'You're all way too old for her anyway.' She smiled proudly. 'You look gorgeous, sweetie. I knew that colour would be fab on you. I wanted you to look your best for Michel. You haven't seen him for ages and if you'd have turned up at the airport wearing that tat . . .' she nodded at the clothes in Cate's hand. '. . . well, he would have turned tail and run for the hills. He is French, after all.'

Cate knew that Michel wasn't the sort of person to care what she was wearing, but still, she was thrilled with the clothes. 'Thanks again,' she said. 'That is so kind of you.'

'Don't worry about it,' said Nancy, turning back to *Hello!* magazine. 'Just don't forget to invite me to the wedding. Anyway, it didn't exactly set me back much.'

Cate grinned inwardly as she sat back down in her chair. You could always rely on Nancy to be brutally honest. And, to be fair to her, at least she had actually remembered the reason why Cate had come all this way.

With just a few minutes left before the plane began its descent, Cate allowed herself the luxury of becoming excited at seeing Michel again. Back in London, she'd tried not to miss him that much. But now she realised she was desperate to see him again, to tell him all her news, face to face.

She had texted Michel to tell him the time of her expected arrival at Passande. She knew that reception at the camp was patchy and she wasn't surprised when there had been no reply by the time she had needed to switch her phone off on board the jet. But still, she was hoping against hope that he had received her message and would be waiting for her at the airport. Could he possibly be as handsome as she remembered?

The noise of the wheels descending from the underbelly of the plane brought Cate out of her daydream. She looked out of her window onto an endless forest through which a narrow strip had been cut for the runway. Parallel to that, she could see the ocean filling the horizon, an impossibly blue backdrop to endless dots of emerald islands fringed with bright white sand.

The Friday Islands, thought Cate, marvelling at the beauty and the colours. *I've really arrived.*

'Welcome to Passande airport,' said the stewardess as the plane drew to a halt. 'The gateway to the Friday Islands. It's been an honour to fly with you and we look forward to seeing you again soon.'

The door at the front of the plane opened and immediately Cate could feel the heat seeping down through the cabin. It felt different from Sydney – hotter, damper. Suddenly Cate couldn't wait to be off the plane, away from the airport, starting her holiday. For now she was going to forget about the IMIA and the Eco Trust and just enjoy the experience of being somewhere completely different. She grabbed her bags and marched past Nancy, who was applying her lipstick, and out into the afternoon heat.

The humidity was almost overwhelming, pressing down on her like a heavy woollen blanket, and within seconds of leaving the jet, Cate was drenched in perspiration. She found herself almost running to the doors of the airport and the blessed relief of the air conditioning.

The band followed her, clutching various bags and instruments. The Aussie soap star was looking decidedly dishevelled, her thick make-up showing signs of running in the heat. Last off were Lucas and Nancy, Nancy already chatting away to someone on her mobile.

'This is goodbye for now then, Nancy.' Cate gave her a hug, even though she was still on the phone. 'Thanks so much for the place to stay and ride. Drop me a text and let me know how fab the island is, won't you?'

Nancy put her hand over the receiver. 'Sure thing, babe,' she said, 'and come and see us, have a bath, take in a massage. Even save-the-world types need a bit of luxury sometimes.'

Cate grinned. 'Honestly, Nancy, I've told you, I'm not saving the world. I'm helping look after some turtles.'

'Whatever,' she said, putting the phone back to her ear. 'See ya, Cate, and say hi to the lovely Michel.'

'Thanks for the lift,' Cate said to Lucas.

'Take my number, kid,' said Lucas, passing a small card into her hand. 'This is my private line. When it rings I know it really is an emergency. Only my close friends and family have this. Only use it if you really have to and, if you sell it to the papers, I swear I'll kill you.' He smiled at her. 'Or I'll just get it changed.'

'Thanks,' said Cate. She was genuinely touched.

'Come on, babes.' Nancy had finished her call now and was impatient to be going. 'The limo is outside waiting.'

As Nancy and the band took a private exit, Cate went into the arrivals lounge, scanning the faces, looking for the familiar blue eyes, crinkly smile and dark floppy hair. Then suddenly Michel was beside her, lifting her up in a massive bear hug and planting kisses on her cheeks and, after a moment's hesitation, her lips. 'Cate! I have missed you so much. You look amazing! I never thought it was possible to want to see someone so badly!'

'Me too,' said Cate, feeling slightly dizzy as he set her back down on the ground. 'Michel, I am just so happy to be with you again.'

CHAPTER 7

Michel led her to the far end of the car park where, under the shade of the sugar canes, a large yellow motocross bike waited, two helmets strapped to the side.

Cate looked at Michel, excitement welling up inside. Her dad had a Harley Davidson which he rode for pleasure, often taking Cate out to the country on it at weekends. She loved those rides, the speed, the thrill of the powerful acceleration and the feeling of freedom they brought with them. She even got a kick out of travelling to school on the back of Monique's powerful Lambretta scooter and she had already put one on her wish list for her seventeenth birthday.

'Michel, is that yours?' She hardly dared ask in case she was disappointed.

He nodded, his grin larger than ever. 'Well, not exactly mine, of course, but I have hired it for the time I am out here. The camp is so remote that this bike makes great sense. It gets me to the most inaccessible of places.'

'Genius,' said Cate, as Michel strapped her luggage onto the back rack and handed her a helmet. 'Let's go!'

The bike bumped and skittered over the rutted track, through endless mango groves. Hanging on tightly as Michel weaved the bike around the potholes and deep furrows, Cate found herself having to duck to avoid overhanging branches. Several flocks of parakeets, disturbed by the engine's roar, rose up in a great shriek, their whirring, flashing wings a kaleidoscope of bright colours. Cate could smell the dry, almost burning intensity of the peaty soil thrown up by the wheels, and the unmistakable tang of the sea breeze.

Soon the mango groves were thinning and the neat rows of tall trees became more erratic and interspersed with other tropical vegetation. As Michel slowed the bike, Cate glimpsed the sea over his shoulder and her heart soared.

Michel steered the bike over the end of the track before coming to a halt by a large timber-framed hut built on stilts. He switched off the engine and, as Cate swung her leg over the saddle of the bike and removed her helmet, she heard the first unmistakable sounds of the ocean. Even on that calm day it was remarkably loud, sucking back and roaring forwards across the shingle sand.

'Welcome to Snapper Bay,' said Michel proudly, draping his arm over her shoulder as they walked around the side of the hut. 'I can hardly believe you're actually here with me, Cate,' he said, pulling her close. 'Thank you for coming all this way. I promise we'll have a great time.'

Cate squeezed his hand. Any anxiety she had had about seeing Michel again had vanished, but for a few seconds Cate's stomach lurched as she thought of how she was supposed to deceive him, spy on his friends, abuse their hospitality. She hoped against hope that it would turn out to be nothing, just over-caution on the part of Marcus and Henri, and that Michel would never have to find out about it.

She gave herself a mental shake. 'Stop thinking about the IMIA,' she said to herself sternly. 'Just for a while, be a teenager and enjoy being here with Michel.'

She looked around her with interest. A dozen or so tents and tepees, in a variety of colours and conditions, were pitched in two separate groups in the sandy soil between the trees, which lined the edge of the beach. In front of them lay a circle of blackened stones, the remains of a campfire, surrounded by sawn off tree trunks, large boulders and a few plastic camp seats.

Several tents had been customised with bunting or flags, one or two were spray-painted in vivid colours, and hammocks were slung between the trees around them. A clear stream ran quietly beside the camp, forming intricate patterns in the sand before fanning out into a deep orange delta as it reached the edge of the beach just a few metres away.

'It's really pretty,' said Cate, as she stared at the peaceful scene. 'So cool. I can't believe that just a few days ago I was in cold, grey London and now I'm here in this paradise.'

Michel laughed. 'I know what you mean. I felt exactly the same when I first got here.'

Cate was suddenly struck by how empty the camp seemed to be. 'Where is everyone?' she asked.

'A couple will be out on boat patrol, keeping the tourists and their speedboats away from the bay, some are down on the beach checking that there aren't any predators sniffing around the turtle nests,' Michel explained. 'Late afternoon is a busy time for us.'

'Hey, Michel!' A tall Japanese girl came out from behind the trees and walked towards them, her smile wide and friendly. She gave Michel an energetic high five before putting out her hand to Cate. 'Hi, you must be Cate. I've heard heaps about you from Michel and Noah. I'm Mitsu. I'm from Kyoto. Welcome to Snapper Bay.'

'Thanks.' Cate shook her hand, touched by her friendliness. 'Lovely place you've got here.'

'Michel, I'm really sorry to do this to you when Cate has only just arrived . . .' Mitsu was smiling apologetically. 'Noah asked if you could come and help him right away. He's trying to move some logs and he needs another pair of strong arms.'

She turned to Cate. 'Sorry to you too, but I'm happy to show you around instead. Unless you want a nap that is?'

Cate hesitated, looking up at Michel.

'Go ahead,' he said. 'I'll sort things out with Noah and bring your bag over in a while.'

'The girls' tents are over there,' Mitsu said, pointing to one of the groups. 'I hope you don't mind being in my tent – no one else will put up with my snoring.' She winked at Cate as she spoke and Cate felt herself relaxing. If everyone was as friendly as this, she was going to have a great time.

'Let's start with the most important place,' said Mitsu, linking her arm through Cate's. 'The loos. Luckily they're not as bad as you might think.'

As they reached the edge of the clearing and headed into the trees, Cate felt rather than saw a movement in the dry grasses and instinctively stood still.

A snake-like head poked out of the grasses, its black eyes darting around furiously before the remainder of its long thick body and even longer tail was hauled out into the sunshine.

'Oh my God,' breathed Cate, hardly daring to move a muscle. 'What's that? Some kind of lizard?'

'It's a lace monitor,' whispered Mitsu. 'Look at the size of its claws. You are very lucky, Cate. We don't often see them this close to camp.'

The body of the creature was well over a metre long, its tail at least half that length again. Broad yellow and black stripes covered its reptilian back, giving it the distinct air of an armoured medieval knight. It was surprisingly graceful, moving with sudden rapid bursts of speed as it snuffled, nose down to the rocky soil, now and again stopping to claw at the earth in the search for yet more bugs to eat.

'It's amazing,' said Cate, completely transfixed. 'Like some prehistoric creature.'

'That's exactly what it is,' replied Mitsu. 'They've been around for literally millions of years. Like those lovely turtles on the beach down there. They've been coming here almost since time began to lay their eggs and hatch their young. They are so precious, so incredible. Yet you'd be surprised just how much protection the turtles need.'

'From what?' said Cate, feeling stupid about asking such an obvious question.

'From fishermen who chuck their lines and nets overboard and don't care if the turtles get tangled up in them and drown,' said Mitsu, all traces of her previous cheerfulness vanished. 'Thugs on jet skis or in powerboats who just charge along at high speed, mowing down everything that happens to get in their way. Not to mention dumb sailors who ignore the warning signs we have put up in the bay and bring in their boats to the beach because they fancy a picnic. Or, worse still, decide to do a spot of night fishing and shine bright lights onto the water. The poor turtles get disorientated and can easily drown.' She shook her head. 'A couple of weeks ago some drunken holidaymakers decided it would be a great idea to take a midnight boat trip from their hotel on Summer Island.' She pointed out to sea. 'They ended up in this bay, dropped their anchor and started to party, complete with lights and music. Somehow they failed to notice that they were bang smack in the middle of a shoal of turtles who were trying to get to shore to lay their eggs.'

She grinned. 'They got a heck of a shock when they found themselves surrounded by several irate eco-warriors in their kayaks. They hardly spoke any English. Luckily Miles is fluent in Spanish and he managed to persuade them to go and party somewhere else. Seriously, Cate, if we weren't here I really believe the turtles wouldn't stand a chance.'

There was a silence as Cate digested this information.

'Sorry,' Mitsu said suddenly with a smile. 'How depressing am I?'

Cate gave her arm a squeeze. 'You just care, that's all. Most people stick their heads in the sand and hope it'll all be OK. You're out here, accepting reality and trying to make a difference. I'm really impressed.'

'Thanks,' said Mitsu. 'Speaking of Miles, I hear you popped into the Eco HQ. How was it?'

Cate felt herself go pink. She hoped that Mitsu wouldn't notice that she had something to hide.

'Errm it was, um, grungy,' she said. Well, that was true, anyway.

'A bit like our bathroom arrangements then.' Mitsu laughed and pointed to three small timber shacks standing close together in a clearing ahead of them. 'There are the composting loos. The waste is digested by a quick-acting bacteria which converts it into a brilliant compost – one that doesn't actually smell.'

'That's a relief,' said Cate, who had had a rather nasty experience with portaloos at a rock festival the previous autumn that had left her feeling nauseous.

'And over there . . .' Mitsu gestured to several large black bags, hung from branches, with hoses disappearing behind material panels. '. . . is the shower area. Each shower is solar heated and then the water drains away to a reed filter bed not far away. We've come here to help keep this place pristine, not to mess it up.'

'You've thought of everything,' said Cate. 'It's a great set-up. I can't wait to have an open-air shower.'

As she spoke, a short, powerfully built, dark-skinned young man came striding up through the trees, clad only in dripping surf shorts and a pair of flip flops.

'Hey, Mits,' he called as he positioned himself under a shower, twisting the plastic nozzle until the water began to run over his hair and shoulders.

'Hey, Jacob,' said Mitsu. 'Good day at the office?'

'Wicked,' said Jacob, as he rubbed the salty residue of the sea off his skin. 'No reported attacks on eggs, no lunatic jet skiers and, best of all, I spotted a small school of hammerheads out there enjoying a tasty lunch of stingrays. Pretty pleased that the hammerheads got to the stingrays before I did. Otherwise – ouch! Even the suit wouldn't have saved me from a pretty nasty jab.'

'Cate, meet Jacob Anderson, our resident shark expert and camp leader,' said Mitsu. 'He's majoring in marine studies at the University of Stockholm, but like lots of Scandinavians, he hates the long winters. So every December, as soon as uni breaks up, he jumps on the first plane to Australia, where he does lots of sunbathing, surfing and, of course, a tiny bit of shark watching.'

'How do, Cate?' said Jacob amiably, tipping his head backwards to keep the water out of his eyes. 'Mitsu, sell me short, why don't you? Clearly my intimate knowledge of the shark feeding patterns and their breeding grounds in this area counts for nothing.'

'It'd count for more if you did your fair share of the washing up,' said Mitsu, winking at Cate as the two of them left him to his shower. 'Honestly, these academics, they're all the same. Think things like that are beneath them.'

They left the last of the trees behind them and walked through a narrow opening in high sand dunes. Suddenly the beach was in front of them, a perfect curve of wide, fine sand framing an almost circular lake of turquoise water, the circle broken only by a narrow mouth through which Cate could see out to the ocean beyond. The sand was so pale it was almost white, the dunes piled up beyond the high tide mark like plump duvets.

'Fantastic,' said Cate, breathing the clean, salty air deep into her lungs.

She gazed down at the milky surf, watching transfixed as

the bright sunlight bounced and shimmered off the ever-shifting surface of the water. As always when she first saw the sea she was seized with an urge to run down to the water and jump over the breaking waves as she used to do with Arthur when they were young children.

Several brightly coloured kayaks floated just beyond the surf and a rack of wetsuits flapped in the wind. To Cate's surprise, two tall fishing rods were stuck into the sand at the water's edge.

'I thought turtles could get caught on hooks,' she said to Mitsu.

'The turtles hardly ever come into the bay in daylight. They wait until nightfall. It's safer for them and their eggs if they lay them under cover of darkness.'

'Wow,' said Cate, looking out at the ocean. 'So right now, out there, are turtles just waiting for darkness so that they can come in and lay their eggs?'

Mitsu nodded. 'Awesome, isn't it?'

They stood there in silence for seconds, enjoying the view. Then the older girl touched Cate on the arm. 'Come on,' she said. 'Let's see if the boys are finished.'

Cate followed Mitsu back up through the dunes to camp. There, two men were sitting on a large log, pouring over a laptop.

'Hey,' Mitsu called out. 'You guys, meet Cate Carlisle. 'She's come to visit Michel and Noah and to help out at the sanctuary. Cate, this is Dan and Tuyen. They say they're doing a PhD in turtle breeding patterns. We think it's just an excuse for them to spend a year out of uni playing computer games.'

'Huh, very funny, Mitsu.' Dan, like Tuyen, looked

Vietnamese, but his accent was pure Australian. 'That's because you're a princess who thinks the internet was invented purely for online shopping.'

Mitsu grinned good-naturedly. 'It wasn't?' she said. 'When the nearest mall is about four hundred kilometres away, well, what's a girl to do?'

Cate laughed. 'What about delivery?' she asked.

'Pick it up at the Post Office at Parsons Rock. The local town. It's only half an hour away by jeep,' said Mitsu. 'Well worth it.'

'You girls,' said Tuyen. He hardly lifted his eyes from the laptop, which seemed to be processing huge amounts of data at a very high speed.

'What's that?' asked Cate, looking down at the laptop with interest.

'An algorithm showing the probability of likely turtle breeding routes in and out of the Australasia maritime corridor,' said Tuyen without pausing.

'This part of Australia is one of the best places to see turtles lay their eggs and to watch them hatching,' explained Dan. 'They've been coming here for hundreds of years, probably along the same routes and using the same tidal currents. That's what we try to work out. If we can find their routes we can get them incorporated onto maritime charts, send out warnings to shipping. Some won't listen, but some will.'

The laptop suddenly beeped loudly, some figures flashed up and the two boys turned as one towards the screen, Cate and Mitsu forgotten in an instant. Cate grinned ruefully. Boys and their computers. Arthur would love these guys.

The thought of her little brother bent over his laptop

working through amazingly complicated programs or playing online games made her feel momentarily sad.

She turned to Mitsu. 'Thanks for the fab tour. I think I'll find Michel and see what he has done with my rucksack.'

Mitsu smiled. 'Any time, Cate. Make yourself comfortable in the tepee – it's the bright green one – and don't forget to keep the mossie nets in place at all times. Otherwise we'll be covered in bites by the morning. They're vicious little so and sos. Oh, and never forget to check in your bed before you turn in. That's the best advice I'll ever give you!'

Cate headed for the tepee, looking out for Michel as she went. She couldn't see him, but her rucksack was now placed neatly on the camp bed and there were welcoming presents of the latest book by her favourite author and a small but beautiful bunch of freshly picked flowers. Seeing them, she smiled inwardly and, unable to resist, she wrote a quick text to Louisa to tell her just how wonderful Michel still was, before finding there was no signal. She thought about Skyping Arthur with the dongle he'd given her, until she realised that it was about one in the morning. She badly wanted to tell him about meeting up with the IMIA and she already had a job or two for him to do. Still, it would have to wait for a few hours.

Realising she was ravenous, Cate followed her nose to the kitchen, the timber-framed building she had seen when she first arrived with Michel. She walked up the steps, looking at the stilts it was raised up on – protection, Cate guessed, against tidal flooding, or possibly even wild animals.

Inside, two girls were singing along noisily, and not very tunefully, to pop music. Their identical faces, with big brown eyes, dark curly hair and freckled skin, turned towards her.

86

'Hi,' they said together, in an unmistakable Californian accent.

'You must be Cate Carlisle,' said one.

Cate nodded.

'I'm Amber and she's Jade,' said the other twin, who was holding a vegetable peeler. 'We're from LA. Don't bother trying to tell us apart. You won't be able to.'

'You must be starving,' said Jade. 'There's some veggie soup left over from lunch if you fancy.'

Cate gratefully tucked into the tasty soup. As she did, a very tall girl, her dark hair tied back in a single plait, strode into the kitchen. Slightly older than the twins, she was carrying a bunch of twisted roots which she was holding carefully away from her body.

'Hi,' she said in a friendly fashion as she walked past. 'Sorry I can't shake hands but I might be poisonous. Well, not me,' she laughed, 'these plants. I'm Maria by the way. As you might have guessed I'm a botanist – my thing is looking for medical properties in native Australian plants.'

Cate smiled to herself. After the squalor of the house in Parramatta she had been expecting the turtle sanctuary to be manned by a bunch of extreme eco hippies who only washed once a month. Instead, there were showers, a proper kitchen, and friendly, caring people. It was more like being on an international university campus.

'Hey, guys.' Mitsu's head popped around the kitchen door. 'Softball on the beach at four. Boys v girls. Losers on bathroom duties. No excuses. No ducking out. Be there.'

'Go, go!' Jacob was cheering as Michel made his third home

run, receiving huge high fives from his teammates.

'Come on, girls.' Maria was their captain and she was clearly in her element. Long-legged and strong, she was a natural athlete and every time she made a hit she easily made a home run, despite Dan's blatant attempts at sabotage. 'Rubbish, Dan,' Maria jeered in her Italian accent as he attempted to rugby tackle her yet again. 'You'll have to do better than that.'

Their other secret weapon was Amber who could bowl like a demon. She had already managed to get Michael and Tuyen out twice, simply by pitching the ball so fast they complained they couldn't see it.

'Honestly, Amber,' moaned Tuyen as he struck out for the second time. 'The thing whizzes past me like a bullet.'

'She played little league,' Jade explained to the others proudly. 'And every single year, she received the most valuable player award. Luckily, I hated softball or I might have been horribly jealous. Way to go, Ambs!' she yelled suddenly as Tuyen was bowled out. That was it. The girls had won! 'If there's one thing boys hate more than losing,' she said to them with a grin, 'it's losing to the girls!'

Cate, who had managed a couple of home runs, looked around her happily. They were such a friendly bunch, she thought, welcoming her as one of the gang. Most were in their late teens or early twenties and had already done so much with their lives. *That's how I want to be,* thought Cate suddenly. *I want to get out there and make the most of what life has to offer. Do something worthwhile.*

'Yeah, well, it's easy to beat us when Noah isn't playing,' said Michel.

'Where is he?' asked Cate. 'I thought we were all meant to be out here, fighting for the honour of our sex.'

'On patrol with Josie,' said Mitsu. 'We all take it in turns to go into the bay and out to sea to check for things that can harm the turtles – plastic bags, old nets, that sort of thing.

'Last week a couple of turtles were washed up dead with really nasty injuries. Shark bites, Jacob said.'

'Wow,' said Cate. 'Isn't that serious?'

'Not really,' said Michel, dropping down in the sand beside Cate and Maria. 'There are sharks up and down this entire coastline. If an unwary seal or turtle crosses their path they'll go for it. It's food to them. But it really upset Josie. She was never that keen on going into the water anyway and this has made things a whole lot worse.'

Beside them, Cate saw, to her dismay, that there were tears in Maria's huge brown eyes.

'Are you OK?' she asked quietly.

Maria nodded. 'It's just that the last time we saw Rafe he had talked about going for a swim. I'm so worried that some-thing awful happened to him.'

'Maria.' Michael spoke kindly. 'His belongings were gone from his tent. You know what the police said. Sometimes people do just go, on a whim, for no reason at all.'

Maria turned to Michel pleadingly. 'I just can't work it out, Michel. He had been really happy – we'd been really happy, and then that morning he had been for a walk and when he came back . . . well . . . he was different . . . distracted. I couldn't get him to tell me what was wrong. Said he had a lot of thinking to do.' She stopped again and chewed on her fingers.

'Perhaps he'd come to a decision, and that's why he was

distracted. Maria, you have to stop going over this.' Michel put his arm around her shoulders and gave her a friendly hug. 'He'll be back in touch – I know he will. When he's ready.'

Maria gave him a watery smile. 'I hope you're right, Michel. I really do. And when he does I'll give him such a telling off! Anyway, Cate, how're you enjoying Snapper Bay so far?'

'It's brilliant,' she said. 'It's just a different planet from where I was a few days ago. I am so glad you asked me, Michel. And thanks for the flowers, by the way.'

'Flowers? So sweet!' said Mitsu. 'How did you guys meet, anyway? You're from London, aren't you, Cate?'

They looked at each other.

'It's a long story,' said Michel, 'but to cut it very, very short we got together when Cate was working on a boat down in Antibes last summer. That's my hometown in France. She stood me up a few times I might add, but I kept trying and, well, here we are.'

'Sweet,' cooed Mitsu. 'Really sweet.'

Half an hour or so later, Cate was helping Amber and Jade prepare supper in the kitchen.

'Could you just take these peelings out?' asked Amber, passing Cate a bowl full of vegetable waste. There's a wormery just outside the door. Stick it in there, would you?'

'No problem, said Cate, taking it from her. 'Back in a second.'

Cate was just lifting up the black lid to dump the waste onto the writhing mass of plump red worms, when the screaming began. A female voice, a sound of almost primeval terror. 'Sharks, sharks!'

CHAPTER 8

Almost before she knew it, Cate was sprinting down through the trees to the beach. Ahead of her she could see Mitsu, her body taut with fear, staring out to sea.

A hundred metres or so away, in the calm waters just beyond the breakers, a small two-man kayak was being tossed and bounced around as if it were on a trampoline. Cate recognised Noah immediately, his long dark dreadlocks flying out behind him as he frantically worked his paddle. In the front seat a large blond-haired girl was hanging on frantically to both sides, her body rigid, as the kayak bucked and swayed beneath her.

Circling around the kayak, like wolves around their prey, Cate counted two, then three, then five dark grey fins, pointed up out of the water like huge rotten teeth. As she watched, one of the shark fins suddenly disappeared into the water only to resurface a few seconds later, right beside the kayak. Cate winced as the power from the shark's blow sent the small craft juddering and rocking violently once again.

From where Cate was standing it seemed highly unlikely that they would be able to force the kayak through the ring of sharks and, worse still, keep it from turning over. Noah was strong and fit, but even he would have trouble keeping the kayak upright if he got another large blow from a shark. Cate looked around her, desperate for any help. Where was Michel? Jacob? The long curved beach was empty.

Cate grabbed her by the arm. 'Mitsu! Mitsu, listen to me. Is there another boat on the beach?'

Mitsu stared at her blankly.

'A boat, Mitsu, a dinghy.'

This time the message got through and Mitsu pointed to the top of the beach, where the sand combined with the dry peat soil of the forest. Cate could see a small two-person dinghy tied to a tree, oars lying beside and, she saw with relief, a small outboard motor fixed to its stern. She grabbed a still-stunned Mitsu and began to run towards the boat. As she did so, the twins finally appeared from the camp, shocked expressions on their faces,

'What's happening?' shouted Amber.

'Shark attack,' said Mitsu, her voice shaking with fear. 'There are sharks out there in the bay, attacking Noah and Josie's kayak.'

'What should we do?' said Jade helplessly. 'What can we do?'

'Help me with the dinghy.' Cate was at the small boat now, her fingers fumbling with the ropes. 'We need to get it into the water now. And someone go back and get a weapon, a spade, a stick, anything. Go!'

Without answering, Amber sprinted back towards the camp while Jade grabbed one side of the dinghy and Cate the other. It was surprisingly heavy, the outboard engine weighing it down at the rear and even Cate, who thought nothing of pushing thirty-kilo weights in her local gym, was struggling to lift it. She shouted to Mitsu who was standing a few metres away, staring, seemingly frozen with shock. 'Come on, help us, Mitsu! Take this side and I'll take the engine.'

The Japanese girl started, then nodded and moved forward.

Somehow, desperately straining every muscle, the three girls managed to lift the boat off the hot sand. It was just by a few centimetres but it was enough, and suddenly they were headed at a brisk trot down towards the water.

Mitsu dropped her side of the dinghy as the first of the waves lapped their feet.

'I can't go out there. I just can't. I'm sorry.'

Cate looked at her partly in exasperation, partly in pity. 'Mitsu, I can't do this by myself. At least help me get afloat.'

'It's OK,' Jade said bravely. 'I'll come with you, Cate.' Before Cate could answer the American girl was knee-deep in the water, holding the dinghy steady for Cate to clamber aboard.

'Sharks! More sharks!' cried Mitsu.

Cate could see that more fins had indeed appeared, moving back and forth parallel with the shoreline.

'Jeez,' said Cate to Jade, as she pulled herself quickly up and into the dinghy. 'What's going on here? It's like an invasion.'

There was silence as they looked at each other, then out towards the kayak again, besieged now by ten or more fins.

'This is madness,' said Jade, her face white with fear. 'If we go out there we'll end up dead too. We have to leave them.'

Just then there was a despairing shout from the kayak. 'Please.' Noah's voice was almost unrecognisable. 'I can't hang on for much longer.'

'Sorry,' said Jade, after a long pause, her face a picture of guilt and misery. 'I'm just too scared. Those sharks aren't acting like normal.' She slowly waded to shore as the small engine spluttered and then revved into life.

Cate's heart sank. There was no way she could see off the sharks and rescue the kayak at the same time, but equally she couldn't just leave Noah and Josie to such a terrible fate.

For a few seconds she could see her father's face, hear him warning her not to jump in too fast, to weigh up the dangers and the likelihood of rescue. 'You can't save the world on your own, Cate,' he had said to her on more than one occasion. 'No one can.'

Suddenly a narrow spade and a sharpened fence post were thrown noisily into the bottom of the boat, which then dipped and swayed alarmingly as Michel pulled himself over the gunwale. He landed heavily in the seat in front of her.

'OK, Cate,' he said, sitting upright and nodding at her in encouragement. 'Let's go.'

Relief swept through her body. 'Michel,' she said smiling at him. 'What took you so long?'

Cate released the engine break, turned up the power and the small dinghy bounced forward through the water. They clutched onto the sides as it swayed and rocked over the first of the breakers.

Cate knew that most of the terrifying stories about sharks

were an exaggeration, and that less than ten people were actually attacked by sharks every year worldwide. 'Sharks get a very bad press,' Tom, a deep-sea fisherman friend of her dad's had said when he took Cate and Arthur fishing off Cape Town one unforgettable weekend two years before. '*Jaws* has a lot to answer for. It demonised a beautiful creature and gave us all this idea that they are some kind of psychopathic killers. The vast majority of attacks are a case of mistaken identity. Sharks have poor eyesight and underwater a diver in a black wet suit can look awfully like a seal. The shark takes a bite, realises his mistake and usually spits them back out again. The trouble is, that one shark bite can do an awful lot of damage.'

As she manoevred the rudder, Cate shook her head. This attack, this army of sharks that she was witnessing right now, it just didn't make sense. Tom said that sharks weren't even pack animals, they were solitary hunters. She remembered his final words of advice: 'If you do happen to come across sharks that seem aggressive and if you can't get away from them easily, then make sure they know you're human. Shout, scream, splash and with any luck you'll scare them off. If the worst comes to the worst, hit them hard with anything you've got to hand. Even a slap around the face with a diving flipper can sometimes be enough to scare them away.'

Cate bit her lip and looked at Michel, who was staring straight ahead, grim-faced. She really hoped they wouldn't have to get that close, but between them and the kayak was a wall of shark fins. As the small boat moved closer, Cate could see with a shudder the first of the huge grey bodies, nosing purposefully through the sea like mini submarines on patrol. Behind it was another shark, its great wide mouth gaping

95

open to reveal rows of large razor-sharp teeth.

'Don't give up,' Michel yelled frantically to the kayak, scanning for a gap in the line of sharks for Cate to steer the boat through. 'We're with you.'

'Hold on,' Cate shouted as she spotted an opportunity, and turned the speed setting to full. The little engine roared and lurched the boat even faster through the waves and suddenly they were through the line of sharks. Cate swung the boat around to the kayak, but the sharks were swarming closer and they could not get alongside it. Michel picked up the spade and handed Cate the fence post. It was light but felt surprisingly solid with a sharp point at one end.

'Poke at their eyes,' he advised, 'or anywhere on their heads.' Michel looked scared but determined. 'Whatever happens to me or Noah or Josie, your job is to keep the boat upright. Stay out of the water at all costs.'

Cate nodded. She could clearly see the black, lifeless eyes of the sharks that were circling, sensing the fear of their prey.

'You're safe now,' she called to Josie and Noah, sounding much braver than she felt. 'We're going to throw you a line and pull you towards us. We'll try and beat the sharks away as we go.'

Just as she spoke, Cate heard a sickening thud just underneath her feet, throwing her to the bottom of the boat. For a few terrifying seconds the dinghy reared up, the engine revving madly, propellers whizzing through the air, before the boat dropped down again on the water with a heavy bang.

'Jeez,' breathed Cate, climbing back to her seat. 'That felt close.' She looked up at Michel who had somehow stayed on his feet. He had a rope and was trying to toss it to Noah who didn't want to let go of his paddle to catch it.

'Come oonnnnn!' Michel was almost screaming now in frustration. From the shore Cate could hear the cries of Mitsu and the twins as they too attempted to shake Noah and Josie out of their shock-induced stupor.

On the third attempt, Josie finally put out her hand to catch the rope and tied it, with shaking hands, to the rear of the kayak.

Just as she did so, another large fin appeared, making straight for the side of the kayak. The head of the shark reared up and out of the water right beside Josie. She screamed and instinctively jerked on the rope. The kayak reared up, tipping them towards the water, where they could see the demented sharks, mouths gaping wide open, a prelude to a nightmare.

Cate felt sick, hardly daring to breathe as Michel began to gently pull on the rope. The kayak righted and slowly, painfully slowly, moved towards them. Suddenly revitalised, Noah grabbed his paddle and began to steer the kayak in and out of the ever-moving fins. Cate stared down into the water trying to work out where the next attack would come from.

'Look out,' she cried in terror to Michel, as another shark began its run into the side of the dinghy.

'Hit it, Cate! Now!' commanded Michel, still pulling on the rope. Cate held the stick out like a spear, watching with horrified fascination as the shark sped towards her. At the last moment it lifted its great head out of the water and Cate struck with her makeshift weapon, hitting it hard between the eyes.

Thrust forward by its momentum, the shark didn't stop, but the thud against the boat was less damaging than before.

This time the dinghy only rocked.

'Gotcha!' yelled Michel, making it sound like a battle cry. 'And again, behind you.'

Cate turned and saw another shark, darker, bigger, headed directly towards the rear of the dinghy. This time she was calmer, waiting until the shark was almost by the boat before hitting out and then, when it reeled back in surprise, fending it off with the fence post.

By now the kayak was just a few metres away. 'Make a noise,' shouted Cate to Noah and Josie. 'Shout, splash your paddles, bang on the boat.'

Slowly at first, and then with gathering speed, the bedraggled couple did as Cate instructed them. By the time Michel had pulled the kayak up close to the dinghy and was lashing the two vessels together so the kayak wouldn't tip, Josie and Noah were both yelling and shouting at the top of their voices.

Beside them, Cate hit the water with the post, watching with relief as the sharks retreated further and further away from the noise.

'Head for the beach,' grunted Michel.

Cate inched the rudder cautiously around until at last the dinghy and the kayak were facing the beach. Everyone on the shore was shouting and hollering in triumph.

Now they were into shallow waters. Up ahead of them, the waves crashed gently onto the beach and finally, thankfully, Cate felt the nose of the boat grinding onto the sand. She turned off the engine and waited while Tuyen and Dan helped a shaken-looking Noah and Josie to safety. Jacob stood staring out to sea, his face pale.

'What the hell happened out there?' said Tuyen, as Cate

finally clambered out of the boat and onto the shore to be greeted by hugs and tears. 'Have the sharks gone crazy?'

Jacob shook his head dismissively. 'It's a one-off, guys,' he said firmly. 'Tiger sharks don't attack like that, not in packs and never so near to shore. They must have mistaken you for a shoal of fish or maybe turtles. Don't panic, it won't happen again. I'll stake my PhD on it.'

Cate looked at Michel, who was very quiet.

He took a deep breath and pushed her wet hair away from her face. 'You OK, *cherie*? You were amazing out there. Incredible.'

'You were pretty awesome yourself,' said Cate, feeling slightly embarrassed. 'We make a good team.'

She suddenly felt exhausted, the last of the jetlag and the aftermath of the intense fear overwhelming her. 'I just have to have a sleep,' she said.

Michel looked at her, then put his arm around her waist, supporting her body weight easily with his strong arms. A few minutes later, Cate was lying on the camp bed in her tepee. A light mosquito net floated gently above her and she could feel a warm breeze coming in through the half open doorway.

'Sleep tight, Cate,' said Michel, kissing her on the forehead. 'Don't worry! I'll wake you in time for dinner.'

Cate just had enough time to smile sleepily back at him before her eyelids dropped and darkness closed over her.

She had no idea how long she slept but, although it was still light when she woke, she could tell from the coolness of the breeze on her bare arms that it must be quite late. She lay still for a minute, listening to the gentle sound of sea, the hum of the cicadas and the squalling and clattering of the forest birds going about their business just a few metres away.

Cate breathed deeply, taking in the clean scent of pine and eucalyptus. She felt surprisingly fresh but in no hurry to get up. Even the drama and fear of the shark attack had receded with the benefit of a good sleep. She was sure Jacob knew what he was talking about – it must have been just a random event. There was no reason to let it spoil her holiday.

There was a light shuffling outside and then the sound of the tepee hatch being lifted back. *Michel*, thought Cate happily. She turned lazily on her pillow towards the entrance and was stunned to see someone entering on hands and knees. The face that was turned towards Cate was a picture of misery. Wet streaks ran down her large dusty cheeks and her huge light blue eyes brimmed over with tears.

'Josie?' Cate asked tentatively. After her deep sleep the events of a few hours ago seemed like a dream or, more likely a nightmare, and she wasn't sure she could even remember what the girl in the kayak had looked like.

Josie nodded, put a finger to her lips and looked cautiously over her shoulder and back out through the door. Seeing that they were still alone she suddenly scurried over to Cate's bed and crouched next to her, fixing her eyes on Cate's.

Cate began to feel distinctly uneasy. 'Josie,' she said again, pushing herself slowly up on her bed. She felt vulnerable and defenceless lying down in front of stranger, particularly one that was clearly very emotional. 'Are you OK? What's up?'

The movement seemed to wake the girl out of her trance. She sat cross-legged in front of Cate and unlocked her gaze from her eyes. 'I wanted to thank you,' she said in a voice so quiet that Cate had to strain to hear it. 'For saving my life. I was so, so frightened. I really thought I was going to die out there.'

The tears began again, silently. It was an unnerving sight, particularly for Cate, who had always struggled with huge displays of emotion. Throughout her life Cate's mum had turned tears on and off at will, using her highly honed histrionics as a weapon to get her own way both with her husband and her children. As a result, Cate had a tendency to see all tears as slightly fake, something to be ignored until they passed. It was a trait she hated in herself and now she fought hard to overcome it.

'Hey,' said Cate, swinging her legs around onto the floor and holding out her hand to Josie. 'Please don't cry. I'm not surprised you were terrified. I was too. I thought you were amazing to hang on for so long. But look Josie, what happened to you today was a freak thing. A one-off. You heard Jacob. Sharks don't hunt in packs, or attack like soldiers. They must have mistaken you for a shoal of fish, or a seal, that's all. These things happen sometimes in this part of the world.'

The girl rocked slightly. It was time to get practical, Cate thought. 'Josie, you need some food and some sleep. Have you had either?'

She shook her head.

'Come on,' said Cate, standing up and gently pulling her to her feet. 'Let me take you to the kitchen. We'll get you something to eat and then you need to get your head down. I feel brilliant for my kip and I can guarantee you that after a good night's sleep it won't seem half as bad as it does now. You'll see it for what it was – a piece of really bad luck that won't happen again.'

They were eyeball to eyeball when Josie spoke again. 'You can't say that,' she whispered. 'You don't know things like I do.'

Cate stared at her first in astonishment, then with a mixture of curiosity and foreboding. 'What don't I know, Josie?' she asked.

'Things aren't right here,' said Josie. Cate felt her hands shaking. 'I mean really not right. First Rafe disappeared, then the turtles were attacked by the sharks, not to mention the lights at night out in the bay.'

Cate looked at her incredulously.

'No one believes me but I've seen them,' said Josie. 'I don't sleep well and sometimes I get up and go for a walk. I've seen them, one night and then not for a few nights, then back again. Not boats, not fishermen, just lights. Blue, purple, coming up through the water for a few seconds, then gone. It's been going on since I got here.' She looked at Cate defiantly, as if willing her to laugh. Whatever she saw in Cate's face must have reassured her for she went on breathlessly, 'I want to go, to leave here, but I can't. I promised.' She sighed deeply.

The girl was clearly unstable, thought Cate. But that didn't mean she should discount what Josie said, or indeed what she had seen. 'Josie,' she said slowly and quietly, so as not to frighten her. 'When was the last time you saw the lights?'

Josie thought for a few seconds. 'Three nights ago,' she said. 'It was dark, no stars. I saw them clearly.'

Cate tried another tack. 'Have you seen strangers around here in the last few weeks? Older men, dark, perhaps speaking

102

Spanish?' She paused. 'South American?'

The effect was electrifying. Josie pulled her hands sharply away from Cate and span on her heel, heading towards the tepee doorway before Cate could stop her.

'Josie,' Cate called. 'I'm sorry. I didn't mean to upset you. Please come back.'

Josie stopped and turned around. 'If I were you,' she said, her voice clear and firm for the first time, 'I'd leave here and never, ever come back.'

And then she was gone, leaving a totally bewildered and astonished Cate staring after her.

CHAPTER 9

Darkness had fallen suddenly and completely, and with it came the noises of the forest at night. The cicadas sounded more urgent than they had earlier in the day, and the regular croaking rasp of the sugar cane toads cut through the chorus as they called to their mates. Up in the trees, attracted by the light of the fire, huge black fruit bats circled and dived back and forth from their perches, and every so often the outraged squawk of a parrot could be heard warning others of a possible night predator.

All of them – apart from Josie who had finally been put to bed by Amber and Jade – were sitting around the campfire munching their way through a quickly rustled-up dinner of crabs, prawns and lobster. For a while the conversation had been all about the shark attack, with Jacob repeating his calm reassurances to the still shaken eco-warriors, but after a while it seemed as if there was an unspoken agreement to change the subject and gradually they broke into small groups, chatting quietly together about this and that in the firelight.

Cate and Michel sat close together on a large flat rock.

'Look at those stars,' said Cate, looking up. 'I had no idea they could be so bright.'

'The first time I saw these night skies I couldn't believe it either,' he said, his warm arm around her shoulder. 'There is so much artificial light in Europe that we never get to see them in all their glory. It's almost unreal.'

'Hey, Michel,' Jacob called from the other side of the campfire where he was perched between Amber and Jade. 'Quit being all French and romantic and get some music going.'

Michel laughed, gave Cate a last hug and disappeared. A few minutes later he was back carrying his saxophone.

'You brought it?' Cate said, surprised.

'I told you, *cherie*, I never go anywhere without my saxophone. A bit like you and your running shoes.'

Cate smiled at him happily as he sat back down next to her, brought the mouthpiece to his lips and began to blow. The soft gentle sounds filled the night air, bluesy jazz followed by a few Beatles numbers, Bob Dylan and then, to Cate's delight, one of her favourite classics, 'Wonderful Tonight' by Eric Clapton. By now everyone was singing, their voices merging with the crackle of the campfire and the sounds of the night forest into one magical chorus. Cate looked around her at the faces. They seemed so relaxed, so laid-back, yet just a few hours earlier two of their number had been facing a shark attack. Was it because they were so used to living in the wilderness, being pitted against nature, that the odd run-in with the wildlife was seen as inevitable? Or was it just their way of coping with the unthinkable?

There was something nagging away at her. Something that Josie had said about the lights. Cate sighed inwardly Tomorrow she was going to have to start work. But tonight . . . She took another look up at the huge stars. Tonight she was going to enjoy herself.

'You played "Wonderful Tonight",' said Cate to Michel as they walked down to the beach, hand in hand, leaving the others to enjoy the hypnotic heat of the campfire. 'You remembered.'

'It's my favourite now,' said Michel, giving her hand a gentle squeeze. 'It's our favourite. Our song.'

They walked silently through the dunes onto the beach. Between the bright stars the moon was a narrow crescent, but still powerful enough to turn the sea and the beach an eerie silvery grey.

Far out to sea, Cate could see endless clusters of yellow and white lights, some large, some small, a few just solitary pin-points in the endless darkness. *The Friday Islands*, she thought.

'Careful here,' warned Michel. 'You have to keep a close look-out for the turtles. They don't hear you or, if they do, they don't care. They are on a mission to get to the place where they need to lay their eggs, and self-preservation doesn't seem to come into it.'

As he spoke, Cate caught a movement down to her left. She focused her gaze intently, then she saw it – a curved dome rising out of the sands, moving laboriously and almost painfully along the beach towards them.

The four flippers pulled clumsily across the sand, but

despite the huge effort, the turtle showed no sign of stopping. Her long neck stuck out at an odd angle from the shell, her wrinkled head and beady eyes giving her an air of an ancient but wise old crone.

She looked at them and then away, disinterested. As Michel said, she didn't seem to be afraid and certainly not distracted from her task by their presence. She started to dig, her powerful rear flippers spraying sand out behind her as she worked.

'It's awesome,' Cate whispered to Michel. 'I can't believe I'm seeing this!'

A few minutes later the nest was ready. With what seemed to Cate to be a sigh of relief the turtle lowered her back end into the newly created hole and crouched, almost unnaturally still.

'There,' breathed Michel. 'Can you see the eggs?'

As the turtle shifted slightly, Cate saw the glistening pile of milky white eggs nestled in the newly dug sand.

'There's loads,' she said. 'She must be laying dozens.'

'Maybe up to a hundred, one hundred and fifty,' said Michel. 'And she will come back three or four times this season. I have seen this so many times already but it still blows my mind.'

'I know what you mean,' said Cate, watching as the turtle, finally relieved of her eggs, began using her front flippers to cover the eggs with a loose layer of sand. 'Will she sit on them?'

Michel laughed quietly. 'She doesn't have much of a mother's instincts, that's for sure,' he said. 'She covers them up, and that's her done. Now it is up to chance. Turtles' eggs are tasty things. Wild dogs, sea birds and even snakes will hunt them out.'

'That's where we come in?' Cate asked, watching as the turtle began to shuffle towards the sea without so much as a backward glance.

'That's right. I will mark the new nest now, and tomorrow we will build a small fence around it to help keep predators out. If we see too many predators hanging around we might dig them up and move them into the nursery at the far end of beach. I'll show you it tomorrow.'

'Wow,' said Cate. 'It's amazing that you all go to so much trouble. Is it that important to keep the turtle population going around here?'

'It's important everywhere,' Michel explained. 'Thousands of turtles are killed each year for their meat, or because they get caught up in nets or boat propellers. Some are still being hunted for their shell, even though that's been illegal for decades. Now every single species of sea turtle in the world is endangered. To lose them would be a disaster – not just because they are so beautiful. They are one of the few creatures who actually graze on the bottom of the seabed, which means that other creatures can live and breed there. And,' Michel continued, his voice less serious now, 'they are one of the few creatures that can safely eat box jellyfish. So with turtles around, there are a lot less jellyfish to give you and me a nasty sting.'

'I'm seriously impressed,' said Cate. 'I've just learned more about wildlife in five minutes that I've learnt all year at school.'

'Perhaps I should give up my dream of becoming a geologist and become a teacher instead,' said Michel, laughing.

'Nah,' said Cate. 'The next David Attenborough more like. You've definitely got the looks for TV.'

'Thanks, *cherie*.' Michel grinned as he pushed a piece of driftwood into the sand next to the nest. 'And you can be my very glamorous assistant.'

The two walked on along the beach. Cate had dreamt about being together alone for weeks, but she couldn't stop thinking about the terrified Josie. And Marcus was no doubt expecting some sort of report in a day or so – she didn't want to let him down.

She sighed inwardly, cursing her own diligence. 'Michel,' she said quietly.

'Yes, *cherie*,' said Michel, his hand tightening around hers.

'Josie mentioned tonight that she had seen lights in the bay – under the water. I was just wondering, have you seen anything like that?'

Michel stopped and looked down at her. 'Here was me thinking you were going to tell me how much you'd missed me and how romantic this was. I should have known better.' Then, to Cate's relief, he laughed. 'You are just so different from any girl I have ever met. I guess that's what I love about you.'

Cate felt herself blushing, but still she ploughed on. 'Is that possible? Lights under the water? Or do you think that Josie was just, well, mistaken?'

Michel sighed. 'Josie is a very unhappy girl,' he said. 'Ask Jacob. He is a good friend to her. She's only been here a few weeks, and she's been neurotic from the start. I don't really know why she is here – she seems to hate going in the water, she's not really that interested in the wildlife. She only really lights up when Miles comes by. She totally hero-worships him! And as for the lights, well, I have been nightwatchman seven or eight times in the last three weeks and only once have I seen something strange. It was like a blue searchlight coming up from the sea, intense, powerful. It happened so quickly, come and gone in a few seconds and, you know, it was a very clear night. It could easily have been a reflection of the moon or a bright star. You see all sorts of weird phenomena in this part of the world,' he continued. 'Phosphorescence, light diffusion, shooting stars, dry lightning. The Blue Mountains near Sydney aren't called that because they look blue. It is because they are covered in trees which give off a blue haze in the summer, so intense that the human eye can see it. So yes, Josie may have seen some underwater lights. So might I. Welcome to amazing, fascinating Australia.'

He sat down on the sand and pulled Cate down next to him. 'A bit like you come to that! And now, Cate, we had better make the most of our few minutes alone together.'

The next morning, Cate woke very early. She lay there trying to gauge if anyone else was up but the only sounds she could hear were that of the sea hissing gently back and forth and the birds singing clearly and brightly – beyond Mitsu's snoring, that was.

Cate silently pulled on a pair of shorts and a T-shirt and grabbed her running shoes. Back home, she made a point of either working out or running pretty much every day and her body was badly missing its regular exercise fix.

The beach was longer than she had realised, and it took ten minutes to run to the far end. While the beach near the camp was flat and soft, here it was rocky, with red cliffs looming up above her. Every few metres, great chunks and gouges had been taken out of the rocks, presumably by rock falls, and at the bottom of the cliffs piles of red earth and stones were gathered like massive anthills.

Cate walked over to one of them and pushed at it with her foot. It broke down easily and she was just about to walk away when she noticed something glinting in the soil. She picked up a handful of earth and ran it through her fingers. It was full of tiny metal shards, as sharp as glass. Puzzled, she checked another mound and then another. Each one was the same. She looked back up at the cliff. Were those gorges really created by nature or had man had a hand?

Just then, through the mist, beyond the breakers, Cate spotted a grey fin, then another, then another. For a few heart stopping seconds she thought she was seeing sharks again, but as the fins rose together out of the sea and up into the air she realised that she was watching dolphins at play. As if they were putting on a performance, the three bottlenose dolphins dived and rose through the sparkling surf, racing each other almost to the shore before swerving away at the last minute and heading back out to sea again.

For ten minutes or more they bucked and reared, their thick grey bodies arching gracefully in the morning sunshine, snouts touching, diving backwards and forwards across each other in an almost human display of exuberance. And then they were gone, leaving Cate alone and smiling. This was the flip side of yesterday's shark attack. Good times, bad times. This was what living with nature was all about.

Cate dropped the soil and headed back to camp. Those metal shards could have been there for years for all she knew. She found Noah in the kitchen, boiling up a large pot of coffee and chatting to Jacob about the day's rota.

'Hey, Cate,' said Noah. 'Been running?'

'Yes, it was brilliant. I saw dolphins. Can you believe it? It was totally wicked. Worth the trip from Europe alone.'

He passed her a mug of the strong-smelling brew. 'Welcome to beautiful Snapper Bay.'

Cate was just taking a sip of the coffee when the twins appeared. They were carrying rucksacks and wearing sheepish expressions.

'We're sorry,' Amber said. 'Jade and I, we've been up all night talking. We're ready to move on.'

Jacob looked at them incredulously.

'It's just that we came here to help out,' said Jade, flushing under his gaze. 'We really did. But you know, things have gotten a bit weird. We're on a gap year, we believe in what you're doing but we don't want any hassle or worries.'

'OK, let's not overreact,' said Jacob, finding his voice. 'Don't make a hasty decision, girls.'

'I think they're right.'

This time all eyes turned to Josie who had been sitting quietly in the corner of the kitchen. 'That shark attack was something else,' she continued. 'It was unreal.'

She clearly hadn't slept much; she had dark shadows under her blue eyes, and her freckled skin was pale and drawn.

'Hey, Josie, chill,' said Noah. 'I'm with Jacob here. I was pretty scared out there too, but when you're dealing with wild creatures they don't always act according to our rules.'

'I know something is badly wrong. First those badly injured turtles and now that . . . that . . . co-ordinated military shark campaign you and I went through. Those sharks – I swear they were deliberately trying to kill us, to see us off their patch.' Josie stopped, looking at the stunned faces around her. 'And let's not forget Rafe.' There was a noise of protest from Maria, who had come in while Josie had been talking. 'Who really thinks he left us all that night, of his own free will, without even a goodbye. Do you, Mitsu? Noah? Jacob? Maria, we all know you and him had a thing going on, and he didn't even tell you that he was leaving.'

'Josie, calm down,' said Jacob. 'We've been through all the wild theories. It's obvious he wanted to leave, but couldn't face telling us. He'll be in contact sooner or later.' He turned to the twins. 'Guys, please change your mind and stay. You're a valuable part of the team and we'd really miss you if you went.'

They flushed bright red.

'I get it,' said Josie, looking around her. 'We'll all pretend it's hunky-dory when anyone can see there's something really crazy going on around here. But let's not talk about it because if we do we might make it real. La la la. Fingers in ears, hands over eyes.' Her voice rose, it was shrill now, almost hysterical. 'Why won't you listen to me?' she said. 'I'm trying to warn you and no one will listen to me.' Her shoulders sagged suddenly and she sat down heavily on a chair.

'She's losing it,' said Dan with what Cate was beginning to realise was his usual lack of tact. 'She thinks the sharks are coming to get us.'

'Josie, you're not well,' said Maria gently. 'You're still in shock from yesterday. Guys, I'll take her back to her tent and make sure she gets some sleep.'

Josie stared up at Maria, fear in her eyes, tears running quietly down her cheeks. Then she stood up and leant

113

against her, allowing Maria to put Josie's arm round her waist and half carry her out of the cabin.

'You've got our mobile numbers. Stay in touch, guys,' said Amber as she and her sister picked up their rucksacks. 'Noah, can we have that lift to the airport, please?'

'I'm sorry about that, Cate,' Jacob said. They were the only two left in the kitchen, the others having gone off to carry out their daily tasks, albeit in a more subdued fashion than usual. 'You've only been here a day and you've already seen more drama than we usually get in a month. Amber and Jade have clearly overreacted and Josie can be a little bit, how shall I say, highly-strung. It's not really her fault. She had a pretty ropey childhood.' He laughed grimly. 'Although that's true for other people round here too.'

'Yeah,' said Cate thoughtfully, boiling some eggs in a pan. 'Michel mentioned she is rather unhappy. He said you and she had become good friends.'

Jacob sighed. 'Well, it's more like I look after her, you know? She doesn't seem to have any friends, or family. Her other life is a rented bedsit somewhere in Sydney. I feel sorry for her.'

Cate was touched. 'Jacob, that's a really amazing thing to do. Not many people would bother.'

He shrugged, embarrassed. 'A few days after she came here, Josie told me her life story. She showed me the news-paper cuttings and everything. Carries them everywhere with her just in case no one believes her, I guess.'

He sat down on a wooden chair, watching Cate as she scooped her eggs out into a pair of painted eggcups. 'It's an

114

interesting tale actually. Her grandad emigrated to Australia as a penniless kid after the Second World War and was given a patch of coastline near Melbourne to farm. It seems the luck of the Irish was with him. He found barite on it.'

'Barite?' asked Cate, puzzled. She did a quick run through the periodic table in her head. 'Never heard of it. What is it? Something like barium? But that's a chemical compound, right, not something you can find in the ground?'

'Barite is a source of barium,' agreed Jacob, 'but is mostly used in weighting heavy equipment in mining and drilling and oil exploration, that sort of thing. Apparently within a few years the worldwide demand was going through the roof and he was a millionaire several times over. In the days when being a millionaire meant something, of course.'

'Amazing,' said Cate, cutting up her toasted soldiers. 'What a story.'

'It gets better,' said Jacob, pinching a piece of toast. 'He had four sons. Josie's dad and her three uncles. A pretty wild lot from what she told me, with no intention of working for a living. The old man died early from lung disease, they bought yachts, mansions, horses, cars, farms. The Lucky O'Learys they used to call them. The biggest gamblers in Australia, welcome at every party in town and throwing the best themselves. Little Josie and her big brother went to the top boarding schools – usually arriving by helicopter or limousine – while their nice gentle mum stayed home alone getting more and more depressed. But it turned out Daddy and his brothers were very bad losers and after a while even their many friends on the New South Wales police force couldn't turn a blind eye any more. A small matter of harassing bookies and kidnapping and half-beating a debt collector to death. The Lucky O'Learys all ended up broke and behind bars, their flash friends gone with the wind. About the same time Josie's mother finally cracked and was permanently committed to a secure unit. Apparently the last thing she did before she was taken away by the men in white coats was to smash her husband's wine collection to smithereens. Josie told me that alone would have funded Josie and her brother through college. Now Josie is broke and pretty fragile, as you can see, and her big brother, Michael, I think he was called, is God knows where. I don't think she's seen him for ten years or more.'

'Poor Josie,' said Cate shocked. 'All on her own. Honestly, some parents really do make the most almighty shambles of looking after their kids.'

She thought of her own mother – glamorous, beautiful and totally selfish, dumping her and Arthur at a moment's notice so that she could disappear off to LA and find herself. Now Cate only saw her once a year, and always on her mother's terms. Even the infrequent telephone calls had to be fitted in around her various yoga or writing workshops and, if Cate ever asked anything remotely motherly of her, she was liable to throw an almighty strop and accuse Cate of emotional blackmail. But at least, thought Cate, she had Arthur and her dad, and Monique was a brilliant stepmother; Josie was totally on her own. No wonder she was highly-strung. But that didn't necessarily mean she was crazy.

'Jacob, are you sure Josie didn't have a point?' Cate said, shaking off the images of her mother and helping herself to freshly squeezed orange juice. 'Those sharks yesterday, they did seem to be acting strangely. They were very aggressive, almost hyper aggressive.'

Jacob shrugged. 'Maybe,' he said, 'but even if they were, what does that mean? Anything could have set them off. A perceived threat, a change in the weather or tides, a shoal of fish enticing them into the bay. I don't believe for one second that any pack of animals – sharks included – are capable of planning attacks against humans. Animals are animals. They don't bear grudges. They live in the moment. That's what makes them so much nicer than us humans.' He smiled. 'The fact is that they were here long before us and they didn't ask us to come. So it's no good moaning when they act like the predators they are. There's nothing more to it than that, no matter what poor, screwed-up Josie might believe.'

Heading back to the tepee, Cate felt her phone vibrating in her pocket. She was amazed she had a signal and was even more amazed when she saw it was Nancy calling.

'Caaatttteee,' she wailed so loudly that a kookaburra sitting on a tree three metres away from Cate flew off cackling in fear. 'Something awful has happened. You have to come – quickly!'

'Nancy!' Cate was alarmed. 'What's wrong?'

She started sobbing again. 'It's Lucas.' She paused for effect and Cate suddenly had a sneaking suspicion that Nancy might have been rehearsing this conversation. 'He's having an affair.'

Cate was shocked. 'Are you sure, Nancy?' she said finally. 'He wouldn't have asked you to come all this way if he didn't want to be with you. And, to be honest, he seems like a busy guy right now, what with the tour and this birthday concert coming up. I could be wrong, but somehow he just didn't seem the type to mess around.'

'They're *all* the type, Cate. Not one of them can be trusted.'

Cate didn't entirely agree with that statement, but she knew that now wasn't the time to argue. 'Nancy, tell me what happened?'

The supermodel sniffed before continuing. 'He's hired his ex-girlfriend to work on his album. The singer, Cindy Spencer. That over-painted midget of a goth. He says her voice would be perfect for a song he's written and he wants her to sing it and nothing I can say or do will change his mind. He says it's just professional but I don't believe him. I knew he'd never got over her, not really, and now she's coming here and she's going to sing at the concert with Lucas. And everyone will say they're back together and it'll all be in the papers and I'll be a laughing stock.'

She began to cry again, so loudly that Cate could almost see the tears running down her cheeks. 'Oh, Nancy,' Cate said, trying hard not to laugh. 'Nancy, you know better than anyone not to worry about what the papers say. And I'm sure Lucas is telling the truth. If he was going to have an affair he wouldn't exactly tell you beforehand, would he?'

Nancy paused. Cate could almost hear her brain whirring. 'Well,' she said sullenly, 'he's still not getting away with bringing his ex-girlfriend here. It's dissing me big time.' Her voice took on a pleading tone. 'Hey, Cate, you have to come out here and give me some moral support for when Cindy arrives. You can stay in our villa and watch the gig. It'll be fab, like old times. Please say you will?'

Cate was torn. It was an amazing offer and she was never one to look a gift horse in the mouth. After all, she was simply mad about Black Noir and how cool would it be to see Lucas live in concert and get to hang out with him before and afterwards? Her friends would be green with envy. On the other hand she had only been here a day. How could she leave Michel so soon?

CHAPTER 10

'Pleeeease, Cate,' Nancy begged. 'Tell Michel that this is a national emergency and I need you. He can come too if he really wants,' she added cunningly.

Despite her good intentions Cate felt herself weakening fast. 'Look, Nancy, it sounds like a fab idea. But I need to run it past Michel. Leave it with me for an hour or so. I'll text you.'

Cate put the phone back in her pocket and began to smile. Nancy really was a one-off. Back in the tepee she headed straight for a large bamboo chest that Mitsu had kindly donated to her for her clothes and belongings.

'It's nice to have some little place you can call your very own,' the Japanese girl had said, taking pity on Cate as she tried valiantly to hang her clothes from the thin poles which held up the tepee. 'I'll use this hanging wardrobe Josie gave me. She inherited it from an Argentinian girl. She was really nice and wanted to stay for longer but her parents insisted that she go home for Christmas and she didn't feel like she could say no.'

Cate looked at her watch. Ten in the morning. Eleven o'clock at night in Europe. There were a few favours she needed to ask Arthur. But first she needed privacy, which right now in this hive of communal activity, was quite a hard thing to find. She thought for a moment, picked up the laptop, and headed back to the beach.

The waves were stronger now, louder, running further up the beach than they had done earlier in the day. She swivelled round a log seat so that she was facing towards camp. She didn't want anyone creeping up on her unannounced and listening to her conversation. Then there was the small matter of whether she let people know that, thanks to Arthur's computer expertise, she had fantastic internet access in a place where it was usually pretty unreliable. But, mean as it sounded, she didn't want people queuing up night and day to use her computer. She inserted the dongle, and tapped in the code to enable the signal-receiving booster to start searching for access. Crossing her fingers, she put on a tiny pair of headphones and switched on the webcam, positioning it so that it faced her directly.

Finally, incredibly, she was online, in touch with the outside world again. 'Hey, Arthur.'

It was fantastic to hear her brother's voice. 'Sis, hi!' There was a scrabbling sound as Arthur activated his webcam and then suddenly he was there, his toothy grin lighting up her screen. 'How's it going down under? We're all fine here except Dad has twisted his ankle on the black run. Monique says it's his fault for trying to beat her over some slaloms. They've had a bit of a tiff.' He giggled and Cate did too. Their arguments never lasted for long. 'Mon says that middle-aged men are over-competitive and shouldn't be allowed on the slopes. She wishes you were here so she could go shopping with you instead of having to listen to Dad moaning.'

'Oh, Arthur, don't,' said Cate half laughing, half serious. 'I'm really missing you guys. I'm having a fab time here, but . . .'

'But what?' said Arthur. He suddenly sounded anxious. 'There's no trouble is there?'

'Errm,' said Cate. 'The thing is . . .' She knew it was pointless trying to pull the wool over Arthur's eyes. He knew her so well, every expression on her face, every tone of her voice, as she did his. They were very close and it wasn't unusual for one to know what the other was about to say even before they had opened their mouth.

'Cate.' Arthur's voice was serious. 'Honestly, you promised. I don't think I can cope with any more drama. I'm just recovering from your last adventure.'

'Arthur, cool it.' Cate smiled. 'No, it's fine. It's just that I wanted to ask you something. Hang on.'

She stopped and looked around her. At the far end of the beach someone – it looked like Tuyen or Dan – was busying themselves with a fishing rod. Through the trees she could see activity around the kitchen but, as long as she kept her voice down, there was no one close enough to hear her talk. 'OK, Arthur. Can you do me a huge favour?'

'Go on.' Arthur was guarded.

'Can you see if you can find any cyber trace of someone called Rafe Schuster? He was staying here until a few weeks ago until he suddenly upped sticks and left. Didn't tell anyone that he was going, didn't say goodbye and no one has heard a word from him since.'

'Have the police checked it out?' Arthur asked.

'Not interested,' said Cate. 'The thing is, as I'm beginning to realise about this country, people go AWOL all the time. It's such a huge place, like a hundred times bigger than the UK. If people want to disappear, they can do easily and it's almost impossible to keep tabs on them.'

'I see what you mean,' said Arthur thoughtfully. Despite himself, Cate could tell he was already intrigued by the challenge. 'Does he have a mobile? You can track one of those pretty easily if you know how. I've got some software I got from a mate in Amsterdam that would do the trick. You got his number?'

'I'll get it from Michel's phone and text it to you later,' said Cate. 'Anything else that would help?'

Arthur thought for a second. 'Well, his email address. His bank account details. But really, Cate, I'll start with his phone.' She could see him grinning happily to himself. 'Did you know that anyone with an iPhone can pretty much have their movements tracked 24/7? You don't even need surveillance equipment any more, just geeks like me!'

Cate laughed. 'Arthur, the geeks will inherit the earth. You just wait and see. In the meantime, guess what? Nancy Kyle is staying on Purbeck Island with her latest squeeze, Lucas Black – you know, the guy from Black Noir? He's playing a birthday concert for the some massively wealthy Arab sheikh.'

'Black Noir?' Arthur wasn't really up with the latest bands unless they happened to have a track on a computer game of his. Cate could see him typing furiously. 'Oh yeah. It says here that they are the fastest-selling indie band of all time. And that Lucas Black is the most influential newcomer in music in the last decade. Respect!'

'Anyway,' said Cate, 'Nancy rang up in a huge state. She thinks Lucas is having an affair and wants me to drop everything and fly to her rescue. But actually I was secretly hoping to see Lucas in concert and they do say Purbeck Island is fab.'

There was a pause. Then Arthur spoke again, a quizzical look on his face. 'There's something else you want to tell me. I just know it. Go on, Sis, spit it out.'

'Ohhhh Arthur, you're too sharp,' said Cate. 'I was building up to that.' She took a deep breath and screwed up her face against a sudden blast of dry, sharp sand from the beach as the wind picked up. 'Promise you won't be mad at me but, well, I've kind of hooked up with Marcus again.'

'Marcus? As in IMIA Marcus? Out in Australia? What on earth is he doing there?'

'I asked myself exactly the same question. Apparently the IMIA is concerned about some undesirables from a tiny South American country called Cotia rocking up in Sydney and headed, as it happens, to the Friday Islands. Which is where I come in.'

'Cate!' Arthur interrupted her. 'You promised me you would just have a regular holiday and here you are already meeting up with the bunch who nearly got you killed last summer.' Then, as always, his curiosity got the better of him. 'What do they want with you, anyway?'

Cate grinned at her brother. 'Actually, the answer is, sadly, very little. There's a very small chance that one of the bad boys they're chasing came to the turtle sanctuary recently and, once the IMIA had worked out that I happened to be spending a few weeks up here, they asked me to keep an eye out for anything unusual or untoward. That's all. Something and nothing probably. Apparently I'm cheaper than sending in one of their own undercover guys. Honestly, they make me feel so wanted!'

'Mmm,' said Arthur. 'Why am I having trouble believing that? Cate, last time you went undercover for the IMIA my heart rate didn't return to normal for at least a week.' He gave a dramatic sigh, almost lost in the noise of the waves. 'I know better than anyone else how useless it is to try and stop you doing something you really want to do. Just, well, don't rush into anything. Remember, you don't owe the IMIA a thing.'

'Yeah, I know,' said Cate slowly. 'But funnily enough, Arthur, it feels right to be working with them again. I've kind of missed it.'

Arthur snorted. 'Weird, Sis, weird.'

'There's another thing.' Cate was talking even more quietly now, even though no one was around. 'I've kind of been sworn to secrecy but you don't count.'

'Go on,' said Arthur, raising his eyebrows as he always did when he was intrigued.

'When I was at the Eco HQ in Sydney, it was attacked by a couple of thugs with strange accents. They set fire to it when someone was inside! How awful is that? I only just managed to get to him in time.'

Arthur went pale. 'Cate! This is starting to sound a bit heavy. Do you think it has anything to do with the Cotians?'

'I really don't know, Bro.' Cate was whispering now. 'I can't see how – yet. But I promise if I find a link you'll be the first to know.'

They said their goodbyes and Cate walked back into camp, noticing the hammocks rocking in the stiffening breeze. The wind had changed direction, from a gentle northerly to a gusty south-easterly and now, in the distance, she could see heavy clouds beginning to roll towards an almost unnaturally bright sky. The air felt different too, moist and heavy, and as Cate headed for the kitchen, she saw Noah and Michel were hard at work securing guy ropes and moving anything that wasn't tied down into the timber hut. Michel had left his phone on a tree stump, and it took only moments for Cate to find Rafe's number and text it to Arthur.

'Hey, Cate,' Michel called over to her just after she's put his phone back in place. 'Your first tropical storm is on its way. Don't worry, it's the leftovers from a hurricane up north so it won't be too strong. But best to be on the safe side.'

'Sure,' said Cate. 'What can I do to help?'

'Can you go and get the showers down and bring them into the kitchen?' asked Noah. 'Then go and give Mitsu and Jacob a hand on the beach. Everything needs bringing up well beyond the high tide mark and tying down securely.'

Three hours later, just as the last of the kayaks had been strapped securely alongside the kitchen, the storm hit. The rain came first – a few heavy splatters developed slowly but steadily into a continuous stream of heavy drumming on the wooden roof. It was only mid-afternoon but outside it was almost pitch dark, the blackness broken only by the occasional whip crack of lightning which was followed by thunder so loud Cate was almost deafened by it.

The eco-warriors sat around the kitchen table, drinking coffee, playing cards and reading. Tuyen had tried to work on his laptop but had been told abruptly to switch it off. 'If we get a direct strike that laptop could explode like a bomb,' Jacob said grimly. 'You'll just have to live without it for a few hours.'

Even the gas cylinders had been disconnected, to avoid the potential risk of lightning causing a spontaneous ignition and explosion and now the hut was lit only by reserve oil lanterns, hung from the ceiling beams.

Funny how quickly nature can make us regress, thought Cate looking around her at the strange shadows. *One minute we're all laptops and mobile phones and then we're reading by oil lamps. We think we're in charge of our lives but we're so not.*

She was trying to catch up on some A-level course work. It was a particularly tricky piece of pure maths and naturally Michel couldn't resist giving her some helpful advice, even though it meant yelling in order to be heard.

'I wouldn't mind, Michel,' said Cate, shouting back, 'but the Baccalaureate is completely different from our A-levels.'

'Not different,' said Michel with an infuriating grin, 'just harder, that's all. Which makes me perfectly qualified to tell you exactly what to do with this particular equation.'

Cate bared her teeth at him in a mock growl.

He held up his hands in surrender, lay back on the bench and closed his eyes. 'OK, OK, let's change the subject. Have you heard from the beautiful Nancy yet?'

Cate stared at her boyfriend in amazement. Was he a mind reader? 'As it happens I got a call from Nancy this morning. She's having a few problems with Lucas.'

'What's the matter? Hasn't he proposed yet?' he joked,

shouting into her right ear as another roll of thunder swept over the camp and off out to sea.

'Don't be mean, Michel,' said Cate, smiling. 'She's distraught because he's invited an old flame out to sing with him. She wants me to go out to the island tomorrow afternoon in time for the concert to give her a bit of moral support. You can come too! It should be brilliant.'

Michel screwed up his face. 'I'd love to, Cate, really love to, but Jacob and I have vowed that we're going to clear those old trees away tomorrow – we keep putting it off.' He smiled then. 'But if you want to go, then go, Cate. It's a great opportunity. And after all, you're on holiday, not here to work.'

'I feel bad leaving you,' said Cate, wincing slightly, 'but she really does need a friend and I think I'm pretty much the only person here she knows. Even before this row I got the feeling that she and Lucas weren't exactly getting along too well. I'm not sure that a supermodel whose idea of classic literature is reading back issues of *Hello!* magazine is going to have that much to talk about with an indie musician who devours Sartre and Graham Greene.'

Michel laughed. 'Does Nancy even know who Graham Greene is? She probably thinks he's a hot new designer. Or a Formula One racing driver.'

'Stop it!' Cate was trying hard not to laugh. 'I'd hate to see Nancy go through another high profile break-up.'

Michel put his hand out to cover hers. 'Cate, go. It sounds great. I'll miss you but, hey, you'll be back in a couple of days. And maybe I can come with you another time.'

A few hours later the wind was still gusting but the worst of the storm had passed. Cate got up and wandered over to the window. The rain was running down the glass in rivulets rather than being thrown against it like shrapnel and Cate could see down to the beach. The waves were fast and low. Creamy foam was breaking right at the top of the beach by the palm trees where she had been sitting just a few hours earlier. Every so often, one would race on and reach the clearing. It was a good job that the kitchen was built on stilts she thought. She was longing to be out of the confined space of the kitchen. The boys were mostly dozing. Tuyen and Dan were back on the laptop again. Mitsu was engrossed in her book and Josie, who had quietly slipped into the kitchen just before the storm broke, was listening to her iPod.

'I'm just going out for some fresh air,' Cate said softly to Michel. He opened one eye and nodded sleepily back at her. 'I won't be long.'

Cate slipped through the door and out onto the porch. She loved storms, the spectacle and the exhilaration of nature at its most unpredictable. She stood there, enjoying the sensation of the warm wind whipping her face, watching the trees bend and twist as the last of the storm moved away from land and out to the vast Pacific ocean.

Cate had been staring out to sea for several minutes before she realised what she was looking at. Lights. Faint, sporadic, but definitely lights – blue and purple, not on the water, but under it. She looked away and then back again, rubbing her eyes to rid them of the salty moisture that was being blown into them. But there was no mistake. The lights were still there. Cate considered going back into the kitchen to ask Michel to come with her, but discounted it almost immediately. She knew that if he didn't try to dissuade her then the others would. In any case, there was no telling how long the lights would be there. She had to take her chance now.

Miraculously, despite the winds, the tepee was still standing firm. Cate went straight to her camp bed and felt underneath it for the washbag Marcus had given her. She pulled out the camera pen and a torch, slinging them into a small, waterproof pouch around her neck before running swiftly towards to the beach. The lights in the water were gone now, but up ahead in the darkness she caught glimpses of the sea pitching and swirling, a very different beast from the calm placid waters of earlier in the day. Suddenly she saw them again, this time at the far end of the beach, where she had run earlier that day. It felt like they were teasing her and she knew she had to try to find out what they were. She set off into the wind, stumbling over unexpected sand hillocks and exposed roots, until she reached the far end of the beach and pressed in behind a wide tree for a breather from the fading storm.

She peered through the darkness, trying to see down to the water, waiting for the lights to reappear but there was nothing until the scudding clouds parted, and the moon appeared, washing the beach with a silvery glow. At first she mistook their shiny blackness for seals, but then two of them stood up and she saw them clearly, five men in the surf, twenty metres away from her. She dodged back behind her tree. What on earth were they doing out in this storm, in a protected bay? They were putting themselves in great danger, not just from the high waves but also – she shuddered remembering the day before – from shark attack. There could be an innocent explanation she supposed, but she had to be sure.

She took the camera pen from the bag around her neck. Cate couldn't see their faces in the low light but maybe the camera could. Henri had said it was infrared. Hardly daring to breathe in case they heard her, she pointed it towards the men.

She had taken a barrage of pictures when another man appeared out of the water, carrying a large bag which he strapped around his waist. He was taller than the rest, thinner and with a confidence about him that made Cate think he was in charge. His face too was a blur in the night but, as he turned and beckoned to the others, she snapped quick pictures of him anyway. The tall man pulled out a torch and seemed to start signalling – a red light flickered across the water and out to the mouth of the bay. A few minutes later a purple light appeared just beyond the surf. It flashed on and off for a few seconds and, without a word, the five men slipped one by one back into the inky blackness.

Cate lay in the wet sand trying to make sense of what she had just seen. Divers, that was for sure, but what were they doing here? And why were they coming at night? They hadn't been carrying harpoons, so they weren't fishermen. And there was an odd noise too – a subdued thudding that stopped when they left. Whatever they had been doing, they had finished. For now at least.

Cate headed back to camp and had just reached the kitchen when she saw someone standing in the shadows. He turned as she approached the door. 'Miles,' said Cate, shocked. 'When did you get back here? I thought you were still in Sydney.'

His face lit up when he saw her. 'Cate! Our hero,' he said,

putting out his hand to give her a high five followed by a huge hug. 'Where have you been on this dark and wild night?'

Cate was about to tell him she had been on the beach but something made her hesitate. If there was one thing she had learnt last summer, it was the virtue of keeping your mouth firmly closed unless you had a very good reason not to. 'Just to the loo,' she said, thinking on her feet. 'Then checked on our tepee. Everything's still standing.'

'That's a relief,' said Miles. Before she could ask him about Matthias and whether he had had any more problems at the Eco Trust HQ he had grabbed her hand and marched her towards the cabin, his soaking wet hair gleaming under the porch light. 'Hey guys,' he said, walking into the room and pulling Cate behind him. 'It took me hours to hitch from Passande airport and walk down that goddam track – in a storm, no less – but I did it. I'm back!'

There was a scream as a blond whirlwind rushed past Cate and threw herself into Miles's arms.

'Thank God,' sobbed Josie. 'I've been so worried.'

Above her head, Miles rolled his eyes at Noah and Jacob who had got up to greet him. 'Come on, Josie,' he said good-naturedly patting her on the back. 'I always come back. You know that.'

CHAPTER 11

Cate slept badly, the sounds of the dying storm disturbing her dreams. She tossed and turned, worrying about what she had seen on the beach. She was glad of Mitsu's company, even though the Japanese girl, true to her word, had snored throughout the night.

When she did finally wake up, her head was pounding and her mouth felt dry. To her amazement, it was gone eleven o'clock and there was no sign of Mitsu now, although there was a note on her bed from Michel. *Gone out on the boat. See you later, sleepyhead.*

Just then, Cate's phone buzzed with a text. *Skype me asap, Sis.*

She quickly got out her laptop. Even though it was late at night in Switzerland, Arthur was still up and running. 'Cate, your Rafe,' said Arthur, his voice squeaking down her headphones. 'He hasn't gone travelling. I don't think he's gone anywhere.'

Cate looked at him in amazement. 'What do you mean he hasn't gone anywhere? Rafe cleared out two weeks ago and took everything with him. That's what everyone says.'

'Well, everyone is wrong,' said Arthur triumphantly. 'His phone is switched off but I was able to track the co-ordinates of its location. And guess where it was coming from all that time?' He didn't wait for an answer. 'For the last two weeks Rafe's iPhone has been located in Snapper Bay. Which means that either he left without his phone or . . .' Arthur paused.

'He never left at all,' Cate finished.

As Cate packed away her laptop her mind was in a whirl from the information Arthur had found out, mixed with a heady dose of jetlag. There was only one thing to do when she felt this rough, Cate decided. She had to go for a run. She threw on her running gear, took a swig of water from her bottle and left the tent.

She passed Tuyen, who was lying in a hammock, reading, and spotted Maria walking down the beach, a bucket in her hand. *Off collecting herbs again,* thought Cate. She had only been there two days but it was amazing how quickly she had come to love the place and the people in it. They were all young but most of them were so committed, so passionate about what they did. Cate couldn't help but compare them to some of her school friends who did nothing but moan about their lives and who had no idea what they wanted to do after university.

At first she followed a wide path that led into the forest from the back of the shower area. It looked as though it had been laid professionally and, making the most of it, Cate increased her stride. Within a few hundred metres, though, the track narrowed. The trees closed over her head, vines tangling around them and hanging down like thick strands of spaghetti, and Cate was in semi-darkness. Even the downpour of the previous night had hardly penetrated the canopy and only in small patches was the ground damp.

As always the run helped clear her mind. Cate decided that her worries were completely unfounded. As soon as she got back, she would tell Michel what she had seen on the beach and he would tell her that they were probably just recreational divers they saw all the time.

After a few kilometres the track narrowed again. Now Cate was running along a small path, less than half-metre wide that twisted and turned through the trees, forcing her to stoop under low hanging branches. The forest was almost silent now, only the odd squawk of an unseen bird flying high overhead and the croak of the ever-present cane toads disturbed the peace.

Now and again, the long, coarse grass beside the track suddenly moved and wriggled as an animal made its escape from Cate's approaching footsteps and once Cate saw the black head of a snake a couple of metres away, his bright beady eyes watching her as she ran by.

She had been running for about half an hour when the track suddenly came to an end in a clearing of dry, red earth. Out of breath, Cate looked down at her GPS. It showed that, although she had run over five kilometres, she was actually less than two direct kilometres from the camp, and only a few hundred metres from the main track that she had come in on. Unless she could get through the bush to the track, her only option seemed to be to retrace her steps for the return leg, something that Cate always hated doing.

Still panting she looked around her at the wall of trees and twisted plants, trying to see if there was another route she could take. She pushed aside a particularly large-leafed plant and with great satisfaction saw a narrow passageway curving away from her through the undergrowth. Flattened leaves and grasses showed it had been used very recently.

The width and condition of the track made it too dangerous to run now and Cate, nervous of twisting an ankle or worse, decided to indulge in a bit of wildlife spotting instead. She moved carefully, quietly, choosing her footsteps with care.

Suddenly she heard the sound of grunting, panting, and then a loud angry curse. Cate stopped dead in her tracks, then instinctively dropped down to a crouch in a section of long grass before crawling very slowly towards the sound. She took cover behind a fallen tree, her heart racing. Through the foliage she could make out a man, half turned away from her. His podgy hands were wielding a small, sharp spade as he tried to make inroads into the solidly packed earth.

He was huge to the point of obesity. Through his T-shirt she could see rolls of flesh hanging over his enormous waistband, his thighs so wide that he was struggling to bend as he dug. He was mumbling to himself and she listened hard, trying to work out what he was saying. He was talking to himself in Spanish. But not the European Spanish she had learnt when she had spent six months in Gibraltar while her dad tried to defuse yet another diplomatic row about the ownership of the colony. This was a faster Spanish, higher, with different swear words from the ones she and Arthur had picked up behind her dad's back. He was speaking the Spanish of South America.

There was a ringing sound as his spade hit something metal and he got down onto his hands and knees to scrape the peat away. A metal handle appeared in the earth and he grabbed it, pulling hard, huge beads of sweat running down his heavily tanned face.

After what seemed like an age of cursing, a khaki-coloured box suddenly shot out of the earth and the man sat back on his heels. He fumbled with the catch, the lid sprang up and the man peered eagerly inside. Still muttering, he pulled out an EU passport, an iPhone and a small stack of clothes. Cate caught a quick glimpse of what looked like a Levi jeans logo on a bright blue T-shirt, a pair of suede RM Williams bush boots and a wide-brimmed leather hat. An akubra, she thought it was called. She shook her head, puzzled. A passport, an iPhone and clothes? He reached down into a small leather bag that lay by his side and brought out a huge wad of money – tens of thousand of dollars, Cate reckoned.

Then her heart jumped. In his other hand, glistening in the sunlight, was a Colt 1911. Cate knew all about these guns. Whenever Cate and Arthur visited their mother in LA, she had insisted that they took shooting lessons. The Colt 1911 was the weapon Cate had practised with and, later on, taking a short cut through a poor part of town, she saw kids carrying them as casually as their British counterparts would carry mobile phones.

The man put the gun and the money into the tin box, shut the lid, raked the soil back over it and stamped down hard. Then he stood up, rubbed his back and, bag in hand, turned and began to push his way back through the undergrowth. As he disappeared from view, Cate made sure she kept low in the undergrowth and began to follow him. It wasn't hard to do. The man made so much noise crashing through the forest that he wouldn't have heard ten Cates coming behind him.

Cate soon heard a car starting up and she started sprinting. She was just in time to see a large jeep disappearing and to catch the numbers on the plate as the black vehicle juddered along the bumpy track. *Gotcha*, thought Cate pulling out her phone and texting the number to Marcus. *Gotcha*.

It only took a few seconds to go back and unearth the metal box. As she flipped open the lid, Cate hesitated. She didn't want the money and she really didn't want the gun. But she knew she couldn't just leave the gun there. She had no idea who it was meant for, but she could take a pretty good guess that whoever was going to pick it up wasn't on the side of the good guys.

As she headed back towards camp, the implications of what she had just seen began to sink in. She had stumbled across some sort of drop-off point, an exchange. The question was, who for? Either it was complete coincidence that it was sited so close to the turtle sanctuary or – and Cate felt sick at the thought – she had to face the almost unthinkable truth: the drop-off point was being used by someone in the camp. She shook her head. For now she had to believe it was the former – was desperate to believe it – and, to be fair, she had no reason to think otherwise. But with a sinking heart Cate knew that the seeds of mistrust had already been sown in her mind. She couldn't risk confiding in anyone at the camp about what she had seen, that day or the night before. Not yet anyway.

Not even Michel – he might talk to someone, or try to convince her to stay out of it.

Just outside camp, she stopped by a large rock. A small, weird-looking tree was growing on top of it, its thick claw-like roots overhanging and reaching down to the ground. A dark moss had grown over the roots, providing a series of arches and tunnels.

Cate picked up a thick stick and wiggled it into one of the tunnels. She wasn't in safe old England now, where the worst thing that was likely to get you was a wasp or a grass snake – this was Australia, the natural habitat for some of the most poisonous creatures in the world. It felt wide and was at least half a metre long and when she withdrew the stick she saw it was still bone dry. It was good place to hide something.

She brought the gun out from her pocket, checked that the safety catch was still on, and pushed it deep into the tunnel. It would be safe there. It would be missed by someone of course, but that wasn't her problem. They wouldn't know who had taken it, and they could hardly go around asking questions. At least for now it couldn't hurt anybody.

Her phone bleeped with a text. *Number check you requested returned. Hire vehicle currently on lease to someone with a Cotian passport. Name to be filed later. Keep me posted. M.*

First the divers, now this. It seemed that Marcus had been right. Something very strange was happening in Snapper Bay. It was probably good, she decided, that she was getting away for a couple of days. It might give her space to think.

The tiny seaplane hovered gracefully over Purbeck Island, the propeller engines humming as the pilot waited for his instructions to head down into the horseshoe-shaped bay that lay beneath them.

The twenty-minute flight from the mainland had been amazing. From the moment Cate had walked out onto the wooden jetty and seen the neat blue and white plane bobbing on its ropes, she had been almost beside herself with excitement.

'Ready for take off, Miss?' The pilot, an affable, gum-chewing Aussie had grinned at her and she nodded happily as she put on her seatbelt next to him.

Cate could see Michel through the porthole, still holding his motorbike helmet and waving at her and then, as the plane began to taxi away from the jetty and out into the bay, he vanished as the glass was covered with a fine spray from the sea. As the seaplane began to power its way across the waves, Cate sat back, feeling the tug of gravity as the plane lifted slowly into the air.

'It's a bit bumpy on the water but once we're in the air, it's just like any other light aircraft,' the pilot said. 'She might be an old girl but she just keeps on going. She's a classic, you see. They don't build them like this any more.'

She looked around at the walnut fittings, the art noveau stained-glass lights on the wall, and breathed in the heady smell of well-polished old leather. Photographs of celebrity passengers boarding the plane hung on the bulkhead walls behind them; black and white pictures from the golden age of Hollywood when people dressed as if they were permanently going to or from an impossibly glamorous party. Cate looked down regretfully at her light blue cotton cut-off trousers and scoop-necked white linen top. Luckily she had the outfit that

Nancy had given her tucked away in her bag for the gig, but still, she couldn't help wishing that she was wearing a long floaty dress, possibly with satin stiletto heels and a dash of red lipstick.

And now the island was beneath her, the large low-roofed villas all but concealed beneath the lush green vegetation, each one beside a swimming pool. Some of the villas were situated on small crescent-shaped beaches, others had their own pristine lawns boasting streams and summer houses. Wooden paths ran from one villa to another, some crossing little lakes and rivers. Dotted in the clear waters, Cate could see yachts sailing lazily along the pristine beaches. As the plane climbed up over the centre of the island, Cate saw the heart of the resort and gasped.

'Some view, huh?' said the pilot cheerfully. 'I've been doing this run for two years now and I'm still not tired of it.'

'I'm not surprised,' said Cate, trying not to get a crick in her neck as she goggled at the view. 'This place is beyond amazing.'

The estate was vast, the pool alone covering, Cate estimated, at least a couple of acres. Small pools merged into lakes and then fell away back into the sea. There were several waterfalls and numerous islands. There was even a small mass of what looked like rainforest. Beyond that, a large cricket pavilion presided over a perfect oval of a green complete with a large scoreboard, while several pristine grass tennis courts nestled in the bottom of a lush green valley.

As the plane headed over the far side of the island, Cate found herself laughing out loud. 'Did I just see a castle?' she asked incredulously. 'With turrets and those crenellation thingies. On an island off the coast of Australia?'

The pilot nodded. 'Amazing, huh? Fifty years ago a mega-rich American decides that he wants to recreate Edwardian England on an island off the coast of Australia, complete with a castle, a stable block, dairy, and working farm. Then when he dies from eating too much, his family sell it to this Aussie newspaper magnate who thinks it would be *the* place to bring all his super-rich and powerful mates to relax, so he builds the pools, and the tennis courts and the yacht marina and all these tropical villas complete with every mod con needed for today's discerning guest. And this . . .' he waved expansively, '. . . is what you see before you.'

'Wow,' was all Cate could say.

'The castle's used as a hotel and conference centre now, but there are still no cars or golf buggies to get around. You walk or take a pony and trap,' he chuckled. 'But make no mistake, the men who stay here are the type of men who run the world. They make decisions over breakfast that can make or break entire economies and governments, all the while having a massage, playing golf or enjoying the finest haute cuisine from around the world.' He sniffed theatrically. 'Smell that?' he said. 'It's the sweet smell of power.'

'Any women allowed in this hallowed bunch?' asked Cate, her hackles rising at the casual inference that all world leaders must be men.

'I think Hilary Clinton has been here a few times,' said the pilot, looking apologetic, 'and Angela Merkel, and your Margaret Thatcher once in the early days. But mostly the wives and girlfriends watch couture fashion shows and get spa'd to within an inch of their lives.'

There was an unintelligible squawk from the radio and then Cate felt the plane shifting and rolling as it slewed back out to sea.'

'Going down,' said the pilot, more to himself than to Cate, as the plane turned sharply again to begin its final descent.

A few minutes later, the plane bounced and slapped down on the water, throwing up a fountain of spray before coming to a halt next to a wooden jetty. The pilot pushed the door and gallantly held it open for Cate.

As she stepped out, she saw two figures standing up ahead of her. Dark and completely bald, dressed, despite the heat, in immaculate black suits and shiny shoes, they were clearly impatient to board the plane. Before Cate had even stepped down from the wooden boarding plank, they were barking orders to the pilot in heavily accented English.

They barely looked at Cate but she looked at them. And then looked again. There was no mistaking that scar that ran right across the top of one of the men's head, the mutilated hand of the other. She had seen these men just a few days before. They had attempted to burn Matthias to death. And now they were right here on Purbeck Island.

CHAPTER 12

'Pleasant dudes, huh?' the pilot said to Cate as he walked down the jetty behind her. 'Security guards. Always the same. Think their muscle gives them the right to push everyone else around.'

Cate slowed down to let the pilot catch up with her. 'Have you seen them before, then?' she asked as casually as she could. 'Are they regulars?'

He snorted. 'No way. Otherwise I might have to have a word with Mr Lake – the guy who owns this plane company. Nah, these guys only turned up here a few days ago. They flew in from the mainland just like you did. You haven't been here before, have you?' he said, his grey eyes looking at her keenly.

'No, I'm visiting Nancy Kyle. She's a friend of mine.'

'Wow,' said the pilot. 'I heard she was here. She's gorgeous! I don't s'pose you could get me an introduction, could you?'

'Maybe,' said Cate, smiling. 'I'll try.' She was keen to keep the conversation going. 'Got far to go with those two guys?'

'Nah, just a bit of island hopping to pick up their bosses.'

The sandy path which climbed up from the jetty led to a circular gravel drive. Ahead of them stood the castle, its granite stone looking almost comical against the background of tropical plants and blue sky.

'They're Spanish, aren't they?' said Cate. She put on her girly expression. 'I thought I recognised the accent. I did Spanish for GCSE. I was rubbish at it.'

The pilot looked at her thoughtfully. 'Close. They're South Americans. From one of those tiny countries no one has really heard of. Patagonia, Catania – something like that.'

'Cotia?' suggested Cate, holding her breath.

'Yeah, could be. Sounds about right.' He gestured over towards a long, low building. 'I'm off to the staff quarters to grab a quick change of shirt before I take the happy pair to pick up their bosses. Nice talking to you.'

'When do you get back?' Cate said desperately, hoping that she hadn't pushed her luck too far.

He stopped still. 'Bit curious, aren't you?' he said, his tone turning unfriendly. 'Why do you want to know?'

Cate felt her stomach curling. 'Oh, just in case Nancy is around and in a good mood,' she said airily. 'I might be able to convince her to say hello. You never know your luck.'

He relaxed, smiled and looked at his watch. 'I'm due back in at around nineteen hundred hours. Maybe see you then? Cheers – Cate, wasn't it?'

'Babe!' The scream reverberated around the vast marbled reception area of the castle. For a few seconds, Cate couldn't see where the sound was coming from but then, looking up, she saw a slash of bright red lipstick topped by a shock of platinum hair leaning perilously far out over the heavy wooden gallery above her head.

'Hi, Nancy,' called Cate as the supermodel came rushing down to greet her as fast as her three-inch platform sandals would allow. 'Great to see you. How's life on Purbeck Island?'

'Weeell . . .' Nancy stopped suddenly and screwed up her face before presenting it again to Cate for a kiss on both cheeks. 'Mwah, mwah, darling. I guess it is beautiful, and the villa is amazing and the food is out of this world, but overall it's a tad, ummm, boring.' She linked her arm through Cate's. 'The problem is, babe, seen one luxury island, seen them all.'

Cate thought of all her friends who would pretty much give their right arm to spend just a few days somewhere as incredible as this place. 'How are things with Lucas?' she asked. 'You two managed to make up?'

'Not sure,' said Nancy doubtfully as she marched Cate past the smiling receptionist and out into the scented sunshine. 'The thing is, I haven't actually seen him that much since we had our massive row. He's been locked away in the basement writing songs. He says he's on a roll and has to go with it.'

'Oh,' said Cate. 'Well, that's musicians for you.' She tried to think of a way to cheer her up. 'Maybe it's because of you, Nancy. Perhaps you're his inspiration. He could even be writing a song about you. Perhaps you might even get a mention on the album cover.'

'Sort of like his muse?' said Nancy, smiling.

'Sort of,' said Cate, encouragingly.

They had walked past the pool area and were now heading along a narrow terracotta tiled pathway through what seemed to be a small rainforest. A canopy of trees and vines with huge leaves provided cooling shade and, not too far away, Cate could hear the tinkle of a waterfall.

As they crossed over a small wooden bridge, a flock of parakeets flew up in front of them and, through a strategically-cut pathway, Cate caught a glimpse of the harbour where she had just landed. A large white motor yacht was pulling away from the island. 'Wow,' she breathed. 'This place is like a film set.'

'I suppose it is,' said Nancy vaguely.

Yet despite the perfection, Cate felt that somehow this version of paradise was nowhere near as lovely as the wilderness of Snapper Bay.

Meanwhile, Nancy had been hit by inspiration. 'Never mind getting a cover mention, Cate. I'm going to be *on* the cover. Actually I will *be* the cover. A great big picture of me looking beautiful. Genius. I'll tell Lucas this evening over dinner. He'll have to forgive me then.'

'Great idea,' said Cate as enthusiastically as she could. Somehow she couldn't quite see Lucas plastering a picture of a girl, no matter how beautiful, on his latest album cover – but then again, Nancy could be very persuasive.

'Here we are,' said Nancy finally, turning under a metal archway which was smothered with large purple flowers. 'Home sweet home.'

Cate had been expecting the sort of villa she and her family stayed in when they holidayed in Greece or Spain – a white or stone cottage with a red tiled roof and perhaps a small swimming pool. Instead, this place was like a Georgian mansion, huge floor to ceiling French doors on the ground floor and large sash windows on the first floor. In front of them lay an improbably smooth, bright green lawn which ran up to the steps of a white pillared porch. An archway at the other end of the building led through into a courtyard where Cate could see a waterfall running down to a layered water feature.

'The pool's round the back,' said Nancy carelessly as she opened the front door. The sound of a complicated guitar riff floated up from somewhere beneath them, followed by a few ripe curses.

Nancy raised her eyebrows at Cate and then opened her wide mouth. 'Valentina!' Nancy yelled at the top of her voice, making Cate jump. 'Visitors.'

A small grey-haired woman scuttled out of one of the enormous doorways which lined the galleried hallway. She looked harassed, her small beady eyes darting nervously at Nancy, but when she saw Cate she gave her a welcoming smile. 'Welcome to Villa Romantica,' she said, rushing forward to pick up Cate's rucksack. 'Let me show you to your room, Miss.'

'Later, babe,' said Nancy as she disappeared off through another door. 'Catch you later.'

Cate's room was vast, with views that overlooked the front lawn at one end. The other end was dominated by a large four-poster bed swathed in acres of pale muslin and behind that wooden blinds covered a huge window. Cate peered through the slats and looked down onto the oval swimming pool where Nancy was already ensconced on a lounger, a waiter serving her what looked like a very large glass of champagne. Opposite Nancy, on the other side of the pool, Pete the drummer and the Aussie soap star were cuddled up

148

on a double rocker which swung out over the water. Next to Nancy, thought Cate, the soap star, with her tiny white and gold bikini and her white stilettos, looked like a supermarket checkout girl.

As she watched, she saw a man with long, dark hair walk into the garden and head for Nancy. She sat up and smiled broadly at him, presenting the side of her perfect face to him for a kiss. He looked familiar and after a few seconds Cate remembered why. The man standing in the garden below her was none other than Wayne Shawn, one of the world's most famous cricketers. He was retired now – Cate knew that from Arthur who had had a poster of Wayne on his wall for years – but he often made the headlines, mainly for his unlikely conquests of the most eligible women in the world.

If I were Lucas, thought Cate as she saw Nancy move over on the lounger to make room for Wayne to sit down, *I wouldn't sulk in the basement for too much longer.*

The windows opened out onto a tiled balcony where Cate found a table and chairs and a couple of teak sunbeds as well as a fridge stocked with mini bottles of water, Coke, and lemonade. She searched in vain for the ensuite, pushing on false doors and opening wardrobes until she finally found a discreet door in the corner of the room. Behind it was a marble bathroom, complete with very wide, claw-footed roll-top bath.

There was a tap at the door and Cate called, 'Come in.' A young maid was carrying a pile of fluffy towels that almost obscured her face. She went into the bathroom and reappeared a few seconds later. 'You need anything?' she asked in a Russian accent. 'Shall I unpack?'

The maid was probably only a few years older than Cate

but she seemed so tired and careworn. Looking at her name tag, Cate felt a pang of pity for the girl.

'Everything is fine, thank you, Marissa,' she said, smiling at her. On an impulse she reached into her purse and brought out a twenty dollar note, placing it gently into the surprised maid's hand.

'Please,' said Cate. 'The room looks lovely and I'm very grateful.'

The maid looked at the note and then at Cate and smiled. 'Thank you very much,' she said as she made her way towards the door. 'You are a kind girl.'

Cate sat down and pulled out her phone. Marcus took so long to pick up that Cate was beginning to think she had made a mistake when she had dialled his number.

'Marcus, the Cotians are coming right here to Purbeck Island.' Cate's words tumbled out in rush.

She heard him take in a deep breath. 'Hey, Cate, chill. Take it easy, will you?' Marcus was clearly in one of his laid-back moods. 'Are you sure you've got the right guys?' He was speaking loudly over a roaring noise in the background.

Cate paused for a second, thinking things through. She hated breaking her word to Miles and Matthias but she'd known that this time would probably come.

'Marcus,' she said, 'I've got something to tell you.'

He listened in silence as she recounted the events of that terrifying afternoon back in Sydney.

When she had finished, Marcus let out a low whistle. 'So you think the two men you saw today were the same thugs who tried to set fire to your mate? Cate, you really should have told me about his before.'

'I know,' said Cate, wincing, 'but I hate breaking my promises and I wasn't sure if there was any link. But now . . .' She stopped again to compose her thoughts. She had to convince him of the importance of what she had seen. 'The pilot told me they were bodyguards, and that their Cotian bosses are arriving this evening. This could be the perfect opportunity to find out what they are up to.'

'Cate Carlisle, I knew I was right to bring you back on board,' Marcus said, trying hard and failing to keep the smugness out of his voice. 'Just wait till I tell Henri. He thought you were a one-hit wonder, that you'd never be able to play to the same high standards as the summer.'

'OK, OK, Marcus,' said Cate stiffly, not quite sure whether to be pleased or annoyed that she had become the subject of a competition between the two IMIA agents. 'Can we get back to the Cotians? So much has happened the last twenty-four hours that I'm not sure I can think straight any more.'

'Sure, sure.' Cate could hear Marcus pulling himself together. 'OK, Cate. We've got a Cotian using Snapper Bay as a pick up and drop-off point for money and guns. And you've just seen two men leave Purbeck Island who are probably, if your pilot friend is right, Cotians who you can definitely place as the thugs who set fire to the Eco Trust's headquarters.'

'With someone in it,' Cate reminded him.

'With someone in it,' agreed Marcus. The line was beginning to crackle.

'Marcus,' said Cate curiously. 'Where are you?'

'On an Australian air force jet flying over New Zealand as it happens,' said Marcus cheerfully. 'They offered me a jaunt up to the Arctic Circle and I couldn't resist it. Sorry, Cate, I had no idea things would move this fast.'

'Marcus,' said Cate sternly. 'At nineteen hundred hours several Cotians, if that's who they are, will arrive on Purbeck Island. You promised me I wouldn't have to get involved. Just keep a look-out, that's all, you said. I was really hoping that I could hand everything over to you now and get back to my holiday.'

'Sorry, Cate, no can do,' said Marcus. 'We won't land in Sydney for another two hours. The earliest I can turn it around up to Purbeck will be for around nine-thirty tonight. Until then it's over to you. You know what to do. Listen in to their conversations, try to work out where they've been hiding. Cheers, Cate.'

'Marcus!' Cate said, exasperated as the line went dead. She threw her phone down onto the sofa beside her, then, after a few minutes, began rummaging into her rucksack for the bag of tricks Marcus had given her. It looked as if she would be needing them sooner that she had anticipated. She looked longingly out at the swimming pool where she had hoped she would be spending the rest of the day and sighed.

Cate was meant to have spent the last few hours sleeping. At least that was what she'd told Nancy when she called up to her room to ask why she wasn't at the pool. But in fact Cate had been very busy indeed.

First stop had been the jetty, now completely deserted as most of the resort seemed to be taking a siesta. Cate stripped off her light cotton dress and sandals and, clad only in her swimming costume, eased herself slowly into the water, using the slats to pull herself beneath the wooden frame. Holding onto one of the damp jetty posts with her left hand to keep herself above water, she fumbled in the waterproof bag slung around her neck. She didn't know much about the Cotians' plans but she did at least know where and when they would be arriving.

The bug was no larger than her little fingernail, and it slotted perfectly into a small crack Cate found in the wood just above her head. As a precaution, she shook the slat hard but the bug stayed firmly put. That done, Cate dropped gently into the water and dived into the depths leaving hardly a ripple behind. By the time she surfaced, she was metres away from the jetty – to anyone watching, she was just another swimmer on a hot afternoon.

The seaplane was bang on time, skimming low through the sunset haze and landing on the pinky water with hardly a splash. Cate was sitting fifteen metres away, halfway up a vast redwood tree in a treehouse that had clearly been designed for a small child.

'Thank God,' she muttered as the plane door finally opened. She had only been there for ten minutes but already her legs were aching from their cramped position and she had banged her head at least five times on the timber roof.

The bald security guards were out first, walking to the end of the jetty, scrutinising the trees and bushes, looking up and down the path and the deserted beach. For a few awful seconds, Cate thought they might spot the treehouse and come to investigate. Cate bit her lip as she watched the smaller of the two men kneel down and stick his head underneath the jetty horribly close to where she had placed the bug, before he stood up and signalled to someone inside the plane.

Seconds later, two men, immaculate in neatly creased chinos and expensive-looking shirts, got out of the plane and were stood on the jetty waiting for their bags. Cate brought out her camera pen and zoomed in on them, photographing their faces. Then she put on some headphones, switched to record on the handheld bug receiver and began to listen. At first she struggled to hear above the gentle hiss of the water. But then she heard voices, which became words and then conversations. She sat up, concentrating hard. Cate wasn't bad at Spanish but she had no idea how close European Spanish would be to South American Spanish.

Five minutes later she pulled off the headphones and sat back on her sore legs, her mind racing. These men were going to be joined by several others for some sort of meeting. She'd heard where, now she somehow had to find out just what was on the agenda.

Room 14 lay right at the end of a very long corridor of conference rooms on the second floor of the castle. Cate strode along the thickly padded carpet doing her best to look as if she was totally entitled to be there, despite the fact she had already passed three signs that said *Entry to authorised staff and guests only*.

The plan was the best Cate could come up with at such short notice. She was carrying a couple of listening devices in the pocket of her cropped trousers, and she wanted to get into the meeting room, plant them and get well away before the meeting began at eight. She had no wish to get any closer than that to these killers.

For now the corridor was empty. As Cate neared the end

she heard the sound of guitar music coming from a room to her left. She paused and pushed on the door gently. To her surprise it opened easily onto a vast room about the size of Cate's assembly hall at school. At the far end was a stage, and on it, Lucas Black was standing, eyes closed, his fingers dancing over the strings of his bright blue guitar, rehearsing for the gig. It sounded amazing and she could have stood there all day listening to him perform.

She pulled herself together. She had other things more pressing to attend to. Cate knocked gently on the door of Room 14 and waited, her heart beating fast. There was silence. She tried again and then turned the handle and went inside. The room was low ceilinged and windowless, lit only by a couple of low level lamps. It was dominated by a long, polished wooden table and rather plain wooden chairs covered in dull brown leather. At the far end, a large screen hung on the wall, ready for use, a projector beneath it whirring away gently.

Cate was inexplicably assailed by feelings of panic and claustrophobia, which she did her best to ignore. She looked around her for somewhere to hide the bugs. Under the table would have been the obvious place but after watching the security guards check out the jetty she was pretty certain they would carry out the basic checks here too. She looked under the lamp and along the wooden skirting board but knew they would check there as well.

She was just about to unscrew the projector casing when she heard a clattering sound outside the door. Before she had time to do more than move away from the projector, a trolley was being pushed into the room followed by none other than

Marissa. She stared at Cate curiously before breaking into a smile as she recognised her.

'Hello,' she said. 'What are you doing here?'

She parked the trolley next to the table and began to unload jugs of water, wine, plates of whitebait and smoked salmon, wafer thin slices of salami, chorizo, hams and bowls of delicious smelling pastas and garlicky olives.

'Errm, I was just exploring the hotel,' Cate said lamely.

To her relief Marissa seemed to accept Cate's feeble excuse. Marissa took a bunch of keys from her belt and walked over to a small door in the corner of the room. It opened to a miniature laundry room and Cate could see stacks of table-cloths, napkins and a couple of the blue and white staff uniforms hanging up.

'I get the room ready, then serve the men food,' Marissa said.

Cate looked at her in horror. There were only a few minutes left before the men started arriving for the meeting. The bugs had to be in position by then to give her any chance of finding out what the Cotians were doing in the Friday Islands.

Cate could have kicked herself. She had left it all too late. Then she heard the faint sound of music filtering through from the rehearsal room nearby.

'Do you know Lucas Black?' she asked Marissa. 'Lucas Black, Black Noir.' Cate mimed a guitar playing, then sang a few bars of 'Trapped', Lucas's latest single.

Marissa's eyes lit up. 'Lucas Black,' she repeated in her Russian accent. 'Yah, I like very, very much. He is cool, really cool.'

'He has asked for help with his rehersal. He needs your help.'

Cate grabbed her by the hand and half dragged her to the rehearsal room and up to the stage where Lucas was still playing the guitar. This time he saw Cate approaching and stopped playing in mid chord.

'Hi, Cate,' he said, coolly, as if he had been expecting her. 'Come to watch the rehearsal?'

'Lucas,' Cate sounded panicky even to herself. 'Lucas, this is Marissa. Marissa, this is Lucas Black.'

'Hi, Marissa,' said Lucas, smiling down at her and strumming on his guitar.

'Hi,' croaked Marissa, gazing at him with total disbelief.

Cate went up to him, looked imploringly, and whispered, 'Lucas, please can you do me a huge huge favour and keep Marissa here until I come to get her? Tell her you need her help. You're so important she'll do anything for you. I know it's a big ask, but it won't be for long.'

He grinned. 'Cate, I don't know why you're in such a state. I could actually do with someone to adjust the amplifiers. The sound system is playing up something shocking.'

He put out his hand to the awestruck maid and helped her onto the stage. 'Fancy checking out my new song?' he said as Cate mouthed a silent thank you to him.

'Take your time,' Cate said to Marissa. 'I'm really happy to cover for you.'

Out in the corridor she paused and rested against the wall for a few seconds to catch her breath. She looked down at her watch. Five minutes to the meeting. Just enough time to nip back and place the bugs. She didn't care where any more. Then she heard a noise and through the glass corridor doors she could see the men assembling. The meeting was about to begin.

Without thinking, Cate ran back into the conference room and headed for the laundry cupboard. By the time the first man was walking through the conference room door, Cate was standing by the table, hair tied back, smoothing down the apron of her maid's uniform, and trying to stop her hands from shaking.

CHAPTER 13

The five men sat around the table, the low level lighting adding shadows to their already sinister faces. The oldest men, greying hair slicked back from their leathery foreheads, sat at either end of the table, one security guard behind each of them. The bodyguards had been first into the room, checking under the table, pulling back the TV screen, even tugging at the door of the laundry room which Cate had just had time to lock behind her. That done, one produced a bug sweeper which he ran over every surface in the room – including Cate's uniform.

Cate thanked her lucky stars that she hadn't managed to plant the bugs or activate the ones on her. She was trying hard not to make eye contact when a guard jabbed her painfully in the shoulder. 'Where is your name tag?'

Cate looked down at her chest and feigned surprise. 'I must have left it back in kitchen – I came here in a hurry. I'm sorry. My name is Marissa,' Cate replied, mimicking the Russian girl's accent.

He grunted and looked at her, his eyes hard and calculating. 'You speak Spanish?' he asked.

Cate took a deep breath and shook her head. 'I am from Russia,' she said. 'I speak little English.'

He seemed satisfied with that. For ten minutes, the men ate and drank as if they had not seen food for a week. The room became hotter, stickier, the smells of the food mingling with the sickly sweet aftershave worn by the men.

Cate stood quietly to one side, removing plates as they were emptied, filling up the glasses with water or wine.

Then one of the older men began to talk and, as soon as he did, the other four put down their glasses and listened intently.

'Friends,' he said in Spanish, raising his glass to the table. 'This is a great day for us all. Today we leaders of Cotian industry are exporting our expertise to another country for the very first time. As you know, we have identified the product that will ensure our success. Now all we have to do is work out which of us takes on what role and rewards from our endeavour.'

Cate hoped that her face didn't betray her understanding and fear. Her eyes moved around the table and she knew she had seen each face before on the screen in another hot and claustrophobic room back on Diamond Island in Sydney Harbour. They were all there: Carlos Ibanez, Fernando Gutierrez, Miguel Lopez. Despite the exaggerated courtesy and respect they were showing one another, she knew these men hated and feared each other.

'These men are ruthless,' Marcus had said, 'and most of all they hate informers. They would kill their own mothers if they got the slightest inclination that they were acting against

160

them.' And now she was stuck in a room with them. Spying on them. Her mouth suddenly dry, she swallowed hard and put her hands behind her back to stop herself from biting her nails.

The clock on the wall opposite her told her that it was quarter past eight. Just how much longer could Lucas keep Marissa away? A man with a scar – Gutierrez – was talking now, and fiddling with the projector. First up on screen was a map of the Friday Islands and the mainland, and then, Cate realised she was looking at a topographical picture of Snapper Bay. The men were talking quickly now; it was harder to understand them. They were also using a lot of slang that Cate was struggling to translate. She could pick up that they were talking about computers, discussing the sales of iPads and mobile phones and mining for . . . What? The word sounded like 'Indians'. Then there were several mentions of 'Indianbe'.

There was another picture of Snapper Bay, this time taken from the sea, and then, to her horror, shots of the eco-warriors. Noah, Mitsu, even Michel. All of them were there. Her heart froze, expecting to see herself, to be caught out, but the pictures must have been taken before she arrived. They moved on to more shots of the beach.

'How is the *sapo*?' the young man with the curly hair suddenly asked. 'Is he encouraged to work faster now?' He laughed, his mean face lighting up, and the two bodyguards sniggered like schoolboys from their shadows.

Sapo . . . Toad? thought Cate wildly. How is the toad? Frustration was taking over. She had risked so much to be here and yet she was learning nothing.

And then she remembered. A long ago insult from a Mexican kid with whom she and Arthur had shared a tutor during her dad's stint in Warsaw. She had been maybe ten or eleven and he thought she had sneaked on him to the teacher. 'Sapo, sapo,' he had shouted at her when lessons had finished. 'Spy. Traitor.' Cate felt as if she had been kicked in the stomach. So it was true. An informer was working for the Cotians. At Snapper Bay.

'The encouragement worked perfectly,' said Gutierrez. 'As it always does.' He put his hands together as if in prayer. 'The *sapo* is doing our work and people are already starting to leave.'

He gyrated his hands from left to right, and began to sing the theme tune from *Jaws*. 'Now we'll see just how much those kids love their precious turtles.'

The whole room erupted into laughter. Cate thought about Josie's terrified face as the sharks had surrounded her kayak and she was seized with an overwhelming urge to push their vicious faces into the dirty plates.

The phone on the side table rang, an irritating beep that silenced the whole room.

'Answer it.' The guard nodded curtly at Cate. Cate's mouth went dry. It must be the hotel kitchen or maybe reception checking to see if everything was OK. They would hear her voice and know she wasn't Marissa. She walked towards the phone slowly, praying that it would stop ringing before she reached it. 'Answer it,' said the guard again, his tone more menacing.

She swallowed hard, picked up the receiver and spoke quietly. 'Hello,' she said. 'Marissa here.'

'Cate, it's Lucas.' Cate felt her knees almost buckle in relief

162

at the sound of his voice. 'Marissa's on her way back.'

'Thank you,' said Cate, her voice expressionless as she replaced the receiver. She looked up and caught the security guard's eye. 'I have to go to the kitchen,' she said. 'Someone else will come to serve you.'

He nodded and opened the door.

Out in the corridor, Cate turned and leant against the wall, her head bowed. Despite her relief at being out of that fetid room, she felt as if she was about to be sick. Further down the corridor, a door opened and Marissa came out, waving and blowing kisses into the room. But when she saw Cate, her smile vanished and she turned white.

'They have been there long?' She pointed a shaking finger at the conference room. 'They didn't notice?'

'It's OK,' said Cate, pointing to herself. 'I pretended to be you. I helped a friend waitress once. How was Lucas?'

The girl blushed. 'He was amazing. It was the best day of my life. Thank you. But now I must go in and do my job. Please, you tell no one?'

'No one,' said Cate firmly, feeling slightly guilty that the girl was so grateful. She bent forward and removed Marissa's name tag and at the same time pushed another twenty dollars into her pocket. 'I said I was Marissa. You need another name.'

'I'll be Claudia,' she said, beaming. 'The name of the other maid on duty here tonight.'

'Sounds great,' said Cate kindly. 'See you around, Claudia.'

Cate walked slowly up the corridor. She reached the rehearsal room and paused. She knew she should go in and say something to Lucas, but she was too tired to come up with a bright idea to excuse her weird behaviour. She would face him later.

'Nice outfit, Cate,' said Lucas sardonically. He was standing in the doorway holding his guitar case and looking at her with an unfathomable expression in his dark eyes. 'I think its time you and I had a talk.'

CHAPTER 14

Cate sat on her balcony watching as the last of the sun's rays were obliterated by the gathering darkness. Beside her, the swimming pool was lit up with a rainbow of underwater lights, their colours reminding her, as if she needed it, of the events at Snapper Bay. She was just about to text Louisa when she spotted the old text from Arthur – the one he had sent her containing the news report on the attempt to buy out Snapper Bay. Of course, how could she have forgotten?

It was too early to call her brother. A text would have to do. *Cn u find out just who ws bhind bid to buy lease on Snapper Bay? ASAP. Xxx*

Half an hour later her phone rang. 'How're you doing?' Michel said sheepishly. 'I really needed to hear your voice.' He paused. 'Things are a bit tense here, Cate,' he continued, all trace of his usual humour gone from his voice. 'When you get back from Purbeck, I want us to take off, just you and me. I just want you to myself for while. I feel like since you got here, well, you've been in another place, if that makes sense. I want us to be close again, like we were in Antibes last summer . . . Cate, I have to ask you . . . Is everything OK? With us, I mean?'

The concern in his voice made Cate want to cry. Especially since she knew that, in part, he was right: her mind had been elsewhere, focused on the IMIA and its demands. It wasn't fair, she thought furiously. They asked too much of her and it was rebounding on poor Michel.

'Michel,' she said, her voice firm, her emotions now fully under control. 'Everything is OK with us. More than OK, I promise. I'll be back at Snapper Bay in a couple of days' time and then I can't wait for us to go off together. It sounds like the best idea ever.'

As Michel hung up, Cate heard the thud of a helicopter flying overhead. Nine-thirty. They may be disastrous for her personal life, but Marcus and Henri were always punctual to a fault.

'What's he doing here?' Henri asked as he and Marcus strode into the room minutes later. He was glaring at Lucas Black who was sitting impassively in an armchair in Cate's bedroom.

'It's Lucas, Lucas Black,' said Cate nervously. 'The pop star.'

She knew the importance that Henri, Marcus and indeed the entire IMIA placed on silence and she hated that Henri may be thinking she was loose-tongued. Or, worse still, that she had become so starstruck that she had confided in Lucas just to get his attention.

'I didn't ask who he was,' Henri was speaking quietly now, always a bad sign. 'I asked what he was doing here.'

Cate took a deep breath. 'He helped me,' she said simply, deciding that honesty was the best policy. 'I needed a miracle and you guys weren't around. Lucas came through but he wanted to know what was going on. Somehow I couldn't manage to fob him off.'

'I worked for British counter-intelligence in Afghanistan,' Lucas said, his voice sounding almost robotic, and his face expressionless. Suddenly he looked like a stranger and Cate shuddered inwardly. 'My brief was to infiltrate the Mujahideen and get information that would allow us to pre-empt suicide attacks. Both in that country and in ours.' He paused and his eyes dropped. 'I wasn't always successful. I lost someone I loved very much and I left the army to build a new life.'

Cate's heart lurched. She remembered his first hit single and felt tears of pity for Lucas pricking at the back of her eyes. No one spoke.

'I can smell a covert operation a mile away,' Lucas finally continued. 'So I was never going to buy Cate's excuses, no matter how good they were.' He sounded more like the cocky, confident Lucas that Cate knew now. He looked from Marcus to Henri. 'Don't worry. I can keep a secret. But in return, I have to know what is going on here on Purbeck Island. I have me and mine to think about, to protect if necessary. And that includes Cate.'

Marcus and Henri gazed at each other, their expressions unreadable. Then Marcus turned his palms up in a gesture of defeat. 'OK by me, Henri,' he said, 'but you're the boss.'

Henri looked at Lucas and then seemed to make up his mind. He turned back to Cate. 'Well, Cate,' he said, as if Lucas had never spoken. 'What have you got for us?'

'Some evidence,' said Cate, heaving a sigh of relief and handing him the tiny memory card she had retrieved from the pen camera. 'I took some shots of the divers I saw last night at Snapper Bay. It may have picked up their faces – it may not.'

'Very good,' said Henri shortly. 'Anything else you can tell us about what is going on?'

Cate shrugged. 'Not really,' she said honestly. 'The Cotians are definitely staking out Snapper Bay. I could be mistaken, but they talked about a *sapo* amongst the eco-warriors.' She looked at the two agents, wondering if they knew what it meant.

'An informer,' said Marcus flatly. He slapped his hands together in frustration. 'Here we are, thinking we were smart putting in Cate as an undercover agent. These guys were ahead of us, maybe have been for some time. But why go to all that trouble? What is it that they want from Snapper Bay?'

There was silence.

'Come on, Cate.' Henri was sounding testy as he always did when things didn't go his way immediately. 'You must have picked up something. These guys are making hundreds of thousands of dollars every week out of their illegal activities back home. It's got to be something pretty phenomenal to bring them all the way here.'

Marcus shifted uncomfortably on the bed where he had taken up residence. 'Cool it, Henri,' he said. 'Cate's doing her best. She's just a kid.'

Cate walked over to the window and stared out at the swimming pool. Dinner over, the band were back in their favourite spot, swigging from bottles of beer, horsing around, pretending to push each other into the pool. There was no sign of Nancy.

She sighed and turned back to the men. 'They talked a lot

about a word that sounded like "Indians" she said. 'Mining Indians, and making huge amounts of money from it.' She thought back to the conference room, her mind running back through the snippets of sentences she had heard from around the table. 'I think one of the men said something about paying,' she said slowly. 'Making the rest of the world pay huge amounts, that's what he said.'

There was silence and then Marcus got up from the bed. 'Look, Cate, that's brilliant. You've done really well. Getting into that conference room was pure genius. I'm sure you understand that, well, for now we still haven't a lot to go on. We can't just arrest people from a perfectly legitimate Latin American country because we don't like the look of them. We need more.'

'Well, you can count me out,' said Cate firmly. She had been waiting for this. 'I'm staying on for the concert tomorrow and then I'm going back to Snapper Bay.'

'Good, that's great, Cate,' said Marcus. 'I think that's just where you need to be, to get to the bottom of this. We have to find out which one of the eco-warriors is working for the Cotians and then we might have a chance of finding out why.'

'No.' Lucas spoke again, this time his tone flat and menacing. 'Cate's done enough now. It's someone else's turn to risk their lives. You, for example.'

Henri and Marcus turned as one to stare at him, shock written on their faces. Cate wished she had a camera. It wasn't often that Marcus let down his cool.

'When she told me what she was doing, I thought she was a complete fantasist,' he said quietly. Lucas raised his hand in apology. 'Sorry, Cate, but I did. But not any more. Can we get this straight? You have a sixteen-year-old schoolgirl working for you as a spy, you send her in, alone, to spy on some of the most dangerous men in the world and then, when she's risked life and limb already, you ask her to keep spying?' He shook his head. 'And people say rock stars are immoral.'

Cate laughed. She couldn't help herself. Marcus was grinning too.

'Mr Black.' Henri was clearly not amused. 'You may like to take the moral high ground but we can't afford to be quite so sanctimonious. The IMIA take on the crimes that just about everyone else – the CIA, MI6, even Mossad – have given up on, and because of that we use every weapon at our disposal.' He paused. 'Even if they happen to be sixteen-year-old girls with a God-given talent for spying.'

Cate knew she was weakening. After all, there was no denying that she was in the right place at the right time. She smiled apologetically at Lucas. 'OK,' she said. 'I'll try to find out who the informer is, but that's it. I'm leaving you guys to deal with them. But after this, I really don't want to hear from you guys again for a very long time.'

'Fair enough,' said Marcus.

Lucas stood up. 'Please, Cate,' he said. 'This isn't some kind of game; it's highly dangerous and I think you're too young to know what you're doing.' He looked at Henri, contempt all over his face. 'I've a good mind to go to the press with this.'

'Mr Black.' Henri's voice was menacing. 'I have to warn you that you are now moving into very dangerous territory indeed. Either you are silent about what you have learnt today or you will be taken out of circulation until this problem is cleared up.'

For one awful moment Cate thought Lucas was going to hit Henri and she knew it would be Lucas who would come off worse in the fight.

'Henri,' she protested, mortified that it had come to this. 'Lucas is only trying to protect me. Lucas, I'm sorry, really sorry. I didn't mean to drag you into this.'

The two men continued to glare at each other. It was Marcus who broke the impasse.

'Hey, guys, chill,' he said. 'No need to stress. Lucas, if Cate doesn't want to do something she won't, believe me.' He put his hand on Lucas's shoulder. 'How about a deal? We give Cate two days in Snapper Bay and then we'll leave her be. Send in someone else. Come on, man, just two days?' Lucas looked at Cate. 'You OK with that?' he asked.

She nodded.

'All right,' he said, turning his gaze back on Henri, 'but I warn you now if anything happens to her, nothing and no one will be able to shut me up.'

There was a loud knock at the door and instantly, miraculously, Marcus and Henri were gone, faded into the dark corner of the room. Cate went to the door and opened it cautiously. There, dressed in bright pink Versace from head to toe and wearing an outraged expression stood Nancy.

'Cate, where is everyone? I've hardly seen you since you got here. And Lucas seems to have gone missing too. You came here to cheer me up, remember? Not go around pleasing yourself.'

'Sorry, Nancy,' said Cate smiling apologetically. 'Don't worry, I'll come and help you look for Lucas right now. Have you tried the basement recently?'

Without a backward glance Cate stepped from her room and shut the door firmly behind her.

The music was blaring, pounding; the heavy beat reached down and shook the very ground that Cate and hundreds of other guests were standing on. They had been dancing for the best part of an hour now, irresistibly drawn to the unique rhythms of Black Noir – part African, part R & B all mixed in with unforgettable melodies. More powerful than anything else, thought Cate, who along with Nancy was standing within the fenced-off VIP area, were the lyrics. She loved Lucas's lyrics. Some were so sad that they brought tears to her eyes, others defiant and angry, others clever, witty plays on words.

Even Nancy was mesmerised, happy for once to play second fiddle to someone else. That morning, at breakfast by the pool, Nancy was clearly thrilled to be reunited with Lucas. 'You'll be fab tonight, darling,' she said, picking out a huge red strawberry from the luscious heap of fresh fruit piled on a crystal stand in front of her and popping it into his mouth. 'I just can't wait and neither can Cate, can you?'

Cate nodded. 'I can't believe my luck,' she said truthfully.

Lucas smiled at her benignly. He was doing a very good job of pretending that the events of the day before had never happened. 'You're welcome, Cate,' he said. 'Enjoy.' He stood up. 'I've got to do a last rehearsal and sound check, then I'll be sleeping for the rest of the day.' He kissed Nancy passionately. 'I'll be looking right at you,' he said to her as he finally turned to leave.

'I'll be right there, babes,' she cooed back at him tenderly.

Cate sat back in her wicker chair, her face to the sun, her feet dangling in the pool and smiled. She had to admit,

Purbeck Island was incredible. Whilst out on her morning run she had spotted an ex-president of the USA, a couple of Hollywood stars and a famous playboy golfer. The place was awash with celebrities.

'Everything OK with you and Lucas now?' she asked Nancy idly. 'I take it Cindy wasn't here to steal him after all?'

Nancy giggled happily. 'Since we last saw Cindy she's put on about twenty kilos and has taken to wearing a burkini. Apparently Cindy is so paranoid that her lovely pale goth skin might get a bit of colour while she's in Australia that she even wears the ridiculous thing at night.'

Cate snorted. It was a brilliant image.

'I could hardly keep a straight face when I first saw her,' Nancy continued wickedly, 'and you should have seen Lucas's expression when he opened the door to her. I think he thought the island had been invaded by large black aliens. He didn't know whether to say hello or call security.'

The two girls dissolved into helpless laughter.

'Told you so,' said Cate eventually, wiping tears from her eyes. 'No competition. If she ever was in the first place.'

Now on the stage, Cindy was belting out a Black Noir number, her powerful, distinctive voice raising high up into the starlit sky, every note pitch perfect.

Lucas was standing behind her, his guitar slung round his neck. Suddenly, he ran across the stage, down the tiny flight of stairs to the VIP section and dragged Nancy on stage with him. She looked amazing, her blond hair glowing like a halo under the spotlights, her perfectly fitted maxi dress both sexy and demure. Lucas pulled her into his arms and, seemingly oblivious to the crowd roaring their approval, began to slow dance with his girlfriend.

'Wow,' said Cate to the Australian soap star who was wearing a gravity defying micro mini dress. 'Those two really know how to put on a show.'

Cindy finished her number, Nancy and Lucas disentangled themselves and waved happily at the audience. Then, to Cate's horror, Nancy was at the top of the stairs beckoning to her. 'Come on, babe,' she mouthed over the noise.

Before she had a chance to think, Cate was up on stage. It was the weirdest sensation to be looking at hundreds of faces of complete strangers who were cheering her on as if they knew her. The lights were hurting her eyes and the smell of sweat and the heat of the energy from the band was almost overwhelming.

She tried to edge towards the back of the stage only to find the bass guitarist tapping her on the back. 'Oh no you don't, gorgeous,' he said naughtily into her ear. 'The good sheikh needs all the friends he can get to sing "Happy Birthday".'

Just then there was a drum roll from Pete, and Lucas struck up the first chords of 'Happy Birthday'. Off-stage, Cate could see a man holding a huge cake in the shape of a skyscraper. Nancy beckoned to her and she and Nancy carried it carefully to a gilt table that had been placed in the middle of the stage.

Standing there was a man in white robes, his red face beaming with pride, his immaculately dressed and heavily made-up wife standing just behind him. 'Thank you,' he said politely, bowing first to Cate and then to Nancy before kissing both their hands. 'The cake is beautiful.'

Cate stood at the edge of the stage as the entire audience erupted into 'Happy Birthday' followed by 'My Special Day' –

a Black Noir hit. The stage lights had dropped to a single spot-light focused on the sheik, and now Cate could actually recog-nise a few faces in the crowd below her. In the second row, she could see Wayne Shawn and some of his old team-mates, each of them with their arm around a stunning girl and exuding a beery happiness. In the row behind sat a couple of Hollywood actors who were clapping along to the music. Then she saw the smile of the seaplane pilot. He was pointing at Nancy and giv-ing Cate the thumbs up. Cate grinned and waved back at him – she remembered she had promised him an introduction – then glanced along the row to see if she could spot any more famous faces.

Suddenly she felt the blood drain from her face. Standing out with grim and angry expressions in the middle of the sea of smiling singing faces, were the two youngest Cotians. There was no mistaking them and, from the look of it, they had no trouble recognising Cate either. The feeling of fear was so rapid, so overwhelming, that Cate thought she was going to be sick. She gasped for air, and stumbled backwards into the wings, frantically trying to marshal her thoughts.

She was really angry with herself. How could she have been so careless as to be dragged up on the stage in front of just about everyone on the island. She might as well have put up a banner telling the world that she was available for ques-tioning if any Cotians would like to ask her just why she had been pretending to be a maid at their meeting.

She was in real danger now and she had to get out of there fast. But who could help her at this time of the night? She scrolled mentally through her options. Marcus and Henri had left the island the night before and the last regular boat left the island at eleven – and it was now nearly midnight.

Then she remembered. The seaplane pilot. He was here at the concert. She slipped through the wings and out down some small steps which brought her out to the edge of the crowd right to where he was sitting. She tugged at his sleeve.

He looked at her incredulously and then at the stage. 'Weren't you up there a minute ago?' he shouted above the noise of the music. Then he grinned. 'Any chance of me getting up there with you and the gorgeous Nancy?'

She shook her head. 'I need to get off the island now.'

He stared at her in surprise. 'Did you say *now*?' he shouted back at her. The band were in full swing, the sheikh and his wife enjoying a birthday dance in the middle of the stage.

Cate knew she didn't have much time left before she would be missed on stage. 'I'm sorry but I'm in real trouble,' she confessed. 'Only you can help me. Please believe me.'

He looked at her and suddenly his smile dropped. 'You serious?'

She nodded pleadingly. 'I'll explain it later. Can you get me off Purbeck as soon as possible? I can pay. A lot.'

He went to look at his watch.

'Don't,' said Cate sharply. 'They're watching.'

'Who?' asked the pilot.

Cate took a deep breath. She could see Nancy looking around for her. 'The Cotians,' she said, praying he would understand.

The pilot shook his head. 'What have you got mixed up in, kid? Then he aded, 'How much?'

'Double your normal rate.'

'Triple it.'

Cate shrugged and nodded. It wasn't her money anyway.

'Meet me at the jetty in half an hour exactly,' he said. 'Be there. I won't wait around.'

He stood and pushed his way into the sea of people who were up on their feet and dancing. The band were working their way noisily through the closing bars of 'My Special Day', the sheikh and his wife finished their dance and waved a final farewell to their friends and family in the audience. The Cotians were still there, but Cate could see from their faces that the show was now the last thing on their minds.

As soon as she could, Cate backed away from the crowd and headed for the cover of the small wood nearby. Away from the heat of the stage the night air was cooler, the stars brighter. She had half an hour to get back to her room and pick up her belongings. She needed the money she'd put in the room safe to leave, and she couldn't go without her computer.

Cate jogged carefully through the trees, trying hard not to be spooked at every strange shape made by the branches and the leaves. It was all she could do not to scream when a large bat flew off noisily in front of her.

She reached the back garden of the villa. The house was in darkness – empty, Cate knew. Nancy had given Valentina and Marissa the night off and everyone else had been at the concert. She glanced up at the windows, her imagination running wild. 'Stay calm,' she told herself. The Cotians had no idea of who she really was, let alone where she was staying on the estate. At this time of night it would take them ages to find out.

She walked past the pool, and the table which had already been laid for breakfast and without hesitation she picked up the sharpest knife she could see. Luckily for Cate, someone had been careless and left without locking up. She pushed at the large French windows, which opened without a sound.

She moved cautiously into the large drawing room and then the hall. Feeling more confident now, Cate took the stairs to her bedroom a couple at a time until she was finally standing outside her bedroom. Her heart was pounding, her mind racing. Every sense in her body was straining, trying to work out if there was danger behind the door. Cate knew she couldn't wait any longer. She turned the handle gently, then threw open the door, flicked on the light and raced back into the corridor as light flooded the room.

There wasn't a sound from the room, yet somehow, Cate could sense danger. Her hand tightened around the handle of her knife and she stepped silently into the room and took cover behind the bed, before leaning down and switching on the lamp beside it.

The room was completely and utterly empty and, as far as Cate could see, undisturbed. Her clothes lay as she'd left them on an armchair, the bed still ruffled from where she had sat to do her make-up a few hours before.

She breathed a huge sigh of relief, went to the safe at the far end of the room and punched in her number. The tiny door swung open and she stuffed the money and laptop into her rucksack.

Cate turned to leave the room. It was then she heard the smallest of clicks away to her left. At the same time the room was plunged into darkness and instinctively she ducked down behind the armchair, knife at the ready. She looked around, weighing up her options. The door was at the other end of the room, too risky to run for, but a few metres behind her was the balcony window. She tried to remember how high it was, what surface lay below it and was just bracing herself to make a dash for it when the bathroom door swung slowly open, light spilling out.

Cate looked up and all thought of escape vanished from her mind. Standing there, with tears trickling down her cheeks and a look of pure terror on her face was Marissa. Her hands were tied in front of her and blood streamed down one side of her head dripping onto her uniform. Just behind her, his gun pointed directly at Cate, was a balding man with a scar across his forehead and a look of satisfaction on his face.

'Welcome, Cate Carlisle,' he said. 'Come and join us.'

Cate knew she didn't really have a choice. She sighed and stood up slowly, sliding the rucksack over her shoulders.

'Leave it,' said the bodyguard. 'The knife, too. Come in here. Be quick about it or your friend will suffer again.' He grabbed the maid by the shoulder, the pressure making her wince.

'OK,' said Cate, holding her hands up. 'OK, I'm coming.'

As she reached the bathroom, the man motioned for her to shut the door. 'Lock it,' he said.

Cate's heart sank as she did as she was told. This was bad. She was trapped in a tiny area with an armed thug with other Cotians very likely to be on their way. She thought about the concert. There was, she reckoned, at least another hour before it ended. Another hour before anyone would come looking for her and by then . . . She shuddered inwardly. Arthur had been right, she thought grimly. So had Lucas. This really was way out of her league.

But Cate wasn't going to give in without a fight. She stood

quietly, obediently, but all the while her eyes flickered around the room, desperately searching for anything she could use as a weapon. Right now, she thought, she needed to buy time.

'What is this?' she asked, her hands stretching out in a gesture of bewilderment. 'Why are you in my room? I'm a guest here but I'm not rich, I've got nothing worth stealing.'

The man snorted. 'Nice try, kid,' he said, 'but guests on Purbeck Island don't dress up as maids and wait on tables, do they? And maids don't end up dancing on stage at rock concerts with the guest of honour, do they, Marissa?'

Marissa shook her head, her eyes wide. 'I am sorry,' she said to Cate. 'I am sorry I told them where you were staying. I had no choice.'

'It's OK,' said Cate. 'It's not your fault.'

'Shut up,' said the man flatly. 'I'm the one talking and I've got some questions. He pushed his gun into Marissa's neck as he glared at Cate. 'Where are you from and who are you working for?'

Cate stared back at him, a plan formulating in her mind. If she went for him, Marissa would be dead instantly and, in all probability, she would be too. She had nothing left but the element of surprise.

'I'm going to faint,' she said suddenly, putting one hand up to her head and swaying theatrically. She put her other hand out to the sink to steady herself and then went down, her knees buckling beneath her.

As she fell sideways onto the marble vanity unit, she heard the man cursing with surprise, heard him coming towards her and knew it was now or never. She slid her hand from underneath her body and groped for one of the crystal bottles of luxury body cream that she had so admired earlier in the day. As the man pulled roughly at her shoulder, she swung the heavy container up and around and smashed it over his head.

He staggered back swearing, blood mingling with broken glass and cream in a grotesque mess that was slithering slowly down his forehead. His eyes met Cate's and in them she saw an expression of murderous hatred, but this time she had the advantage. Before he could bring his gun up, she had grabbed his wrist, twisting it round and backwards, paralysing his grip. The gun dropped uselessly from his hand.

By now the gunge had reached his eyes, and he was staggering half blinded around the tiny space. Dodging him, Cate grabbed at the thick cord that held the shower curtain back, and coming up behind him, threw the rope over his body and pulled it tight behind his back, trapping his arms by his side. He bellowed and kicked as she knotted it and then tied the ends of the cord around some pipes. *It will take him a while to get out of that one,* thought Cate.

Marissa was already by the door, valiantly trying to undo the lock with her tied hands. Cate slid the lock open and the two of them were free of the room, slamming the door behind them.

Cate grabbed the knife and slit Marissa's bonds. 'Quickly,' said Cate. 'Help me.'

Cate pulled out a heavy chest of drawers and together she and Marissa pushed it against the bathroom door. 'I'm sorry I got you into this trouble,' said Cate, grabbing her rucksack, 'but now we have to get out of here.'

Marissa nodded. 'You rescued me. I trust you,' she said bravely. 'Let's go.'

They crept down the stairs in darkness, Cate not daring to put the light on or even use the torch she had in her rucksack. They had just reached the drawing room when they heard noises outside. Cate grabbed Marissa and pulled her into the entrance of the corridor that led to the kitchen.

It was just in time. Cate saw a flickering torch light appear, then the two young Cotians walked past them, talking in low voices. Cate and Marissa stared at each other, clutched each other's hands. The two men moved on and up the stairs and Cate nodded encouragingly at Marissa.

'Now,' she breathed, and they slipped silently into the drawing room, and out into the sweetness of the night, running in the shadows all the way to the jetty.

'You cut it fine.' The pilot was standing at the doorway of his seaplane, his hand tapping impatiently on the wing. He glanced at Marissa in surprise. 'Two of you now?'

Cate took a wad of money from her bag and handed it to him. She could hear Black Noir in the distance, the crowds still cheering. 'Just a quick flight to the mainland and then you can forget you ever saw us this evening.'

The pilot looked down at the money, back at Cate, and then he shrugged. 'Fair enough,' he said. 'Kids nowadays. More money than sense.'

CHAPTER 15

Cate was woken by sunlight spilling into her tepee. Slowly she opened her eyes, looked down at her fully clothed body and finally, remembering what had happened the night before, at her watch. Ten in the morning. By now Marissa would have landed safely in Sydney, enough money in her pocket to keep her going for several months. 'Just forget you ever saw me,' whispered Cate, hugging Marissa as she stepped into a cab bound for the airport. 'And thank you for being so brave.'

Michel had arrived, without a fuss, to collect Cate from the jetty on the mainland, as she'd arranged.

'I decided to come back early,' Cate had said quietly, clinging onto him. 'Nancy and Lucas are all lovey dovey again, so I didn't see the point of staying away another day.'

Michel had put both his arms around her, resting his head on hers. 'I'm glad,' he'd said. 'I am sick of missing you. I feel like everyone else gets a bit of you and I don't.'

Now a bleep came from one of her pockets. Still sleepy,

Cate scrabbled around until she found her phone and looked at her screen.

U OK? Where R U?

Cate groaned with guilt. In all the excitement and exhaustion of last night she had completely forgotten about Nancy. Immediately she texted back. *Fine & dandy. Had to rush back to Snapper Bay early 2 C Michel. Soz. Hope al OK at yr end and C U soon?*

Her phone bleeped again. *Charming! Still, as long as yr Ok. Lucas worried too. C u soon xxx*

Cate grinned at that. *Tell him not 2. Gig was fab. Big thnx. Will bring M to c u nxt time. xxx*

She suddenly stopped smiling. The Cotians must have stayed around long enough to clean up her room and remove all the evidence of the fight. They were professional all right. And that meant they weren't going to give up their search for her easily. But they had no way of knowing she was at Snapper Bay. She was safe at least for now.

She lay back on her bed dozing in the sunshine, her eyes closing again. She felt a shadow cross her face and reluctantly forced her eyes back open. Standing in the doorway of the tent staring down at her was Josie – a smiling, happy Josie. A far cry from the quivering crying mess of just a few nights before.

She walked into the tent and plonked herself happily on the floor next to Cate. 'Miles said you were back,' she said cheerfully. 'I heard you went to a Black Noir gig. I love Black Noir! It must have been so cool to see them live.'

Cate sat up in bed and looked at Josie. Something was stirring in the back of her brain, something to do with Josie's awful childhood, something to do with her grandpa.

'Josie,' she said gently, 'Jacob told me the story of your grandpa's life. He was a miner, wasn't he?'

'He was more than a miner,' Josie said proudly. 'He was a businessman. He made a fortune. He always said mining was the best and quickest way to make huge amounts of money. All you needed was hard work and a bit of luck. It's still true, even today. There are lots of things in the ground, things that most people haven't even heard about. Things we need for computers and satellites up in space. Things for hospital equipment and medicines.' She dropped her voice. 'Even right here at Snapper Bay. There's something I've seen here.'

Cate stared at Josie, trying hard not to betray her excitement. 'What have you seen?'

'Josie.' Someone was calling her from just outside the tepee. It was Miles. 'Hey, Josie, you in there? Noah wants your help on the beach.'

Before Cate could stop her, Josie jumped immediately to her feet, putting her fingers to her lips in a shushing gesture as she went backwards out of the tepee.

'Hey, Cate.' Miles popped his head into the tepee. 'Good to see you back. How was the gig?'

Cate smiled up at him. 'Bit of a late one but worth it.'

With a friendly wave Miles was gone and Cate lay back in her bed, uncertain whether to be thrilled or terrified at what she had discovered. She thought back to the meeting on Purbeck Island, to the men sitting around the table, so cold, so calculating. Men vicious enough to cut two men to death by propeller, and to somehow engineer a shark attack on the eco-warriors.

There was something at Snapper Bay that the Cotians wanted badly enough to fly halfway around the world for, enough to kill for. She had some pieces of the puzzle, but certainly not enough to provide anything like a clear picture of what was going on.

She could hear Marcus's voice now, the last time they had spoken. 'The truth is that right now, Cate, we don't even know where they're hiding out. We need to know what these guys are after before we have a hope of getting in there and stopping them.'

Maybe Josie was onto something. It was definitely a lead worth following. She was going to have to speak to her again.

Cate pulled out her laptop from under the bed and began to Google. She tried *mining*, *Australia* and *Friday Islands*. Two millions entries popped up, but as Cate scrolled down the top few there was no mineral mentioned that was so rare and so valuable as to interest men who already made millions of dollars a week out of crime.

With a sigh of frustration she flipped the lid down, grabbed a change of clothes from her trunk and headed out for a shower. She had just changed into fresh clothes when Michel arrived.

'Hi, *ma belle*,' he said, giving her a huge kiss as she emerged, her hair still soaking wet.

Cate smiled at him, hoping he couldn't see her turmoil. Half of her was desperate to confide in him, tell him everything about her fears, her narrow escape. But the other half just wanted them to stay boyfriend and girlfriend, untainted by all the intrigue and the danger. Maybe she shouldn't think about what Josie had said. She could simply hand everything over to Marcus the next day as planned, forget all about the IMIA and the Cotians and go off with Michel. Hang out at the beach, swim, drink coffee and eat takeaway just like thousands of other couples backpacking up and down the country.

'Could we just take it easy today, Michel? Just us two,' she asked.

'*Mais oui, cherie,*' he said, ruffling her wet hair. 'I cannot think of anything nicer. I'll make us a picnic lunch, bring some books and we'll go and find somewhere quiet to be alone. Who knows . . .' He grinned at her. '. . . I might even bring my saxophone.'

'Don't do that,' laughed Cate. 'You'll frighten the wildlife. I need to grab some breakfast. You coming?'

He shook his head. 'I'm helping out with the nesting count this morning. I'll meet you back here at midday.'

Maria was on her own in the kitchen, sporting a paper mask and latex gloves, grating a strange herb that smelt so strongly of peppermint that it made Cate cough.

'Sorry, Cate,' Maria waved over at her. 'Josie found this for me. She said it was right at the far end of the beach. It's weird, isn't it? I can't find any reference to it anywhere. It could be a world first. It might even be a medicine. Anyway, first up, I'm going to boil a bit of it and see what happens.'

'Wow,' said Cate, impressed, helping herself to a cup of freshly made coffee and a bowl of muesli. 'That would be so cool. Let me know how it goes. But, if you don't mind, Maria, I'll think I'll eat outside.'

From her seat at the top of the steps, Cate had a view of just about the entire camp, and this morning it seemed as if

187

just about everyone was out and about. She spotted Noah and Jacob walking down to the beach carrying a couple of spades, chatting and joking as they went. Mitsu was lying in a hammock reading a magazine. Over by the fire circle Tuyen was training a pair of binoculars on the water whilst Dan tapped away on his laptop. To her left through the trees, she could just catch a glimpse of Miles under the shower. She hadn't known any of them for long but they had all made her welcome, treated her with respect and consideration. Each of them had their own separate passion for the environment, and especially for Snapper Bay, and it seemed almost inconceivable that any of them would help people like these Cotians.

Her breakfast finished, Cate took her bowl and mug back into the kitchen. After the bright sunlight outside, the room was dark and she could only just see Maria standing over the pan, steam rising up from the lid and surrounding her head and shoulders.

A shaft of sunlight came through the window, throwing its rays onto Maria. Cate put down her mug and stared, and then rubbed her eyes and stared again. There was no mistaking what she was seeing. Maria had an aura, a purply blue glow edging the outline of her body. The same purply blue that Cate had seen in the night waters of Snapper Bay. For a few seconds, Cate was transfixed as the colours bent and danced in a ghostly display.

Finally she found her voice. 'Maria,' Cate said quietly.

The girl turned round and smiled, completely unaware of her strange transformation. 'Hi, Cate. Sorry, is the smell still getting to you? I won't be long now.'

'No, it's fine,' said Cate, trying hard to keep the excitement out of her voice. 'Maria, can I have a closer look at the plant of yours, please?'

'Sure,' said Maria. She picked up the chopping board that lay next to the stove. 'Help yourself. I think it looks just like your English parsnip to me.'

Cate cupped the soil-encased root in her hands, marvelling at the weight of the plant. She squeezed it gently with her hand and the soil crumbled lightly away between her fingers. And then Cate understood. It wasn't the plant that was heavy or even the soil around it. In her hand Cate was holding shards of a bright silvery metal.

'It's indium,' said Arthur, his voice squeaky with excitement on the screen of Cate's laptop. 'It's a very rare metal that is in increasing demand in technology manufacturing. It's perfect for LCD technology.'

'Speak English, please, Arthur!'

After Cate had left the kitchen, she had taken her laptop and headed out to her favourite spot on the edge of the beach to talk to the one person she could really trust.

'Liquid Crystal Display. Flat screen TVs, tiny watches, wafer thin phones . . . The use for indium is endless but the supply isn't.' He Googled furiously. 'It says here there's a mine in China, one somewhere in Bolivia, Canada and, if I'm not mistaken, they found some recently in a disused Cornish tin mine. And that's about it.'

'Are you sure, Arthur?' Cate asked. 'I mean, this is really important.'

'Of course I am,' said Arthur a tadge crossly. 'Every techie knows about indium. It was discovered by two German scientists who were searching for different metal ores using spectroscopy. They didn't find what they were looking for but they spotted this weird blue emission instead, indicating a new element. They named it after the colour indigo.'

'Jeez.' Cate was seized with an almost irritable urge to jump up and down with glee. 'I couldn't understand why they were wittering on about something that sounded like Indians.' She thought back to the hot sticky room. 'It was indium they were talking about,' she said almost to herself. 'Indium B.'

'Sorry Cate, could you repeat that, please?' Arthur's voice sounded strangely quiet.

'They were talking about indium B.'

'I thought that's what you said,' said Arthur. He ran his hands through his hair, making it even more spiky than usual. 'Cate, this is mind blowing. Indium is pretty rare and expensive.' He did another quick Google search. 'Ten years ago it was worth sixty dollars a kilo, now its over a thousand. But indium B. That's just a concept really, it hasn't even been discovered.'

Cate stared at the screen. This time her brother had really confused her. 'What on earth are you talking about?'

Arthur sighed. 'I'll try and keep it simple, Sis,' he said kindly. 'Basically we've got as far as we can go with new technology in terms of power and size. If we make things any smaller, we lose effectiveness. So now everything you see – your phone, your watch, your laptop – is a compromise between the two. But indium B gets around that problem. It would be a thousand times stronger than indium, which means you can use much less of it and still get the job done. But indium B has only been produced in a lab in tiny quantities and the process was far too expensive to make it in any commercially viable way.' Arthur was really excited now, his dark head bobbing and weaving on the screen. 'If you have found a natural source of indium B, then believe you me, you have just discovered the next stage in our technological evolution. We can send spaceships further, make computers much smaller, create bigger and faster planes. It's amazing. Stupendous. It could revolutionise the world.'

Cate tried to digest the news. So was that what those divers had been doing on the night of the storm? Checking out the cliffs, the beaches, looking for indium B.

'But if it gets into the wrong hands?' she asked, already knowing the answer.

'Then it could be disastrous,' said Arthur, his excitement subsiding. 'This stuff needs to be carefully monitored, shared fairly across the countries and the industries that can develop it properly. If it gets into the wrong hands or just put up for sale to the highest bidder, then it's a nightmare scenario.'

'That's what they said they wanted to do,' said Cate with a shudder. 'The Cotians want to make loads of money from it – they don't care who they sell it to.'

'Cate, Michel, have you seen Josie recently?' Dan flopped down onto the beach beside them, wriggling under their parasol to escape the worst of the mid-afternoon sun. 'I've been looking for her for ages. It's her turn to collect wood for the fire and she's vanished.'

Cate and Michel exchanged exasperated glances. They had walked for a good fifteen minutes down the beach in the hope of finding a place where they wouldn't be spotted.

'I saw her this morning,' said Cate, trying to be helpful. 'She popped in to see me in my tent. Just before Michel and I planned this *private* picnic!'

'Did she?' said Dan, missing the hint. He stood up, brushing sand from his shorts. 'Oh well, if you see her then tell her to get to the kitchen. This is the third time this week she's forgotten she's meant to be helping out. It's just not fair on the rest of us, especially now that the twins are gone. We all have to share the load.'

Michel and Cate looked at each other and grinned. 'Another Diet Coke, *cherie?*' asked Michel, reaching into the cold box. 'Oh, and here are the prawns. I knew I'd put them somewhere.'

'Who's that?' Dan asked. He was staring up the beach towards the camp, his hands shading his eyes.

Exasperated Michel sat up. 'Look, Dan, much as we love your company, Cate and I, well, we just want to be on our own. By ourselves. Just the two of us. *A deux.* Can I be any clearer?'

Cate giggled. She checked her mobile. She had texted Marcus as soon as Arthur had hung up but she hadn't had a signal since.

'Someone's running towards us,' said Dan, ignoring Michel. 'Fast. It's Noah.'

A feeling of foreboding swept through Cate's body as Michel jumped to his feet and began to jog towards his cousin. 'Noah?' he shouted. 'Noah, *qu'est que c'est?*'

Noah was panting, struggling to get the words out, his face grey with shock. 'It's Josie,' he said. 'I found her over there.' He pointed towards the far end of the beach. 'She must have been climbing up the cliffs and fallen. She's unconscious!'

Holding hands tightly, Cate and Michel watched in silence as the air ambulance lifted off into the sky. On board was a still unconscious Josie, and Mitsu, who had volunteered to go with her.

'I won't be coming back, guys,' she said sadly, hugging them all goodbye as Josie was being loaded onto the helicopter. 'Bad things are happening. I don't like the vibe any more.' She looked at Jacob. 'I know what you're going to say, Jacob, but all the logic in the world won't change my mind. In any case, this isn't about logic, it's about gut feeling.' She paused. 'Don't worry, guys, I'll stay with Josie until she's OK. I'll keep you posted.'

Cate nodded mutely, tears pricking the back of her eyes. She was really going to miss Mitsu.

'Hey, Cate,' said Mitsu, trying to smile. 'Think about it. You've got a whole tepee to yourself now. No more snoring!'

'Time to go!' A middle-aged doctor in green fatigues strode over to them.

'How bad is it?' Miles asked. His hands were shaking.

'She's had a head injury but the rest of her body seems relatively uninjured, apart from a few bad bumps and bruises. Nothing broken that we can see,' said the doctor, 'but she's in a coma and we won't know until we've done a CT scan on her brain what sort of damage has been done. Even then it will be another forty-eight hours before we have any idea of whether or not she will recover quickly or take longer – or maybe not at all. Head injuries are a nightmare to call.'

He put up his hand in a farewell gesture and shepherded the waiting Mitsu into the helicopter. The propeller turned slowly, then faster and faster, until the chopper was above their heads and gone.

Cate couldn't help but wonder if that reduced her list of informant suspects down by two, or if the insider had just got away.

In the silence that followed, Cate turned to Michel. 'I need to get out of here, just for a few hours,' she said quietly.

Michel smiled weakly and squeezed her hand. 'Great idea, Cate.' He turned to Jacob. 'That OK, buddy?'

'No problem.' He looked so down-hearted, so miserable that Cate felt like giving him a hug.

'It's OK, Jacob,' she said. 'Don't worry. Accidents happen. I'm sure Josie will be OK.'

'I guess,' said Jacob, trying to look cheerful.

It took them less than half an hour to get to Parsons Rock, a small town just up the coast from Snapper Bay. It was market day and, despite the heat, the long high street was buzzing with noise and energy.

Cate and Michel parked the bike in the centre and walked slowly along, browsing the stalls which sold everything from fishing gear to waxed jackets and steel-capped boots.

It was clear that it was a day out for many people. Greetings and jokes were shouted across stalls and a steady stream of red-faced farmers and their jean-clad wives weaved in and out of the several pubs that dotted the long street.

Cate soaked up the atmosphere. It reminded her of the little Yorkshire market town she had visited every year as a child.

'Where's all the food?' grumbled Michel good-naturedly. 'I was hoping for some nice cheeses, maybe a stall selling good bread and olives.'

Cate laughed then. It felt like the first time she had done so for a very long time. 'Michel, we're not in France now.' She pointed to a stall selling books and CDs. 'Come on, let me buy you a present.'

It took them nearly an hour to work their way along all the stalls. The far end of the high street forked into two narrow roads, one edged with houses, the other with shops and a few cafés.

'Fancy an ice cream?' said Michel, pointing at a booth.

'You bet,' said Cate. 'With everything on top.'

As Michel waited in the queue of cheerful teenagers and children, she wandered along the street, peering into the shop windows. Suddenly Cate spotted a small metal sign for something called Washers Quay. The name seemed familiar although she couldn't think why. Then she remembered. She put her hand into her purse and pulled out the card the seaplane pilot had given her last night. 'Just in case you need a lift anywhere,' he had said. 'Don't hesitate to call me.' Cate stared down at the card. *Scott Foster. Pilot. Washers Quay.* It was where he moored his plane.

An idea was forming in her mind. He had picked up at least some of the Cotians who attended the meeting. He might just know where they were hiding out. She shook her head. Why on earth hadn't she thought of that before?

She pulled out her phone and rang his number. It flipped to voicemail, the pilot's cheerful voice instructing her to leave a message. *He might be working on his plane,* she thought. It would be no trouble to quickly ask him what he knew and pass it on to Marcus.

She ran back to Michel who was still in the queue. 'Michel,

195

can you give me a few minutes? That seaplane pilot moors here. I think I might have left something in his plane last night.'

Just then, her phone vibrated with a text from Arthur. *Taken me all day but think I know who bid for S Bay lease. Does the name Carlos Ibanez mean anything to U? PS. Take care.*

Cate walked down the hot street, her mind in a whirl. The pieces were finally coming together. Now she knew how badly the Cotians had wanted to get their hands on Snapper Bay. And she knew why. But what she didn't know was what they were going to do next – and how to stop them. She really was going to have to hand this one over to IMIA.

As if on cue her phone rang. 'You took your time, Marcus,' she said, looking at her watch. It was nearly three o'clock.

'Sorry, Cate,' he said, not sounding sorry at all. 'I've been out in the field, or should I say, the ocean. The Aussie navy have been tracking a large Cotian yacht in the Pacific, just east of here. We boarded and searched it but there's nothing untoward going on that we can see. We're probably going to have to let them enter Australian water.' He sighed. 'Another frustrating lead gone nowhere. Oh and your pictures of the divers. Cotians for sure. We ran them through some recognition software and two of them are on the CIA's most wanted list. How about your end?'

Cate took a deep breath. 'Marcus, I think I've found out just why the Cotians are so interested in Snapper Bay. Can we talk?'

'Not like this. We'll meet today if you want. Me, you and Henri. Where are you now?'

'Parsons Rock – just north of Snapper Bay. I'm at the quay

to be precise and I'm just about to go and see if the seaplane pilot is home.'

'Why?' said Marcus puzzled.

'He ferried in a couple of the Cotians for their meeting. He might just know where they are based. It's a long shot, but I might as well try.'

'Brilliant, Sherlock,' said Marcus gleefully. 'Once you've spoken to him, call me back and we'll arrange a meeting. Henri's down in Sydney at the moment pleading for more troops but he should be back by this evening.'

Cate put her phone back into her pocket and followed the signs down to Washers Quay. It was quieter there, less commercial, with just one small shop selling sailing equipment and a scruffy-looking pub.

To her delight, Cate spotted the seaplane moored up at the far end of the quay, its paintwork as shiny as ever. Behind it stood a large wooden shack with a small boardwalk leading up to it. Cate knocked a couple of times and then, getting no reply, turned the handle and opened the door. She was in some sort of workshop. The air was cool and dank, the concrete floor covered in oil patches and littered with tools. To her right, a door smeared with greasy stains stood slightly ajar. She knocked again and pushed it open.

The pilot was sitting on the lino floor, his back pushed hard and straight against the corner of a filing cabinet, his face chalk white, his eyes closed. A small hole in the side of his head was almost obscured by a rim of concealed blood which had run in a neat stream down onto his white T-shirt. An overturned chair lay in pieces beside him, a metal waste paper basket had strewed its contents over the floor.

Almost as if she was in a dream, Cate went slowly over to the pilot and touched him arm. It was stiff and cold and it was all she could do not to scream.

Scott Foster was dead and had been for a while.

CHAPTER 16

'Get the hell out of there, now!' Marcus was shouting down the phone in a tone she had never heard him use before. 'You're not safe. Don't call the cops, don't do anything. Go back to Michel and pretend that this never happened. I'll send someone in now to clean it up, do you hear?'

Cate was standing outside the shack, her back to the sunshine, trying desperately to get some warmth into her body, to stop herself from shaking. 'Marcus, he was a nice guy. He flew me and Marissa out of danger when he could have just stayed at the concert.' She felt waves of guilt washing over her. 'If I hadn't asked him to do that perhaps he wouldn't be dead now.'

'Cate, listen to me.' Marcus was speaking urgently now. 'We don't know why he was killed so don't go jumping to conclusions. If anyone is to blame it's us – the IMIA. After he got you off the island we should have offered him protection but we were too busy concentrating on working out what the Cotians were doing to consider him. We took our eye off the ball. I'm sorry, Cate, really sorry. It must have been a terrible sight.' Marcus sighed. 'I know. It's a really hard thing to deal with. The only way to cope is to keep going, to keep the bad guys in your sights. At least that way Scott's death won't have been in vain.'

'OK,' said Cate, trying hard to keep her voice steady. 'Where can we meet? I can't leave the camp tonight, not again. Even Michel will begin to smell a rat if I do that. And you can't come to me. No way.'

'That's true,' Marcus said. He paused. 'If we bring a boat over to Snapper Bay late tonight can you get out to meet us? In a kayak, perhaps?'

Cate thought for a while. 'Don't come into the bay,' she said finally. 'It's too risky. Stay just outside it and look for me. I'll sneak out after dark and aim to be at the mouth of the bay for one a.m.'

'It's a deal, Cate. We'll go through everything then. In the meantime, stay on your guard.'

'Yup,' said Cate, hanging up. She was calming down now, pushing away the image of the seaplane pilot's bloodied face. She stood in the shade of an alleyway and took some deep breaths and spoke sternly to herself. 'Come on, pull yourself together, Cate. You did it last summer and you can do it again.' She squared her shoulders and turned onto the street and saw Michel, coming towards her, waving an ice cream.

'Hurry up, Cate,' he called to her happily. 'It's about to melt.'

'It's very quiet here,' said Michel as they dismounted back at camp. 'Where is everyone?'

Cate pulled her helmet off and listened. Usually there was the sound of music coming from someone's tepee, or a clattering from the kitchen. But now only the birds singing their evening chorus and the cicadas revving up for a night of calling to their mates filled the almost eerie silence.

'The others must be on the beach,' said Michel. 'I'll go find them. Thanks for a lovely afternoon. It was a great idea.'

Cate headed back to her tepee but, as she passed Josie's yellow tent, she heard a movement from inside. She lifted up the mosquito net and peered in. There was Miles, sitting on Josie's bed, bits of paper strewn around him like confetti. He looked up at Cate, his face a picture of pure misery.

'I thought I'd better see if there was any address for her family,' he said. 'It was the least I could do.' He picked up the papers and shoved them into a small chest at the bottom of Josie's camp bed and slammed the lid shut.

Cate nodded. 'Good idea. Miles, I'm going to dump my bag and then start on supper. It looks like no one else is doing it.'

'I'll come with you,' said Miles, looking around the tent. 'There's nothing useful here.'

Surprisingly, supper was a lively affair, with the remaining eco-warriors seemingly determined to enjoy themselves. Cate and Michel had searched through the cupboards in the kitchen and managed to rustle up a huge bowl of pasta with anchovies and olives.

'Homemade bread,' said Michel proudly, dumping a large bowl of warm rolls onto the kitchen table which he'd carried outside and set for seven.

'How long have I been your cousin?' asked Noah, slapping

201

Michel on the back. 'And I never knew you could make bread.'

'Good news, guys.' Maria appeared through the trees, holding her phone. 'Mitsu just called – I had a signal. They've scanned Josie's brain and there's no damage that they can see. They think its just a question of time before she wakes up and, fingers crossed, there shouldn't be any lasting damage.'

'That's brilliant,' said Jacob, who had just arrivedfrom surveying the beach.

'Ta-daahh.' Tuyen arrived, carrying a large black bucket which was full to the brim. Cate peered into the water and yelped as a large pincer waved back at her. 'Crabs,' said Tuyen proudly, his black eyes sparkling. 'Great big juicy ones. The nets were full. We're going to have a feast.'

'This is where I resign as chef,' said Cate firmly, taking off the tea towel that had been serving as an apron and passing it to Tuyen. 'I can't put those poor creatures into boiling water. It's the sound they make. Horrible.' She shuddered.

'Honestly, Cate, you're too soft-hearted,' Dan mocked her gently. 'If you think that's bad, don't even think about going backpacking in south-east Asia. It'd give you nightmares the way they treat their animals.'

That started everyone off with tales of their travels, and soon people were laughing and joking around the table. Only Miles stayed silent, his face morose and anxious. Cate watched him out of the corner of his eye. He had really taken Josie's accident badly, she thought.

When it was almost dark, Michel stood up to light some candles. Cate, used as she was to long lingering twilights, still found it a shock when the day and night met so abruptly.

'Jacob, we're struggling with our internet connection,' said

Dan. 'It's a bit of a pain to be honest. It's been fading in and out all day. Even worse than usual.'

'Strange,' said Jacob. He pulled out his phone and checked his signal. 'Must be going through a bad patch. Maybe the storm moved a satellite a bit.'

'Maybe,' Tuyen shrugged, unconcerned. 'Anyway, we know you're a bit short-handed but Dan and I wanted to head into Parsons Rock tomorrow. We need to file some reports back to uni and to pick up some data for our PhD. We don't want to take any chances with dodgy reception. Is it OK if we take the jeep? We only plan on being gone a couple of days.' He laughed at Jacob's stricken face. 'Don't worry, we're not doing a runner and we're not worried about sharks. We are, however, utterly terrified of what our college professor will do to us if we don't get our PhD papers finished on time.'

'Fair enough.' Jacob smiled. 'We should be OK here. There's enough of us to carry out the basic tasks for the next few days. Just don't stay away too long, that's all.'

Cate looked at her watch. It was nearly nine o'clock. Just under four hours before her meeting with the IMIA. 'Do you know, guys,' she said. 'All the excitement of the day has worn me out. I think I'll turn in. Do you mind?'

'No problem, Cate.' Michel stood up with her. 'We'll all soon be in bed.' He took her hand and kissed it. 'Will you be OK without Mitsu's snoring?'

Cate laughed. 'Michel, I'm looking forward to my first good night's sleep since I left London.' She looked around the table. 'In fact, if anyone disturbs me between now and ten o'clock tomorrow morning I swear I won't be responsible for what I do to them.'

Curled up in her bed, she set her phone alarm to vibrate and tried to get some sleep. But there were too many thoughts turning over in her head, too many images she just couldn't erase. The seaplane pilot's bloody head, Josie's body lying crumpled on the beach at the bottom of the cliffs, Miles's stricken face as the helicopter took Josie away.

With a sigh, she switched on her torch. She tried to read but her brain was too full to take in the words, so she got out of bed and began to potter around the tent. Nothing like a bit of housework to take your mind off your troubles, as her grandmother used to say. Save for Mitsu's wetsuit, the hanging wardrobe was empty. She may as well make use of it. She took a few items of clothing from the chest, shook them out and began to hang them up, the torchlight shining through the thin plastic, making it virtually transparent in the darkness.

Except, Cate realised, it wasn't see-through. Not all over anyway. On the bottom of the wardrobe she could see a large shadowy rectangle, the size of an A4 envelope. *Perhaps Mitsu has left some documents behind*, thought Cate. She slid her hand underneath the wardrobe and into a small slit that had been cut into the plastic. A few seconds later, she had the envelope out. She sat back down on the bed and pulled out some faded newspaper cuttings. Old pictures stared out at her. A little girl holding the bridle of a huge racehorse, a silver cup almost as big as she was clutched in her chubby hand. A big sandy-haired man standing behind her with a huge smile on his face, holding what looked like a pint of Guinness. *Little Josie O'Leary receives the Melbourne Cup whilst her father looks proudly on*, said the caption.

Of course, Jacob had told her about the newspaper cuttings

and Mitsu said Josie had given her the wardrobe. Josie must have forgotten she'd left them there.

Cate flipped carefully through the yellowing paper. There were pictures of huge houses, a yacht, then, more ominously, two men in handcuffs. One picture had been taken in front of a large, official-looking building and showed Josie and another child, an older boy, standing on either side of woman, each clutching at her hands as if they were clinging on for dear life.

The woman was beautiful, with an oval face and huge mesmerizing eyes, and auburn hair which tumbled around her slim shoulders. But the look on her face was one of desperation. Cate found the image almost unbearably sad, even before she read the text. *Bella O'Leary, wife of the convicted fraudster David O'Leary with their two children, Josie and Michael leaving court after he had been sentenced to eighteen years in prison.*

Cate peered more closely at the boy. His oval face, long nose, tight red curls . . . They all looked terribly familiar. She looked again, realisation slowly dawning. She had been looking into those eyes earlier that evening. Unless she was very much mistaken, Michael O'Leary was now going by the name of Miles Finlay.

Cate lay down on her bed, her mind racing. What was it Jacob had said? That there was an older brother, Michael. No one knew where he was. Cate bit her lip. Josie had known. But why keep it secret from everyone else? What was the point?

Unless he wanted to hide his identity. Cate thought back to when the Cotians had tried to burn down the HQ. Why would they do that? Miles had turned up, said he had received a warning. Supposing he knew about the indium B and he

205

realised what it was worth. His grandfather was in mining – maybe Miles knew something about it too. Could Miles have alerted the Cotians? His family were broke, so he'd need funding to mine. Had he sold the secret of Snapper Bay to the highest bidder?

It made sense. It was the Cotians who had tried to buy Snapper Bay. When that failed they had decided they were going to take what they wanted anyway. Had Miles's job been to clear the coast of all the eco-warriors? Had he brought his sister Josie in to try to scare everybody too? Except that hadn't worked so well – Josie was so highly-strung no one had taken her fears seriously. She had been genuinely scared of the water though. Did she know something about the sharks, and why they were attacking everything? Cate thought back to the attack on Matthias. Miles had seemed genuinely distressed then – but had it been the Cotians' warning to Miles to get everyone out of Snapper Bay so they could get on with their mining?

Cate's hands were shaking as she pushed the cuttings back into the envelope. It looked very much as if she had found her *sapo*. The last person anyone would suspect of selling out his eco-friends at Snapper Bay.

Long before her phone vibrated its alarm, Cate was ready to go. She put on Mitsu's wetsuit and packed her phone, her penknife and a torch into her waterproof pouch and strapped it firmly around her waist. She was worried about her phone. The signal was fading in and out, she found. Typical for this to happen just as she was going to be out at sea. The last thing she wanted was to lose her only means of communication with Marcus and Henri.

Quietly, she pushed aside her mosquito net and put her head out into the still night. The camp was in darkness. Everyone, it seemed had turned in for the night. Above her, clouds moved slowly over the sky, a sliver of moon providing just enough light for her to see by.

Slowly, gently, she stood up and, careful not to stand on any twigs or gravel, began to make her way down to the beach.

The kayaks were lined up on the wet sand like sleeping seals, their paddles underneath them. Cate pushed at the dark blue one. Clutching a paddle in one hand and the kayak in the other, Cate hopped in and pushed off, paddling out towards the mouth of the bay.

She looked up and fixed her eyes on the point where the bay opened out to the ocean. As soon as she headed around the point, she felt the water change beneath her. In the bay, the waves had been choppy but relatively gentle. Now they were higher, rearing up above her head one moment, and then rolling and lurching away underneath her kayak a few seconds later. She didn't fancy being on the open ocean for too much longer.

She was just about to try her phone again, when a small, black dinghy materialised out of darkness, two dark figures sitting up high on either side. There must have been an engine, Cate reasoned, but it was so quiet she couldn't hear it at all.

'Hey, Cate, fancy seeing you here.' One of the black figures stood and threw her a rope. 'Here you go,' said Marcus. 'Tie that to your kayak. We'll tow you in.'

The small naval boat was cloaked in darkness. Cate sat in a warm cabin below deck, wrapped in a blanket and drinking a mug of frothy hot chocolate.

'Take your time, Cate,' said Henri. He was perched on the edge of a table, his arms crossed, his face even more stern than usual. Marcus was lounging on an uncomfortable-looking grey sofa.

'Have you heard of indium?' Cate asked them eventually.

They looked surprised. 'Yep,' said Marcus slowly. 'The stuff they use in micro technology, LCDs, iPads, anything that needs to be small yet powerful. Quite rare but not desperately so. A relatively valuable commodity.'

'Blimey,' said Cate. 'I had to get Arthur to explain all that to me. Well, here's another question. Have you heard of indium B?'

Henri frowned at her. 'That's classified information, Cate. How did you find out about indium B?' His face cleared. 'Of course. Your brother. We really are going to have to employ that boy one of these days. Cate, only a handful of people in the world know about indium B. The only reason I was told was because the IMIA is at the forefront of satellite tracking technology and, right now, that technology is going nowhere fast.' He turned to Marcus. 'We've basically got as fast and as accurate as we can without a major leap forward in the strength of the component parts. Unless we can improve them we'll be stuck in a technological dark age. The problem is, Cate, indium B doesn't really exist.'

'Oh yes it does,' said Cate, quietly putting down her mug. 'I've seen it. And so, I think, have the Cotians.'

Henri stood up and stared at her, his eyes wide and shocked. For once his composure had vanished. 'My God, Cate, are you sure?'

'As far as I can be. Do you remember I was telling you that

at the meeting the Cotians were talking about Indian mining. I though they meant a mine somewhere in India or something. But they didn't. They'd said indium. I only realised when I saw it in the kitchen at Snapper Bay. Maria was trying to boil up some sort of root than had been growing in it and she got surrounded by this like purply blue aura.'

'Er, Cate,' Marcus said sheepishly. 'Are you sure you're feeling OK?'

'Marcus do be quiet,' Henri said sternly. 'I know exactly what she's talking about. Indium gives off a purply blue haze when viewed through a certain light structure, but i ndium B is only detected through its aura, which can appear in sunlight, moonlight – even through water. That's what Cate saw.'

'I thought about it and suddenly I realised it all made sense,' Cate went on. 'The Cotians wouldn't come halfway around the world for something that cost a few thousand dollars a kilo. Nor would they go to all that expense to try to get their hands on the land surrounding Snapper Bay. It had to be something incredibly rare, incredibly precious. It had to be indium B.' She reached for her bag. 'I've got some here if you want to look at it.'

The effect on Henri was electric. His mouth fell open and his outstretched hand was shaking. Cate reached into the small pouch and brought out a small handful of the dull metal, still brushed with red soil. She put it into Henri's hand and he looked at it silently.

'We'd better get it checked out,' Marcus said. He walked over to the door and opened it. A smartly dressed naval man sprang to attention. 'Can you send the captain to us, please? We need to get an urgent message to HQ in Sydney.'

'How on earth did the Cotians find out about this?' said Henri, finally pulling himself together. 'We didn't know about it, the Aussies didn't know about it.'

'Someone told them, of course,' said Cate. 'It was their *sapo*. Their informer. And I think it was a guy called Miles Finlay.'

'Miles Finlay? The dude who heads up the Australian Eco Trust?' Marcus was incredulous. 'You can't be serious.'

'That's what I thought,' said Cate. 'In fact, I never, ever, considered him. After all, everyone knows he is the ultimate eco-warrior: passionate, committed, trustworthy. Except he isn't. Trustworthy, or even called Miles. He's actually Michael O'Leary, the son of David O'Leary, otherwise known as one of the Lucky O'Learys. Google him. His sister Josie was here at the camp. Been here for a few weeks. I can't be sure, but I think Miles must have found the indium B. He knew immediately what it was worth, and had contacts in Cotia. He's gone travelling round the world before. And you can bet your bottom dollar that his passport will have a few South American stamps in it.'

There was a knock on the door and Marcus opened it, speaking quietly to the person outside before turning back. 'They're sending a scientist to pick up your stuff now, Cate. They'll analyse it and have the results back by tomorrow.'

Henri spoke. 'If this is true, Cate, do you know what this means? The Cotians are going to try and get to the indium B illegally. Which means all of you at Snapper Bay could be at risk at any time.' He drummed his hands on the table. 'We're going to have to shut the turtle sanctuary down. I'm sorry, Cate.' He raised a hand to her protest. 'We can't risk harm coming to any of you.'

There was a long silence.

'If only we knew where the Cotians were hiding out,' said Marcus finally. 'We could go in and arrest them. We'd find something to link them to the seaplane pilot's death and Cate here got a good look at the bodyguard who threatened to kill Marissa.'

'But we don't know where they are,' said Henri testily. 'They all met up at Purbeck Island, so maybe the base is near there. Somehow they've managed to get under our very extensive radar.' He thumped his hand down on the table. 'They're outwitting us at every turn. They've got us on the defensive and I don't like it.'

Cate felt her phone vibrating in her pocket. 'Hi, Arthur,' she said. 'Great timing. What's going on?'

His voice was excited, jumping with enthusiasm. 'I've just checked Rafe Schuster's phone. You know how the signal was at Snapper Bay? I've just checked it again and it's moved.'

Henri swiftly left the room and Cate heard him barking orders to connect Arthur to the ship's communication system.

'Cate, can you please explain again who Rafe Schuster is?' Marcus asked as they raced to the bridge. Henri and the captain were poring over a chart of the Friday Islands.

Arthur's face was up on a large screen, directing operations from his chalet bedroom.

'Rafe? He's the boy who went missing from the camp a week or so before I got there,' said Cate. 'Everyone said he must have done a runner, even the police. But there was always something suspicious about him disappearing without saying goodbye. And his girlfriend, Maria, had said his mind was on other things before he disappeared – he was going to talk to her, but never did.' She stopped suddenly.

'Go on,' said Marcus quietly, his dark eyes never leaving hers. Henri too was very still.

'The thing was that if he hadn't done a runner, that meant that someone had cleared out his belongings. I didn't want to admit it, but the more I thought about it, the more likely it was that something bad had happened to him. I just couldn't work out what or how. The other day, Maria was admiring my blue T-shirt. She told me she'd bought one just like that for Rafe as a present when they went to the market at Parsons Rock. And guess what? The Cotian at the drop-off point was collecting a passport and clothes. Including a bright blue T-shirt. It has to mean they had Rafe.'

'And the phone?' Henri asked.

'Not everyone knows they can be tracked when switched off,' Arthur chipped in. 'You can bet it's with his clothes. Which are most likely now in the same place as Rafe.'

'But why kidnap the boy?' Henri was speaking almost to himself. 'Why go to all that trouble?'

'Perhaps he had stumbled across something that meant he was a danger to the operation,' said Cate. 'Maria did say he was distracted. Or maybe he just got unlucky.' She didn't voice her real concern: that these people hadn't worried about killing when it suited them.

'Don't worry, Cate,' said Marcus, reading her mind. 'The fact that the Cotians bothered to collect his clothes suggests Rafe is alive. Perhaps they think they can use him as a bar-gaining tool, should things go wrong.'

'Either way,' said Arthur, 'that phone will probably lead us straight to the Cotians.'

Marcus and Cate looked at each other and shook their heads in admiration. 'Arthur, man,' said Marcus. 'Double, no, triple respect. When all this is over, I am going to buy you any piece of computer kit your heart desires.'

'Done,' said Arthur. 'Actually, I could do with an introduction to the guys who are creating Geronimo – you know, the new generation of satellite positioning. I've heard they're a really cool bunch.'

'No problem,' said Marcus, smiling back up at him.

Henri looked up from the chart. 'Those co-ordinates, Arthur. They're for a place called Razor Island, about twenty kilometres from here. According to our captain, it was used as a submarine base in the Second World War when the Aussies were terrified Japan was going to invade from the North. It's been wired off and abandoned for years.' He seemed to come to a decision. 'Marcus, you'll head up a surveillance team tomorrow morning and we'll check it out. If the Cotians are there, I'll take a team in. All being well, we'll go in tomorrow at nightfall. In the meantime, Cate, you get back to camp before you're missed. I take it you haven't told Michel about your secret life and it's best you keep it that way.'

'Well done, Cate.' Marcus was sitting ahead of her in the dinghy, the kayak trailing out behind them. 'Yet another amazing result. I honestly think you have the luck of the devil. And that's a compliment, by the way.' He paused. 'This time tomorrow it will all be over, hopefully with as little fuss as possible. Once we've arrested the Cotians, we'll pick Miles up quietly and you and the guys at Snapper Bay can go on doing your thing, whatever it is eco-warriors do nowadays.'

They had reached the mouth of the bay and Marcus pulled up the kayak and held it steady whilst Cate clambered into it. Her job was done now, the danger over. She could leave everything to the IMIA and go back to being a teenager. She should be relieved. So why then did she feel so miserable, so cheated?

'Marcus,' said Cate as she picked up the paddle. 'I don't suppose I could come with you guys tomorrow, could I? Just to watch the action.'

Marcus laughed. 'Don't even think about it, Cate. It could get very nasty. And let's not forget your dad. He wasn't very pleased with us last summer. If he thought we were taking you into another risky situation, I don't like to think what he would do.'

'Marcus, come on,' she wheedled. 'I'll just stay on the boat and watch from a distance. There's no harm in that and my dad will never know. I won't even tell Arthur – well not until it's all over. I've done all the hard work. I've practically led you to the Cotians. And now, just when the fun starts, suddenly I'm a little kid and told to run along. I thought better of you, I really did.'

Marcus shifted uneasily in his seat. 'OK, OK, Cate,' he said. 'I'll speak to Henri. But I'm not promising anything, mind. I'll text you later.'

Cate had just got back to her tepee when her phone bleeped. *You win.*

Yeeees, thought Cate triumphantly. She lay back on her pillow, a huge grin on her face and thirty seconds later was fast asleep.

CHAPTER 17

'And then there were six.' Jacob and Cate stood at the edge of the track watching the jeep carrying Dan and Tuyen into the distance.

'There's going to be five for a while, I'm afraid,' Cate said. 'I'm meeting my friend Nancy in Parsons Bay this afternoon. Michel is dropping me off and she and I might just stay put for the evening.'

'*The* Nancy Kyle?' asked Jacob enviously. 'Can I sneak along and join you? I could do with a break for a few hours.'

'Sorry,' said Cate, feeling guilty that she was lying so efficiently to such a nice guy. 'There's only room for two on Michel's bike. Another time. I'll arrange it, I promise.'

Cate lay in the hammock, looking out to sea. Michel was surfing with Noah, their black wetsuit hoods standing out sharply against the morning haze. She waved to him and he waved back, then turned to catch a wave that was rising behind him.

He really had no idea what she had been doing these last few days, Cate realised. How was that possible when in many ways they were so close?

She was desperate to tell Michel about the Cotians, about the IMIA, about last summer. But she knew that it wasn't fair to put such a burden on him. Henri was right. It was best that he didn't know.

'Hey, Cate, how are you doing?' It was Maria, carrying a large fishing rod in her hand. 'I thought that as our two fishermen had gone I would give it a go myself,' she said. 'Just how hard can it be to catch a few fish?'

'I might join you in a bit,' said Cate, suddenly in need of company. 'My dad showed me how to cast a line. It's not too difficult, as long as you haven't got any trees to get it caught up in.'

Maria laughed. 'I'm glad you're here, Cate,' she said, 'and not just because you're the only girl. You're such good fun.'

'Has anyone seen Miles?' Jacob was stomping crossly along the beach, carrying a clipboard in one hand and binoculars in the other. 'He was on turtle watch last night and he hasn't left any records of nestings. Honestly! It's bad enough that we're so shorthanded without him going flaky on us as well.'

Maria and Jacob wandered off along the beach leaving Cate to her thoughts. She was glad she hadn't seen Miles that morning. She still couldn't work out how someone could be so duplicitous, so evil. The Cotians with their blatant crimes and thuggery were awful, dreadful people, but at least they didn't pretend to be anything else. Miles had fooled everyone into thinking he was some kind of eco hero when in fact he was selling out his friends and the environment.

She pictured Josie, driven to despair by her brother. And how did he thank her for her help in trying to get everyone away from Snapper Bay? She was pretty sure he'd overheard Josie talking to her, got worried Josie was going to tell all, and pushed her off the cliff.

Cate sighed and walked towards the tepee, checking her phone for about the twentieth time that morning. This time there was a signal but still nothing from Marcus. She hoped he wasn't going to go back on his word. She grabbed a towel and shampoo and headed for the showers. She may as well make the most of all the unused hot water.

She was just towelling off her hair when she heard a noise behind her. It was Miles, looking flustered.

'Hi, Miles,' said Cate, trying to keep her voice as casual as possible. 'Been for a walk?'

'What?' he said irritably. 'Yeah, yeah. See you later.'

Maybe he's been looking for that gun that was left at the drop-off point, thought Cate, suppressing an urge to giggle hysterically at the thought of Miles wandering around the clearing searching for a misplaced gun. *When all this is over I'll retrieve it and get it to Marcus. He'll know how to deal with it safely.*

Cate was checking her phone yet again, when she heard a commotion coming from the beach. It was Jacob, sounding panicky.

Michel, Noah and Jacob were near the turtle nursery. At their feet were three black shapes, lying horribly still on the wet sand.

'This is really bad.' Jacob stood up and pointed at the dolphins. Blood seeped slowly, endlessly, from them. 'Shark

217

bites.' Jacob turned the ravaged creatures over with his foot. 'These poor creatures have been half eaten alive by sharks. It's the worst attack yet. I'm sorry, guys, but that's it. Until further notice we're all staying out of the water.'

The boat had floated in on the tide, its lights dimmed, almost invisible in the rapidly gathering gloom. Up on the deck, Cate watched Henri looking through heavy-duty binoculars, sighing and tutting impatiently. He turned to Marcus, who was standing behind him, a wire trailing from his left ear giving him, Cate thought, a slightly untidy air.

'Anything back from the divers?' Henri asked him.

'Not really.' Marcus sounded frustrated. 'They've been around the island several times and security is very tight. There seems to be no way in apart from the one main entrance, and there's absolutely no way of getting through there except with a ton of explosives. And that might just alert the Cotians to the fact we're coming. That's if they're there at all, of course.'

'They're on that island all right.' Henri spoke confidently. 'And not just because Cate and Arthur say so. I've just been sent some aerials taken at first light this morning. They're a bit hazy, but there's definitely been some sort of activity there recently. Some vegetation has been cleared around the entrances to the underground bunkers.' He snorted angrily. 'It looks as if they've been there for a while and we didn't even notice.'

He turned to Cate. 'You wanted to see some action. I'm afraid that this time you might well be disappointed. If that boy Rafe is in there, and I'm pretty sure he is, then if we try to go in all guns blazing we're risking a hostage situation. We've been in touch with his father and he's flying out here as we speak. Apparently he's the personal doctor to the German chancellor. She's already been onto the Australian PM and rattled her cage.' He rubbed his forehead. 'I hate it when politicians get involved.'

Marcus held up his hand and pressed the other to his ear. 'Shh,' he said. 'I'm getting something on the wire.'

Henri glared at him.

Cate tried hard not to giggle. Henri hated being told off.

'One of the divers has found a tunnel entrance in the seabed twenty metres out from the wall,' said Marcus. 'It looks like some sort of wastewater chute. The boys have put an underwater camera up there and, as far as they can see, it's clear. Goes straight through.'

'Brilliant,' said Henri cheerfully. 'That's more like it. Tell them to let us know as soon as they are on the island.'

'There's a problem,' said Marcus slowly. 'It's narrow. Our divers are big men. None of them can even get their shoulders into it let alone swim up it.'

Henri and Marcus looked at each other and then at Cate.

'No,' said Marcus sharply. 'No, Henri. Not this time. I promised her father.'

'Cate,' said Henri, smiling at her. Like a crocodile, she thought. 'Have you done much diving recently?'

Henri and Marcus argued almost non-stop for twenty minutes. At one point Marcus actually threatened to resign. It wasn't until Cate stepped in that things calmed down.

'Look, Marcus, if I didn't want to do this, I would say. All I have to do is get on the island, do a recce, check out where Rafe is and then report back to you so you can get all the glory. Don't worry.' She gave Marcus what she hoped was a reassuring smile. 'You'll be able to guide me every step of the way.' She pointed at the pile of equipment lying on the table in front of her.

Finally a technical advisor was summoned. 'Kit her out,' Henri said to the short rather plump man who suddenly appeared in front of her holding a large plastic box. 'Make sure she has everything the other boys have.'

The man nodded. He had a brilliant way of explaining how his gadgets worked and best of all, from Cate's point of view, he completely ignored the fact that she was young and female.

'This is the portable sonar/radar device.' He picked up a small black box the size of a cigarette packet. 'You strap this onto your belt and it sends out a sonar pulse when you are underwater and a radar signal when you're not. It gives you the position of just about everything within a two hundred metre radius. Put these on.' He handed Cate a small pair of black-tinted goggles. She put them obediently over her head and stared into blackness. 'Now switch on your pack.'

'Wow!' said Cate as she pushed down on the tiny button. Her goggles were suddenly lit by red lines which danced across her vision like tiny fireflies. After a few seconds, they settled down and Cate realised that she was seeing an outline of Marcus, Henri, the sides of the boat and even out to sea.

'It's called Personal Positional Vision,' he said proudly. 'Be careful. It costs a lot of money. Now press the switch again and you get normal vision – even in the dark and underwater. Now, most importantly of all – make sure you activate this green switch as soon as you are in the water. It's a sonar cloak. That's what those divers down there are using right now. If they weren't, the Cotians would have spotted them by now. And here's a hypermagnet. It can scramble most computer security systems. And one more thing.' The techie reached into his rucksack and brought out what looked like a circle of miniature fireworks and began to strap them to her arm. 'Waterproof flares that work with the night vision mode. Point it upwards, pull a tab and the whole area will be lit up like bonfire night – but only if you're using night vision mode. As you – and we – will be.' He smiled at Cate's amazed expression. 'Now that's me done. Good luck, young lady.'

'Is he always like that?' Cate asked Marcus, who was strapping a small bottle of oxygen to her back and fiddling with the valve at the top, checking the pressure.

'He's the best,' said Henri, 'and of course, Cate, you'll be carrying a communicator. You'll be able to talk to us and us back to you. But not too often. We don't want to risk the Cotians picking up the transmission. Now, are you ready?'

Suddenly Cate felt sick. She looked over the edge of boat down to the tiny dinghy that was waiting for her, the black water sucking and sliding like some sinister alien slime. The last thing she wanted was to go down into its depths; she'd just wanted to see these crooks being brought to justice.

'You can still change your mind, you know,' said Marcus gently.

She took a deep breath and forced herself to think of Rafe, a young man, not much older than her, who had been held captive for weeks, not knowing if he would see his family ever again. How scared he must be, how desperate. However she was feeling, he must be ten times – one hundred times – more scared. If he was alive, that is, but Cate knew she had to believe he was. 'It's OK,' she said. 'I'm ready.'

'The divers will be waiting for you at the chute entrance,' said Marcus, as the small dinghy bounced silently across the dark waters. 'They'll wait there until you come out. If you get into any trouble we'll see via the videocam in your headtorch and we'll think of a way to get to you. Whatever you do, don't panic.'

She nodded.

'When you're on the island just concentrate on locating Rafe. Once you find him, get the hell back out again.' He turned to face her, his eyes wide and serious. 'That's all you're there for. No heroics, Cate, you understand?'

She nodded again.

Right at that moment, with the chill coming off the ocean biting through her wetsuit, the last thing she felt was heroic.

The boat was rocking and rolling as the pilot fought to keep it in position using just oars, and through the darkness Cate could see the island looming up above them. It was smaller than she had imagined; wilder, emptier.

'The buildings are mainly underground,' said Marcus. 'Easy to defend. I guess that's pretty much why the Cotians chose it.'

Marcus looked over his shoulder at the silent sonar screen. 'We're over the chute entrance now,' he said in a whisper. 'Good luck.' Cate put out her hand and in the darkness he grabbed it and squeezed it tightly. 'You can do it,' he said.

She clicked on the sonar cloak, pushed backwards off the spongy side of the dinghy and felt the water embrace her.

Then she was diving down, down into the inky black waters.

The water was surprisingly warm and, as she switched on her headtorch, she could see that it was also relatively shallow. Roughly twenty metres below her the seabed shimmered in the thin light, lumps of brightly coloured rocks and coral surrounded by waving fronds of a myriad of sea plants. Hundreds of tiny fish swooped and swarmed around them, dodging and weaving in a mass of colour and movement. Cate was so entranced that for a few seconds she almost forgot why she was there but then, up ahead of her, she saw a diver beckoning. As she got closer, he pointed to the chute. It was much smaller than she had expected. Half a metre square, she reckoned, enough for her to go forward or backwards. There was no way she would be able to turn around.

'You can do it, Cate.' She heard Marcus's voice in her ear, crackling so much that it hardly sounded like him at all. At least it meant he was watching.

She swallowed hard, signalled OK to the other divers, said a silent prayer, and pushed herself into the chute. It was quiet, deathly quiet – the only sound coming from the valve as she sucked oxygen into her lungs and from her flippers as they occasionally banged onto the metal sides of the chute.

As she swam, slimy gobbets of grime and mould that hung down from the rusting walls brushed against her face, making her gag.

Cate had been swimming for a couple of minutes when she felt the walls beginning to close in on her. She fought to control herself, concentrating on her breathing, on moving her flippers up and down, up and down, but the bitter taste of panic was rising in her and she tried to turn around.

Her flippers banged hard against the metal, and one edge stuck in a crack. For what seemed like an eternity she thought she was trapped for good, doomed to run out of oxygen and die in that fetid, filthy drain. Then, bizarrely, an image of Nancy flashed into her head from last summer. She was sitting on the top deck of her yacht, telling Cate, 'My mum always says too much imagination can be a curse.'

Despite herself Cate smiled. *It's only my imagination doing this to me.* She forced her body to relax and her breathing to return to normal. She tugged her foot more calmly and suddenly she was free and swimming rhythmically again through the water. She looked at her watch. It felt like hours but she had only been swimming for around five minutes. She must be nearly there by now.

A minute later she was gulping in open air, the light from her torch bouncing off the walls of a small concrete chamber. She had made it. She was on Razor Island.

Cate climbed silently out of the chute and looked around her. The room was dark and airless, two metres high, wide and long. By the look of the grubby tidemarks, the walls had once been used to hold some kind of liquid. On one side of the wall a metal ladder led up to a wooden trapdoor in the ceiling.

She could hear Marcus in her ear again, anxious, questioning. 'Where are you, Cate? Talk to me.'

'Through the tunnel safely,' she whispered. 'In some kind of tank. I'll let you know as soon as I find an entrance to the island.'

Cate removed her flippers and mask and slid her oxygen tank quietly to the ground. After a few seconds' deliberation, removed her earpiece as well. She worked better on her own, no matter what Marcus and Henri might say. Keeping her eyes firmly fixed on the wall in front of her, she began to climb the ladder. She reached the trapdoor and gave it a cautious push then, as it stayed put, another stronger push.

It moved outwards, just a tiny bit, but enough to spur her on. She switched off her torch, climbed another step up and put her shoulder to it. This time it shot upwards and Cate felt a rush of fresh air hitting her face. She peered through the gap, her heart beating fast. There was nothing but darkness and silence. She pushed the door again, just enough for her to slither out from under it, and she found herself lying on her front on a rough patch of earth.

She lay there, enjoying the luxury of the fresh breeze playing over her face, waiting for her heart rate to return to normal. Then she lifted her head a few centimetres off the ground and looked out over the island. It was almost pitch black. The moon was too young to provide anything other than a watery light. Cate reached into her belt for the night vision goggles, feeling a thrill of amazement as the darkness cleared and night became day.

Razor Island was a desolate place: flat, devoid of vegetation and trees. The only variation in the scenery came from a few small mounds into which small, steel doorways had been sunk. Some of these had been filled in with what looked like rubble, others had been freshly painted. Cate looked about for cover. There was none. Only darkness was on her side.

She picked out a route to a green door twenty metres away and made a run for it, zigzagging across the dry earth, terrified that she would hear a shout or, worse still, a bullet whizzing towards her. She reached the door and paused, listening. It was

225

still eerily quiet. Had she and Arthur sent the IMIA, not to mention a few members of the Aussie navy, on a wild goose chase? Her cheeks burnt at the thought. She forced herself to concentrate. No lock was visible, the door was secured fast from the inside. She reached into her pouch and brought out the hyper magnet. Slowly and methodically, she moved it over the door from top to bottom and halfway down she heard the click that told her she had found the lock. She pressed the small button in the centre of the magnet and felt the power surge. Suddenly the door was free, opening to her gentle push.

Cate stood in the cold darkness of a concrete tunnel that led down into the bowels of the earth. The door shut firmly behind her. There wasn't much to see – just grey walls either side of her, a low ceiling above her and endless concrete steps in front of her.

She cautiously began to move down, her hands outstretched to either side feeling along the walls as she went. She counted twenty, then thirty steps, then turned a corner and ahead of her saw a light so faint that at first she thought she was mistaken.

She pressed back against the wall and listened. She could hear a low murmuring of voices, regular and monotonous. Someone was watching TV. The light brightened and she saw it was coming from a slit under a doorway.

She reached for the door and turned the night vision off. She could hear another noise now – snoring. Cate pushed slowly at the metal door. It opened soundlessly to her touch and there in front of her, sitting on a low beige chair, she saw the source of the snores. She knew him well. He had a bald head and a scar running from his scalp to his left ear. And next to him, his hands tied tightly to the wooden arms of a chair, his grey eyes wide open and staring at her with a mixture of fear and relief, was a boy. He was not much older than her, thin, with a shock of white-blond hair. His legs were bare beneath his shorts and Cate could see a large jagged wound on the front of his right calf that was oozing pus. She stared back at him, her heart pounding. She had found Rafe.

CHAPTER 18

Cate put a finger to her lips. Rafe nodded in return, then rolled his eyes sharply above her head. She followed his gaze and her heart sank. In the shadows, a CCTV camera was casting its eye over the room, clicking and whirring as it changed position every few seconds. Cate watched the sleeping guard carefully, alert to any sign of awakening and she could see that Rafe was doing the same.

She reached up beneath the camera and, standing on the tip of her toes, pushed it just enough to change its trajectory. Despite herself, she grinned. For the time being at least, whoever was watching was going to get a pretty continuous view of the bald head of a snoring bodyguard. She ducked under the camera and knelt beside the boy.

'Who are you?' The boy was speaking German, his voice low and hoarse as if he hadn't spoken for some time.

'I'm Cate.' She knew she was whispering but in her heightened state it sounded to her as if her voice was booming. 'I've come to find you, Rafe. Help is on its way. I'm going to leave you now, but you won't need to wait long.'

He looked at her pleadingly. 'Don't leave me. I'm so frightened. They have been talking about whether or not to kill me every day. Do you know how that feels? It's like torture. I've been trying to convince them that I'm worth more to them alive than dead . . . Please, Cate, take me with you now!'

'I can't,' Cate said, trying to sound reassuring. 'I'm sorry, really sorry. It's just too risky. If he wakes up and finds you gone we'll both be in danger. Just hang on – an hour or so, that's all. Half the Aussie navy is just off the island, waiting to come and rescue you. I just have to get back to them and give them your location.'

They gazed at each other for what seemed like minutes.

Cate sighed inwardly. She knew what Marcus had said, knew that it made sense to follow his orders, but it felt like the height of cruelty to turn her back on Rafe, to leave him frightened and isolated in this cell.

He seemed to sense her indecision. 'Cate, please. It could be that they have decided to kill me now. It could happen any time. Before your friends get back to me even. Then how would you feel?'

Cate shook her head, both at his audacity and her weakness. She did a quick calculation in her head. She could free Rafe and with any luck they would be up the stairs and down to the chute before anyone realised something was amiss. But what if the Cotians saw them and came after them before they could escape? Then they would both end up prisoners. She shuddered – it didn't bear thinking about.

Even as the worst case scenario whizzed through her mind,

she knew that there was no way she could leave him. Cate had never had been able to turn her back on someone in need and she knew she wasn't about to start now. She sighed and reached into her bag for her penknife.

'Shhh,' said Cate, pulling Rafe down onto the ground. They were back at the trapdoor to the tank. So far they had gone undetected, despite a hairy moment when Rafe got giddy from standing up after sitting down for so long. If Cate hadn't grabbed him around the waist and kept him upright he would have fallen straight onto the outstretched legs of the guard.

He had been limping too, his leg wound clearly painful and Cate had no idea how she had managed to get him safely up the narrow stairway without incident.

'Rafe, listen to me.' She spoke urgently, gesturing at the ground in front of them. 'This is our exit route. Under here is a drain that goes out to the open sea. There are men waiting for us who will help. Michel said you are a strong swimmer.' She pulled back the trapdoor and felt for the ladder.

Rafe gazed down into the hole in the ground and then back at Cate. 'I can't,' he whispered, his eyes wide with fear. 'I'm sorry. I'm afraid of dark enclosed spaces. Terrified. It makes me think of hell.'

Cate looked at him in disbelief. 'Rafe,' she said firmly. 'You begged me to bring you. Any minute now they are going to discover you are missing. And when they do, well, this island is so tiny they'll find us in seconds. We have to go now.'

He shook his head slowly, tears in his eyes. 'I'm sorry,' he said again. 'You'll have to go without me.'

With a sigh, Cate pulled off the goggles and shoved them

at Rafe. 'Put them on,' she said, flicking the *On* switch. 'Quickly.'

Seconds later, Rafe smiled for the first time. 'It's fantastic,' he said. 'I can see everything.'

Cate bent down over the gaping dark hole, hoping her natural night vision would kick in fast as Rafe swung his legs painfully over the side of the pit and down onto the ladder. Just then, Cate heard the ominous sound of a siren sounding somewhere deep inside the island. Cate and Rafe looked at each other in horror.

'They know you've gone,' said Cate, her stomach knotting. 'Go, Rafe, go! It's our only chance.'

She pulled the trapdoor down over her head and, a second later, she heard the sound of footsteps pounding the hard soil above them. The hunt was on.

The pair of them stood in the corner of the tank looking down at the chute. Cate had her headlamp on now, taking care not to shine it at Rafe, and she could see the filthy water lapping and swirling around the edges of the metal walls. The chute looked smaller than she remembered. Rafe was thin, but he was still bigger than her and she had been a tight fit. What if Rafe couldn't fit? What if he got trapped down there in the darkness of the tunnel? Most worrying to her was how they were going to get through the tunnel with only one mouthpiece for the oxygen tank. She hadn't even considered that when she rescued him.

'I'll go first. If you get stuck I can go for help.' She looked up nervously. Above her she could hear men shouting, boots thumping on the ground. They were getting closer. It could only be a matter of time before the chamber was discovered. 'Come on.'

Cate slung the oxygen tank back onto her shoulders and passed him the mouthpiece. 'We'll have to take it in turns with the oxygen. I'll need some after a minute, OK?'

He nodded, his face a mask of fear. Cate knelt down at the edge of the chute and turned to give him what she hoped was a reassuring smile. 'We'll trust each other.'

She took three deep breaths to fill her lungs and then pushed down into the dank, dark water. With no oxygen to hand, she was relying on a complete stranger to keep her alive. And if Rafe lost his nerve . . . She shuddered and pushed the thought out of her mind. For a few seconds she concentrated on her flippers, making sure she wasn't moving too far ahead of Rafe. She counted slowly up to a minute. She could cope with that. She had held her breath for that long in her swimming lessons at school since she was about ten.

She looked behind her to see if she could spot Rafe. But all she could see was darkness. Her heart lurched. Where was he? Had he chickened out, left her to die in this horrible place?

Another minute passed and she exhaled slowly, watching the bubbles leave her mouth and then fought against the need to take a deep breath. Her chest began to hurt, her lungs straining, and then she could hear her heart pounding in her ears. She was running out of time.

Still nothing. She was feeling light-headed now, the pain in her chest taking over her entire body, the roaring in her ears almost deafening.

Then she felt a tug on a flipper. Rafe's hand was reaching alongside hers with the mouthpiece, and suddenly she was breathing again, taking great gulps of oxygen, and feeling it rush through her body. The pain receded and she could hear herself think once more. It was the most wonderful feeling in the world, like coming back from the dead. Somewhere in that tiny cramped space she saw Rafe's hand give her the OK sign, and somehow she found the strength to give him one too before passing back the mouthpiece. They were going to make it out alive.

The speedboat surged through the waves towards Snapper Bay. Cate was wrapped in a blanket, silent while Marcus and Henri took turns in telling her off. They hadn't even allowed her back onto the ship, insisting instead that they take her directly back to camp.

'Cate, that really was the dumbest thing ever,' said Marcus for about the eighth time. 'Not only did you put your life at risk in the tunnel but Rafe could have got stuck and drowned.'

'And you broke your word to us,' said Henri, sounding remarkably like her least favourite teacher at school. 'As an agent you have to be trustworthy.'

'I thought you had to think on your feet, be proactive,' said Cate. She'd had enough of being told off. 'Rafe was on the edge of cracking up. He was in agony from a wound on his leg.' She played her trump card, an excuse she had thought of whilst Rafe had been hauled to safety onto the naval boat. 'And I was worried that he might tell his guards that I had been down there so I thought the best thing to do was get him off the island. I bet if you asked him he wouldn't care about me not keeping exactly to my word.'

'True,' conceded Marcus after a pause. 'I suppose you do have a point about needing to bend the rules now and again.' He turned to Henri. 'After all, if we weren't prepared to bend the rules, we would have never have worked with Cate in the first place.'

Henri harrumphed, looking at his watch. 'I suppose everything has turned out for the best. Rafe is safe and on his way to meet his father and, in precisely one hour, twenty or so of Australia's finest will be going in to Razor Island to flush the rats from the trap. And, Cate, before you ask, there is no way you are coming too. I'm not giving you any more chances to get yourself into trouble. We've got your kayak waiting for you at the mouth of the bay. Get yourself back to your camp and we'll call you tomorrow when all this is over. Let you know how it went.'

Cate wasn't up for arguing: the thought of her camp bed was now very appealing. Soon Cate was back in the kayak and she waited as Marcus passed over her rucksack.

'I've slipped you the night vision stuff,' Marcus whispered as he put out his hand to push her off. 'It's a thank you present from me. You did good, Cate, you did good.'

Cate looked up at him in surprise as he winked at her. 'Thanks,' she mouthed. She dipped her paddle into the still water and headed the kayak back towards Snapper Bay.

She was just a few hundreds metres from the beach when she felt a soft bump against the rear end of the kayak. She turned round, and for a few seconds it was all she could do not to scream. There, floating in the water just a few centimetres away from her, was a large, mutilated head, lumps of bloody flesh hanging off the skull, wide eyes staring lifelessly back at her.

For a few terrible seconds, Cate was convinced that a human head was floating beside her, but then she noticed the pointed ears and the large snout, and gave herself a mental shake. What on earth was a pig's head doing floating in a beautiful sea like this one? Had someone thrown it overboard from a yacht, or was it the remnants of a very strange barbecue? Then she saw another chunk of flesh, a pig's trotter, then a leg, and she understood. Someone had just dumped a large bloodied animal carcass into the water.

Not that long ago there had been a series of unexplained shark attacks off the coast of Egypt. Unexplained, that was, until someone had pointed out that live sheep being exported from Australia to North Africa were dying and being dumped overboard just about where the shark attacks were taking place. If there was one thing guaranteed to encourage sharks it was meat, particularly fresh bloody meat. Cate's heart was racing. The creatures were being encouraged to come to this spot to feed and, if they didn't find the meat they were expecting, they would look for it elsewhere. It was little surprise that the turtles and dolphins were being attacked with such ferocity, and no wonder the sharks had been so aggressive towards Josie and Noah.

Slowly, cautiously, she dipped her paddles gently into the water, keeping them close to the surface in a desperate attempt to create as little water turbulence as possible. Logic was telling her that if there were sharks around they would be concentrating on the easy meat, but even so, every splash of water and sudden movement of the kayak made her stomach lurch.

It seemed like hours before she finally heard the sweet sound of the waves breaking on the shore. She was nearly there. Only when she felt the nose of the kayak grinding onto the soft sand did she allow herself to step out into the ankle-high water, before sprinting up through the fizzling foam to the safety of the high beach.

She threw herself down onto the ground, panting with fear, adrenalin pounding through her body. She lay there for several minutes, looking up at the night sky, marvelling at her narrow escape.

The camp was silent although it wouldn't be long before morning. She reached her tepee and dumped her rucksack on the floor then stripped off her wetsuit and changed into shorts and a T-shirt. Too fired up from her near miss, she knew she wouldn't be able to sleep for a while. She felt sticky and dirty from her time in the chute and wondered if she would wake the camp if she had a shower.

She grabbed her toiletries bag and torch and headed out as quietly as she could to the shower area. On the way, she passed Michel's tent and paused. She was so desperate to see him, to talk to him about normal everyday things. And most of all she really wanted a hug.

'Michel,' she whispered quietly. 'Are you awake?' There was no reply. Cate pulled back the net and crept slowly into the tent. 'Hey, Michel, it's Cate. Wake up.' There was no sound from his bed. Feeling slightly foolish, Cate felt up and down the bed. It was empty. She shone the torch up and down the tent, puzzled. Where was he? A few metres away Cate stood outside Jacob's tent listening, but she could hear no breathing there either. Feeling more and more worried she checked them all. Every teepee and tent was empty. *It's like the Marie Celeste*, she thought. *Where would they all go at this time of night?*

Cate glanced over to the kitchen and saw a tiny gleam of light pushing out from under the door and a feeling of anxiety took hold of her. This was wrong, very wrong. If the lamps were on in the kitchen, the light would have been spilling out from the windows as it always did. But for some reason all the blinds had been closed so tightly that not a drop of light was getting through.

She thought for a few seconds and then headed to the shower area and beyond to the outskirts of the forest. If this was as serious as her instincts were telling her, she was going to need a weapon. Keeping the torch beam low on the ground, she began to search for the pathway she had run down a few days before.

Cate walked as fast as she dared, doing her best to dodge roots and cracks, but even so, once or twice she stumbled and fell to the ground. Then she was in the clearing, the large rock as she remembered it, almost blocking her path. She shone the torch around slowly, the pile of coloured stones she had placed as a makeshift marker showing up clearly in the narrow beam. Carefully, she pulled them away and slipped her hand into the tunnel. She felt something small and hairy running over her fingers and shuddered, but bravely persevered. Then she was touching the gun. She pulled it out and inspected it. It was still dry, the chamber full of bullets. She checked that the safety catch was still in place and then stuck the gun into her belt. At least she had some sort of protection for whatever battles lay ahead.

Just then, she heard a dull boom and the ground beneath her rocked and bucked as if it was suddenly alive. Above her, birds flew out of the trees, squawking into the night sky, and then there was silence again. What was that? An earthquake? She crept towards the rear of the kitchen.

As she got nearer she could hear a loud, angry voice. It was Jacob.

'Stop this madness. This will destroy everything. The turtles, the beach, the marine eco structure. Miles, I demand you stop this right now!'

'You can demand away.' Miles's voice was low and menacing. 'But you can't stop anything now. Over the next few days the entire cliff and beach will be blown up and mined by my good friends from Cotia who are working away as we speak. By the time anyone realises what has happened they, I and several tonnes of indium B will be on a ship somewhere in the Pacific, in international waters. No one will be able to stop it.'

Cate was almost rigid with horror. She, Henri and Marcus had made a massive, dreadful error. They had assumed that the danger was on Razor Island, but it wasn't. It was right here in Snapper Bay.

'Miles, you're one of us.' Noah sounded shell-shocked. 'You've been our leader, for God's sake. We look up to you, dude. What are you thinking?'

'What am I thinking?' Miles was suddenly shouting. 'I am thinking that, unlike all of you spoilt brats who have rich parents who pay for your flights and holidays and universities, I have nothing, not a penny to my name. I worked for the Eco Trust for years and what did I get in return? A filthy house to live in and a battered old car to drive. Did any of you think for one minute that *I* might need a bit of help?'

'Mate,' said Jacob. 'Calm down.'

Miles carried on. 'When I accidentally found a very valuable commodity right here on Snapper Beach I wasn't going to overlook it. It was my lottery ticket, come up right there and then. And I sold it to the highest bidder.'

There was another boom. The kitchen swayed and rocked alarmingly and Cate heard Maria cry out in fear.

'Don't worry, Maria. It'll soon be over,' said Miles, more cheerfully this time. 'I must say I'm looking forward to getting my payout and clearing off around the world. First class all the way.'

'But what about Josie?' It was Michel talking now, his voice calm and even. 'You said she is your sister. She has no one else in the world. You can't leave her.'

'Be quiet,' said Miles, his voice menacing again. 'You don't mention my sister's name, you hear? Not unless you want my gun in your mouth.'

Cate felt sick. It was all she could do not to rush into the kitchen in a mad attempt to rescue Michel, but if Miles was armed then this would be the worst course of action. She felt for the gun in her belt. Was she ready to use it? She had no idea, but one thing was for sure: somehow she had to get Miles out of that kitchen, away from her friends.

Suddenly Cate heard the crunch of footsteps coming up from the beach. Instantly she moved away from the window and crouched down behind a bench.

She recognised his face through the gloom. It was the Cotian bodyguard, who had held a gun to the head of Marissa, who had probably had a hand in killing the poor seaplane pilot. And now he was heading for her friends. It was time to act.

As soon as he passed her, she walked calmly out of the shadows and pushed the gun into the small of his back.

Immediately he raised his hands.

'Lie down and stay quiet,' she whispered in Spanish.

He grunted quietly in surprise but did as she said. With her left hand still pushing the gun into his back she used her right to search him. A pistol was attached to his belt, and Cate pulled it out with a shudder. This man had come armed to kill.

Cate was desperate to smack him hard over the head with her gun. Instead, she contented herself with jabbing her gun even harder into his back as she pushed his gun into her pocket with her free hand. 'Keep your face down and put your hands behind your back,' she hissed into his ear.

'I knew we should have killed you,' grunted the Cotian as she tied his hands tightly with her belt.

'You can talk when I tell you to,' Cate said. 'In fact, you can talk right now. And this is what you are going to say . . .'

Cate stood at the side of the kitchen door, her gun pointed directly at the bodyguard in front of her. Not taking her eyes from his face, she slid her arm out and rapped hard on the wooden door. 'Now,' she said, jabbing the gun into his stomach. 'Talk now.'

'Hey, Miles, it's me, Paco.'

'Louder,' said Cate. 'Louder.'

'Miles,' he shouted. 'It's Paco. Let me in. I've come to take over. We need you on the beach.'

'If anyone moves they're dead.' Miles sounded very much as if he meant it.

Stay still, Michel, she prayed. *Don't try anything stupid.*

Cate heard footsteps and then the door opened, bright

light spilling in a pool onto the porch. Still holding his gun, Miles stepped out and peered into the night.

'Hey, Paco man, where are you?' he called.

In one swift movement Cate brought her gun up and cracked it over the back of his head. Miles staggered and fell as Michel and then Jacob were up out of their chairs like greyhounds out of a trap, making sure that Miles wasn't going to get up again any time soon.

'We don't have long,' said Cate. They were all standing behind the shower blocks, away from the powerful searchlights that had now appeared at the far end of the beach. Cate could see small figures moving around, like ants between the cliffs and the shore. 'If we don't get help soon the beach will be blown to smithereens. Has anyone got a phone on them?'

'They're not working.' Maria was almost sobbing with fear. 'When Miles started to round us up I tried to use mine and there was no signal. It's been down all day.'

'What about the bike?' Cate turned to Michel, who was staring at her, a strange expression on his face. 'Michel, why don't you take Maria and head for the road? Try and flag someone down. In the meantime, the rest of us will stay here and do what we can to hold up the Cotians.'

'The bike went up in flames earlier this evening,' said Michel grimly. He was holding Miles's gun in his hand, gingerly, as if he didn't quite know what to do with it. 'We thought it was an electrical fault, but now I know differently. We have no jeep, no bike, no phones. We have no way of getting help.'

Another explosion rocked them, louder this time.

'The turtles . . . the beach . . .' Jacob was nearly in tears. 'All that work, all that beauty destroyed forever.' He pulled himself together. 'We have to save ourselves now. We'll go into the forest. It'll be harder for them to track us there. And with any luck they'll be more bothered about getting their precious treasure out to sea than hunting us down.'

Cate paused. There had to be some way of of stopping this carnage before the entire eco-system of Snapper Bay was lost forever. She remembered Arthur sitting in her bedroom on that last day before he went skiing and she went Australia.

'The boosted dongle doesn't just work for your laptop, you know,' he had said handing her a small piece of rubber with a tiny lead sticking from it. 'This is an adapater to allow you to use the dongle from your phone as well. I've downloaded you an app – see? Just plug it in like a charger, click on the app and your phone will bypass the usual network and link straight to the most powerful one available in a one hundred mile radius. It comes in handy if you're in an area with dodgy reception – or if the usual networks have failed for any reason.'

'Arthur, you're a genius,' Cate said to herself. She looked up. The four of them were staring at her. 'You head into the forest,' she said. 'If you follow that track you'll come to a clearing with a large rock. Wait there for me. I promise, I won't be long.'

'Not this time, Cate,' said Michel. 'This time we're staying together. I'm not going to risk losing you again.'

She looked at him and nodded. The two of them jogged quietly back to her tepee. Michel stood guard outside whilst Cate searched for the adaptor in the side pocket of her laptop case.

She brought it out of the tent in triumph and, grabbing

242

Michel's hand, the two of them began to run back towards the forest. As they did, they heard shouts from the kitchen and her heart sank. Their escape had been discovered already.

Jacob, Noah and Maria were huddled together at the foot of the rock waiting for them. 'OK. Here goes,' said Cate, catching her breath. She slotted the dongle into the side of the phone and gazed down at the tiny screen as she activated the app. 'Fingers crossed everyone.'

For a minute or so, there was nothing. Then there was a quiet bleep and the signal leapt up to maximum.

'Yeess.' The collective hiss of triumph ran through the group.

Cate punched in Marcus's number, then Henri's and then, her hands shaking, Arthur's. No one answered.

Her eyes filled with tears of frustration. Marcus had said she was lucky. Well, just when she needed it, really needed it, her luck had run out.

'Call the police,' said Michel quietly. 'The local police. Tell them we're under attack.'

Cate shook her head. 'We need helicopters, the navy, fire power. We need it now.'

Who else did she know? Who could she call who had that sort of influence? And then she remembered and dialled his personal number.

'Cate, is that you?' Lucas Black sounded alert. 'I've been worried sick about you. You left so suddenly without saying goodbye and that maid, Marissa – she's vanished! No one here has heard from her since you left the island. What's going on, Cate?'

'Lucas, I need your help. I need it now, urgently,' said Cate. 'Listen. Please just listen.'

The first deep thudding of a helicopter swooping in over the tops of the trees minutes later had them all on their feet, screaming in delight. It was followed by another and then another. Out at sea, a huge light was throwing a beam so powerful that the entire beach was lit up like day and, as the five of them ran out of the forest into the camp, they could see swarms of black-clad men disembarking from small dinghies, racing up over the shore.

There was a crackle of gunfire, a few small explosions and then silence. Michel picked Cate up and swung her round and round in delight and then Jacob was doing the same to Maria and Noah was jumping up and down as if he was on a trampoline.

Cate's phone rang. Michel stopped his whirling and, smiling up at him, she reached into her pocket to answer it.

'Cate,' said Henri wearily. 'I thought I told you to stay out of trouble. Why Lucas Black had to say quite those things to the Australian Prime Minister, I'll never know. That young man really has no manners at all.'

EPILOGUE

'I called Lucas because I couldn't think of anyone else who had his influence,' said Cate to Henri. They were sitting near the stage on Purbeck Island, watching as Black Noir tuned up for an impromptu gig in aid of Snapper Bay. Word had spread across the resort already and holidaymakers and staff were filing into the arena, happily making a donation as they came in. 'He's a popstar. He's huge. As big as, well, the Rolling Stones were in your day. And you know he used to be in the army. So when I couldn't get hold of you or Marcus I thought he'd be the next best person to get us the help we needed. Apart from my dad, of course. And I didn't think you'd want him to know what we'd been up to.'

'No indeed.' He paused. 'Cate, you were right. It was indium B that Miles had found and he took it straight to the Cotians. Rafe witnessed them collecting their own samples one night to confirm it. They must have been delighted. They knew that, if they got their hands on it, it would be enough to pretty much give them carte blanche to demand what they wanted from the rest of the world. In any case, they were happy enough to give him a down payment of several million dollars. We found it sitting in a bank account in the Caymen Islands.

'But there was one flaw in their plans. The one thing the Cotians couldn't know in advance was how much of it there was in Snapper Bay. They must have thought it was worth the gamble.' He smiled. 'Turns out they were wrong.'

'Oh no,' groaned Cate. 'Don't tell me all this was for nothing.'

'Well, not quite nothing. There is enough indium B to power about a hundred computers. Enough for research purposes but hardly enough to warrant all that destruction. Still, the report will mean no one else will try the same thing here.'

Cate sighed. 'Poor old Arthur will be horribly disappointed,' she said. 'He's been getting very excited about the thought of a new era of technology just around the corner.'

On the other side of Cate, Marcus was gazing at Dave the drummer. 'I've always fancied a go on the drums,' he said to Cate quietly. 'Do you think he'd mind?'

Cate looked over at Dave who was canoodling with Maria. 'I don't think he'd notice,' she giggled.

In the seats behind them Noah and Jacob were vying for Nancy's attention. As she saw Cate looking at her, Nancy waved with the air of one who was completely used to having men fight over her.

'What will happen to Miles?' Cate asked Henri.

'You mean Michael O'Leary?' Henri said. 'Well, he's managed to distance himself from the murder of the seaplane pilot

Scott Foster – but Rafe has told us that he saw him on Razor Island. He'll be charged as an accomplice to kidnap as well as a whole host of other crimes.' He shook his head. 'Actually, Cate, I don't think he cared what we were going to do to him. He was so terrified that the Cotians would come after him to try to shut him up that he practically begged us to take him into custody there and then.'

'Poor Josie,' said Cate thoughtfully. 'He drove her almost to madness.'

'We think it was probably Miles who pushed her over the cliff but unless she or he admits to it there's no proof,' said Marcus, still eyeing the drums.

'She was trying to warn me,' said Cate sadly. 'I'm pretty certain that Miles overheard her talking to me about mining. But how could he do that, to his own sister? How can people be so wicked?'

There was silence.

Lucas put down his guitar and jumped off the stage and sat down next to Cate. 'You OK?' he said quietly, not taking his eyes off the roadies who were making last-minute sound checks. 'You know for that hour between you calling me and hearing that you were OK. Well, it was a very long hour.'

Cate smiled at him. 'Lucas, thanks, for everything. You saved us, really you did. Actually, more importantly, you saved Snapper Bay from utter destruction.'

'How bad is it?' Lucas asked.

'Jacob doesn't think it's as bad as it looks,' replied Cate. 'Most of the explosions were at the far end of the beach away from the turtle sanctuary. They brought down a bit of the cliff but that's about it.'

'Good.' Lucas put out his hand and gave hers a squeeze. 'You're a very brave kid, Cate Carlisle. If I'm ever in trouble I know who I'll call first.' He stood up and smiled over her head. 'Hey, Michel? You ready, buddy?'

Cate turned around to see Michel stride proudly onto the stage, his saxophone in hand, and stand next to Lucas. A few quick sound checks later and he was actually playing live with Black Noir, his wailing tenor saxophone cutting through the band and rising high above their music.

As the crowd cheered and applauded, Cate was almost beside herself with pride. She beamed at Henri and then Marcus who gave her the thumbs up, and suddenly she was up on her feet dancing, waving up at her amazing boyfriend, happy just to be alive.

'Hey Cate,' Nancy was tapping on her shoulder. 'I know it doesn't feel like it but this time next week it'll be Christmas Day. So Happy Christmas, babe.'

'Happy Christmas, Nancy,' said Cate. 'Happy Christmas.'

ACKNOWLEDGEMENTS

Another huge set of thank yous are due. To Brenda Gardner, Ruth Williams and Andrea Reece at Piccadilly for their encouragement and enthusiasm for *The Cate Carlisle Files*.

To all my friends and family who have so generously supported me, spread the word and bought the books. You have been incredible.

To my sons George, Conrad and Lucas, for all your brilliant suggestions and advice and to Graeme for his love, support and determination. I simply wouldn't have done this without you.

And finally to all the readers, of all ages, who so enjoyed *Trapped* that they have come back for more. It means so much. Thank you.

The **CATE CARLISLE** Files

TRAPPED

ISLA WHITCROFT

School's out and sixteen-year-old Cate Carlisle lands a job
on board a gorgeous yacht, moored in the south of France.
She's working for the glamorous supermodel,
actress and pop star Nancy Kyle!

But mysterious, terrifying events keep
happening around her. Soon Cate's resourcefulness
is the only thing keeping her, and the smuggled animals
she discovers, from a terrifying fate.

An exciting, fast-paced thriller.

'Combining a glamorous setting with a fast-paced plot
involving endangered animals, this is a great teen read.'
The Guardian

VIPER'S NEST

ISLA WHITCROFT

Watch out for the exciting new installment of
The Cate Carlisle Files –
Viper's Nest.
Coming 2012.

Sign up online to be the first to know when
Viper's Nest is released!

www.piccadillypress.co.uk/CateCarlisleFiles

piccadillypress.co.uk

Go online to discover

☆ more exciting books you'll love

☆ competitions

☆ sneak peeks inside books

☆ fun activities and downloads

☆ and much more!